"I wonder if you could help me," Brad said thoughtfully. "There's someone I'm trying to locate."

"Maybe I can," said Kylie.

"It might be just coincidence, but the day you went to the agency for a job was the same day they were expecting another young lady—who never arrived. I can't help but wonder if by any chance she recommended it to you. Her name is Rosemary Bentley."

Kyle didn't move a muscle, but her brain was whirling. Should she confess in order to clear ghosts of the past and end vain searches on the part of lawyers? Should she tell Brad that she was really Rosemary Bentley—or would she stay buried, where she belonged?

NOBODY READS JUST ONE LUCY WALKER

Published by Ballantine Books

FOLLOW YOUR STAR

Lucy Walker

BALLANTINE BOOKS • NEW YORK

ISBN 0-345-24741-8-125

Manufactured in the United States of America

First Ballantine Books Edition: January, 1971
Fifth Printing: July, 1976

CHAPTER ONE

THE SMALL FEEDER PLANE flying inland from the main airline set Kylie Brown down on the Harveys' station airstrip. She had been flying all day, since before sun-up; more than a thousand miles up the west coast to the cattle port, then changing planes and flying inland towards Rock Hill Station. She had to spend the night at Harveys' because this was the nearest station to Rock Hill that had an airstrip.

She was tired, yet her tiredness was not great enough to take the edge from a sharp feeling of anxiety, now she was nearly there.

What would life on Rock Hill be like?

Kylie was a slender girl of twenty-two years of age. There was something a little guileless about her pretty fresh face. Her grey-green eyes were so clear that Mrs. Harvey, going hastily through the homestead gate to meet her, felt a pang of compunction.

"Why, she is charming," she thought. "But so inexperienced——"

She shook hands with Kylie and as she did so she noticed the simple sun-dress and that the only ornament the girl wore was a wide gold bracelet on her left arm. Kylie did not wear her hat and Mrs. Harvey noticed that her dark brown hair, coiled in a loose knot on the crown of her head, was beautiful.

"No room for a sun hat on that," she thought. "Poor child, she will have to learn to wear one up here. Dear me, if they'd only try to keep this one out at Rock Hill. . . ."

She greeted Kylie kindly and brought her into the homestead where she was able to have a rest and a bath before sitting down with the family to dinner.

"You're special," Mrs. Harvey said with a smile. "We can't take everyone in because people are coming and going all the time. That is why the airways line built that 'Two-way' cottage over there by the home paddock. But Mrs. Coulsell from Rock Hill is my nearest neighbour, even though we are a hundred and twenty miles apart. She asked me to take care of you."

"Thank you so much. You are very kind," Kylie said

5

with real gratitude in her smile. She felt relieved at this request from Mrs. Coulsell who, she thought, must be a kindly, thoughtful person.

" You will probably be called in the small hours of the morning, specially if Tom Flynn comes for you," Mrs. Harvey warned. " He generally comes in about four o'clock. Then you can get out to Rock Hill in time for morning tea. Don't be alarmed if you're wakened by loud thumps on your door. Get up and dress quickly, for Tom is an impatient fellow. He'll show you the breakfast arrangements."

Kylie said good night and thanked her hostess warmly for her kindness. It was the first real kindness Kylie had experienced since long before Horace Bentley, in whose home she had lived since she was a child, had died two months before.

*

Later that evening as Kylie tucked herself away in the narrow bunk-like bed in Two-way House she thought of all that had happened to her in the last eight weeks.

Outside the wire-screened window she could hear the night wind brushing gently over the red-brown plains that had looked sunburnt and treeless as the aircraft had flown over them. The country had seemed so vast, with no town or sign of habitation for hundreds of miles. An empty land, she had thought, a little frightened of it. Then, once down on the ground she had met with this hospitable friendliness, when all the Harveys need have done was direct her to the airlines' cottage.

Lying in her bunk, listening to the mild warm wind, Kylie thought again of her farewell to the house down south which had once been her home.

Only yesterday she had stood by the window of the upstairs drawing-room and taken her last farewell of the garden, the wide green lawns, the hedges, the camellia beds.

She had been standing there, twisting the bracelet on her arm, when the tall man arrived in the blue car.

Kylie had had one of those spontaneous thoughts that seem to come from nowhere and have no connection with reality.

" What a pity ! You have come too late !" she had thought as she looked down and saw him get out of the car, then stand a moment looking up at the façade of the big house. Kylie had a strange feeling that this man was someone she might have been waiting for without knowing it. Sometimes someone walks across one's horizon like *that*, Kylie thought.

He was tall, with a face brown-weathered by a life in the sun. His hat was broad-brimmed, as the pastoralists wore them. His eyes were probably grey for Kylie could not see them quite clearly.

It wasn't his eyes or his hat or his height that struck her. It was the man himself. He had a good-looking face that was strong, firm-chinned and firm-browed with an expression that had a reserve of dignity and quiet assurance about it. He would be quite thirty years old. His whole bearing, as he crossed the distance between his car and the porch of the house, was like that—strong and assured. Someone who knows what he wants, and gets it the quiet way. Yet, to Kylie's bemused eyes, there was something magical about him.

Perhaps it was out of her loneliness that she thought this way. Partly it was regret that no man like this had ever come nearer to Kylie than in dreaming. In truth, no man had come near her at all for Horace Bentley, selfish and authoritarian in his ways, had never given his wife's niece the opportunity to meet young people at all, let alone meet anyone of this stranger's calibre.

*

Kylie had been given a home by her aunt, Horace Bentley's wife, when she was five years old. Her parents had died in a boating accident while fishing on the reef.

Mrs. Bentley had romantic ideas about names and she tacked " Rosemary " on in front of the Kylie because she liked it better. Kylie was an Australian native name meaning boomerang and Mrs. Bentley was strictly formal in her outlook. She didn't approve of odd names for girls so she had called Kylie " Rosemary." It was not until Horace Bentley's death a few weeks before the day Kylie stood at the window that she discovered her name had never been changed legally, as she had supposed. She had always been Kylie Brown. Rosemary Bentley had been no more than a fantasy of her aunt's. Rather a cruel fantasy, Kylie thought, now that she was left both penniless and alone. Had she stayed Kylie Brown all her life she might have been earning her living out in the world with lots of other girls instead of housekeeping in a house that was rich in everything except companionship.

She had had only a bare allowance, for Uncle Horace did not believe in frippery, or girls going out for their pleasures. He considered she had a good home; the best of food, enough clothes, a comfortable bed and a very nice room. What more could a girl, his wife's orphan niece want? As for bringing anyone to the house—it was unthinkable!

Kylie had looked after the big house, and looked after Horace Bentley, for though he was a hard man, and an unapproachable man, she felt he too was a lonely man. Something in her heart was sorry for him.

She didn't want to sacrifice her life, yet she would not have left him while he needed her. Why this was so she could not tell.

Then he had died, suddenly in his sleep, and left no will. This seemed unaccountable to his financial colleages, but when Kylie thought about it, not so strange to her. Uncle Horace had never intended to die. It was as simple as that. He had not been able to visualise a world in which he did not have a directive part to play.

It was when his papers had been sifted that it was disclosed to Kylie for the first time that Mr. and Mrs. Bentley had never changed her name legally. She was Kylie Brown and related to his wife and under the laws of the country his entire estate had to go to his next of kin, three sisters, of whom Horace Bentley had never spoken. One was in England, the whereabouts of the other two was not yet discovered.

Kylie was penniless. That is, penniless except for her gold bracelet, her clothes and a hundred pounds in bonds which her aunt had purchased for her on her tenth birthday. She didn't even have the right to continue living in the house which had been her home, lonely though it was, as long as she could remember.

Wherever Uncle Horace's sisters were they appeared to make no attempt to get in touch with the girl who had been their brother's ward.

*

When Kylie stood at the windows of her room, watching for the taxi to come and take her away, this tall stranger had come to the house. He had rung the door bell and been admitted by the caretaker who had been put into the house by the estate trustees.

At the same time Kylie's taxi came sweeping up the drive

and she turned away from the window, picked up her two cases and crossed the carpet to the door. There she stood quite still for she heard the stranger's voice in the hall below as he spoke to the caretaker.

" I am sorry to trouble you. I have some inquiries to make. My name is Brad Coulsell—from Rock Hill Cattle Station."

Kylie took a step back and put her cases down. She shut the door noiselessly and, turning, stood with her back to the door, leaning against it.

Brad Coulsell—from Rock Hill.

She rested her head against the door and closed her eyes.

It seemed to her as if a challenge, like a meteor, had rocketed across her sky. It wasn't only the firm, attractive voice, it was his name and the name of his station that had startled her.

Two days earlier Kylie had gone to a pastoral agency in the city. The agency had been recommended to her by Horace Bentley's lawyer and she had gone there to find some kind of a post, preferably in the country, where she could earn a living.

There had been two places suggested to her. One a small farm in the southern districts where a housekeeper was wanted; the other in the far north, on a cattle station. A companion was required for a *Mrs. Coulsell.* The station had been called *Rock Hill.*

At the moment, as Kylie stood against the door, she could not ask herself if this was coincidence, or something more. She was too preoccupied with seeing again the figure of that tall man, his sun-tanned face, and the way he had walked towards the house; and of hearing his voice saying, " Brad Coulsell—from Rock Hill Catte Station."

He had not come to see her, of course. He didn't know she existed. The agency people had not been told the Kylie Brown who had come seeking a job was the same person as Rosemary Bentley of Number 22 Bay Drive, Mosman. He would be one more of the many people, agents, valuators, public trustees, who had come to the house since Uncle Horace died. He would be one of those concerned with one or other of Uncle Horace's pastoral interests. Rock Hill was probably one of the stations in which Uncle Horace had held a financial interest.

Kylie put the back of her hand against her closed eyes and

tried to think. She had wanted to take that station job but it had seemed so far away. In another world. It would be lonely and she was tired of loneliness.

The job on the farm in the cooler southern latitudes would give her a better chance of meeting other people, she had thought. Farms were smaller than stations and they were nearer towns. There would be neighbouring farms nearby. A station, up in the far north, was sometimes hundreds of miles from another station.

She had hesitated, but then she had agreed to arrange an interview for the farm job in the south.

Now . . .

Kylie dropped her hand, opened her eyes and stood up straight. Sometimes something happens only once in a lifetime. Why run away from it? Why not do what other girls do? Follow their luck? Follow their star?

She ran across the carpet to the telephone on the bedside table. Uncle Horace had had that put there in case he brought one of his business acquaintances home after dinner at night. If Kylie had gone to her room he needed her to dress and come down and make coffee. Now it was an instrument of fate to Kylie.

She had her handbag over one arm and as she sat on the side of her bed she opened it and took out her small pocket diary. She leafed through it madly. She had to do what she was going to do *now* because if she paused to think she knew she would never do it. Her courage, or if it wasn't courage then whatever it was, would ooze out of her shoes.

She dialled a number and a minute later a voice came on the line.

" Good afternoon. Samson and Gilitt, Pastoral Agency."

Kylie spoke softly:

" It is Kylie Brown speaking. I was in the agency the day before yesterday. May I speak to Miss Harrison, please? "

One foot beat a nervous tattoo while she waited for the connection to be made. Miss Harrison must answer quickly. If she delayed, Kylie's moment would be gone. She would put down the receiver. . . .

" Yes, Miss Brown. What can I do for you? "

Kylie sighed with relief. She felt as if her life, some kind of unknown future life that just might be happy, had been saved.

' Please. Miss Harrison, if it is not too late, I would like to

change my mind and take the Rock Hill job. You haven't
filled it yet? . . . Oh, thank goodness. . . . Oh, I beg your
pardon. I must sound stupid but you see I suddenly remembered I like *hot* weather best. It is hot at Rock Hill, isn't it?
The farm might be cold. . . ."

How stupid she sounded! Kylie thought that in a minute
she would begin to cry. Miss Harrison would think she
was mad.

Miss Harrison, on the contrary, was so relieved to find yet
another companion, especially a young companion, for Mrs.
Coulsell, who never seemed to keep companions long, that
she asked no further explanations. Yes, she would cancel
the interview for the farm job. Not to worry. It was easier
to fill farm jobs. No trouble at all. Could Miss Brown take
the plane to-morrow morning if the agency arranged the
tickets? Would she call? . . .

Kylie put down the receiver in its cradle.

Would Miss Brown call?

Miss Brown would. Miss Brown, unconscious of companions that came and went on Rock Hill, might even sing a
song for the unknown Mrs. Coulsell. She might even blow
kisses across the ether to Miss Harrison who had said Mrs.
Coulsell was a middle-aged woman . . . a very nice woman
. . . who was exceedingly lonely in such a remote place as
Rock Hill. The doctor had said she should have a companion. A young one. Youth made older people feel young
and energetic again.

Kylie, sitting on her bed near the telephone table, made a
cat's cradle with her fingers and swung her feet to and fro.

She'd never been gay herself. Little did Mrs. Coulsell
know *that*. There had been nothing to be gay about in Uncle
Horace's home. But now . . . well, just now she felt gay.
Perhaps in a little while the bubble would burst, but for the
moment she would hug a sudden little ray of sunshine to
her heart.

All on account of a tall sun-tanned man she had seen from
her bedroom window.

She must be mad.

*

Kylie hadn't seen that man again. She had picked up her
cases, softly opened the door and slipped downstairs, past the
office where the caretaker was talking to *him*, and so out to
the taxi.

She had had only one night to spend in the city hotel.
There had been an hour or two for shopping and that meant
she was able to buy some sun-dresses, straight from the peg.
This was easy for Kylie was stock size; besides shopping,
even from a meagre purse, was fun in itself. Sun-dresses were
extra fun to buy because this year they were extra pretty.

Somehow everything at the moment seemed to Kylie to be
extra pretty. She stopped worrying about the dwindling of
her hundred pounds—all she had in the world except her
gold bracelet. And now the sun-dresses, of course.

*

All this Kylie thought of as she lay in her small bunk in
Two-way House. She blinked her eyes in the darkness and
thought that if she didn't hurry up and go to sleep she would
be too tired to get up at four o'clock in the morning and
begin that long car drive of over a hundred and twenty miles
to Rock Hill Station.

Mrs. Harvey's kindness had touched her heart with gratitude. She wasn't used to being noticed; to being the subject
of attention. Vaguely, as she fell asleep, Kylie realised it was
just as well. Now, nearing her destination, she was afraid
she had done a foolish thing—following her star.

*

True to the warning Kylie was indeed awakened next
morning by a heavy thumping on her door. She sprang out
of bed at once and, after quickly dashing water over herself
from the shower in the alcove of the bedroom, pulled on her
clothes. That thumping had been peremptory enough to
be a command from the gods.

When she opened her own door and went along the tiny
lean-to veranda to the kitchenette it was to find someone
there before her. A man, probably about twenty-five years
of age, was frying eggs and bacon on the small paraffin stove.
He turned his head and gave her half a grin.

" Two eggs and three rashers for you, Miss Brown—same
for me? "

" Oh, thank you," said Kylie, anxious to please and quite
incapable of admitting she had never eaten two eggs and three
rashers of bacon for breakfast before.

" Okay. You get out the knives and forks. They're in the
drawer there and keep your eyes cocked on that clock. We
leave in exactly twenty minutes. Washing up done." He
turned his head and looked at her again. Kylie had the

impression of a youngish yet fatherly school teacher temporarily dressed up in bowyangs and drill shirt but full of paternal guidance and authority.

" You put the sheets off your bed in the box, as it says on the notice? " he asked.

Kylie nodded.

" I did everything it commanded on the notice."

With dexterity the man whipped the bacon and eggs on to two plates, put them on the table and added as he put the frying-pan into a sink :

" Well, hop to it, Miss Brown. If we get away early that's better than getting away late." He sat down and began his breakfast without ceremony.

" You are from Rock Hill? " Kylie asked. She too began her breakfast.

" Nowhere else. You don't mind if I put my bread in the bacon fat? Trouble about these two-way shakedowns you can't choose with whom you eat breakfast." He smiled. " Meaning *you* can't choose, of course."

He looked at Kylie over the piece of soaked bread with bright mischievous eyes.

She smiled back.

" It's rather fun, isn't it? " she said.

" Good job you think that way. You ought to see some of the people who come this way when they find me flipping eggs at 'em without by-your-leave, and before the crack of dawn. They all but faint. You heard that word ' faint ' before ? Useful out there at Rock Hill and don't forget I told you to use it. Now hop into that breakfast while I make the tea. Then you wash up while I fill up the bus at the bowser. *See notice*."

He pointed with the back of his fork to the notice tacked on the door.

PLEASE LEAVE AS YOU FIND—
CLEAN AND TIDY

Kylie smiled as the bright slightly wicked blue eyes watched her to see how she was taking his way of doing things.

" Nice to get someone young and pretty, this time," he said. " Girl, you ought to see what comes in and out of Rock Hill some days."

" Nice of you to appreciate it," said Kylie. " I think I'm

going to enjoy my drive. A hundred and twenty miles, isn't it? Are you a stockman, or driver from the station? "

The man put down his knife and fork. He appeared to be about to choke but then changed his mind.

" Listen, Miss Brown! " he said severely. " I understand from higher authority that's your name. Well, listen, Miss Brown! Don't jump to conclusions up this way by the way a man eats, talks or wears his clothes. He might just be a millionaire."

" Oh," said Kylie. " Are you a millionaire? Or even the owner of Rock Hill? "

" I am not. I run Rock Hill, it is true. I'm the book-keeper. You know what a bookkeeper is? Jack of all trades, and the station can't run without him. It can do without the manager, or the stockmen, or even that high panjandrum, the rouseabout. But without the bookkeeper? Never. You know why? He does everything. When anyone else is away he does that fellow's job as well as his own." He added lugubriously, " On Rock Hill, anyway."

" Oh, I'm sorry," said Kylie. " I thought, by the way you dressed, you rode a horse."

" So I do, and drive a car and out-muster the stockmen and out-swear the bullock drivers. Now spring to and wash those dishes while I fix the car. You got your cases outside? "

Kylie nodded.

Whatever the bookkeeper's name she was going to like him. If he was a fair sample of the staff on Rock Hill she was also going to like the station. Why had she had those unexpected doubts last night?

Dear stars in the sky, how you had twinkled! Specially my one.

All the same she did wonder why he had to have his trousers tied round the calves of his legs with string, and wear high-heeled stock boots. Perhaps what he said was true and he did do everybody else's job when required.

She thought about him as she rinsed the dishes in the sink. He had a square-cut face with a dark mat of black hair and very striking eyes above a slightly bent nose. His mouth had a small upward scar at one corner but it made him look as if he was smiling, even when he was not.

She wondered how the " people " of whom he had spoken liked washing up the greasy plates at his command. She thought this was a very levelling experience to be flying about between stations and two-way transit houses *en route*. Everyone had to do for themselves.

By the time the lights in the small cottage had been put out, the doors shut and Kylie ensconced in the front seat of the enormous dusty but luxurious station wagon she was beginning to enjoy station life in advance.

" Would you please tell me what your name is? " she asked.

" Tom Flynn. Now hang on while I race her up this hill. No track. Short cut, you know. Takes too long going round the stock route way."

Kylie did indeed have to hang on. The car must have taken miniature gullies as well as plateaux and rock falls in its next half-hour of travelling. There was no opportunity for talking. Tom Flynn had both eyes glued on the lighted way being revealed to him by the powerful headlights of the car.

" I suppose he knows where he's going," Kylie thought anxiously.

At last they reached the stock route, and presently they settled down to a level eighty miles an hour, travelling with only an occasional bump or side-slip.

She wanted very much to ask him about the personalities living on Rock Hill but she thought it wiser to wait and see for herself. She wanted very much to ask him about Brad Coulsell.

Tom Flynn in the course of that long drive told her a few things without invitation.

" The boss went down south," he said. " Should be back any tick of the clock. Coming home the back way. Left his big car out at Sam MacDougall's station and flew down in a private plane. Some of those chaps out there near the border got their own planes. Plenty of money and plenty of flat ground for strips. Not rock-strewn like this place."

" Rock Hill sounds rocky," Kylie said, then after a pause she asked the sixty-four dollar question. The one she was longing to ask.

" What is he like? The boss, I mean? "

Tom Flynn grinned as he looked at her.

" He's okay," he said. " You'll like him, only don't go falling for him. That's an awful complication with the girls that come here. They don't last any time. Someone marries them off to someone else, or sends them home. Just warning you."

Kylie's heart was beating unusually fast.

"I won't," she said. "But why do they fall for him? You mean *fall in love*, I suppose. He's not married then? He's not the only man around, is he?"

What traitors were her words to her thoughts! So casual, and she wanted to know so much.

"There's myself, of course, but he's the only one with a lot of money, a lot of acres, a lot of nice looks—no, he's not married." Tom Flynn changed his tone to one of quiet sorrow. "He's got a kinda way with him, if you understand me."

"But I thought he was the manager. The agency that took me on spoke of him that way. He doesn't *own* Rock Hill, does he?"

"Listen, Miss Brown. He all but owns it, if you understand English. He's called the manager because the one or two others in it—well, one now old Horace Bentley's dead—have got to pay someone to run the whole thing, including their share. Get me? Hence the glorious title of manager. That's company law for you. If you got a company you got to have a manager, see? And they have companies instead of partnerships these days because that way they don't pay so much taxation. He's got to pay himself a salary out of his own profits. See?"

"I see," said Kylie humbly. She didn't quite see but she thought she might work it out for herself by and by. So Uncle Horace *did* have a share in this station! That was why Brad Coulsell had called at the house in Mosman. She took in a deep breath and said:

"He's nice, I'm not to fall in love with him and he's the manager as well as the owner. Go on."

"Well, nearly the owner. His mother, Mrs. Coulsell, is the other owner now old Horace Bentley's gone."

Kylie realised she would have to be careful every time that name was mentioned. She didn't want the Coulsells ever to know she had had any connection with Horace Bentley. It would be too confusing and embarrassing for everyone.

Dawn came, grey and uninviting, and Tom Flynn, without stopping or decreasing his speed, offered Kylie a Thermos flask and extra mug from the box in the dashboard.

"You pour," he said. "I'll drink."

The farther Kylie went with Tom Flynn the more she liked him. Already there was a friendliness between them that warmed her heart. One moment he was brash as she imagined the stockmen to be. The next moment he was chivalrous and kindly. Five minutes later he was talking to her about the cattle run, the seasonal occupations and the hazards, in a quiet voice that showed he was really a well educated and well informed man.

More than everything else she liked the challenging expression in those eyes above that slightly crooked nose and under the square forehead that carried the black thatch of unruly hair, now covered by an old army hat. He was quite a personality, she decided. Privately she felt he would be a friend if she needed one on the station. She had never been alone in the company of a young man before. She was relieved to find she was not too shy or awkward.

" What do you do with the other ' people ' when it comes to washing-up time at Two-way House? " she asked.

" Give 'em some sandsoap and tell 'em to polish the bottoms of the frypan and the kettle," he said.

" And do they? " asked Kylie.

He looked at her sideways and grinned.

" Sandsoap and the bottom of a saucepan is a challenge to any woman, isn't it? " he said. " What would you do? "

" I would probably do as I was told, and polish," said Kylie gravely.

" That's what they do," he said. " I've never missed yet."

" And all the time, you're laughing? "

" No. Just practising psychology. Meantime I'm filling up the bus with petrol. I don't watch women at their profession."

" There's more to a housewife's pride than the bottom of a saucepan," said Kylie firmly.

" When you get to Rock Hill you prove it," said Tom Flynn with a laugh. " Ray will certainly be keen about that aspect of our new arrival."

" Ray? " asked Kylie curiously.

" Ray Coulsell, Brad's sister. She comes and goes. Comes back to the station because she really loves it. Goes, because she gets bored. The girls all do that, you know: grow up on a station and then leave it for the bright lights of town. That's why Mrs. Coulsell likes someone she can *pay* to stay. She's lonely when Brad's out on the run and Ray's way down south. She likes someone young in the house; then she can pretend to herself she's not afraid of becoming useless."

" What a shame," said Kylie. " And is Ray on the station now? "

" Yes, came back three weeks ago. She'll go as soon as she gets bored, which might be any minute now." Tom slewed his mischievous eyes round to look at Kylie. " She's come back to look you over, I guess. Make sure you don't run off with that precious brother of hers."

Kylie had the most mixed of feelings as she heard Tom announce these facts of life on Rock Hill.

" Why should she think . . . well, think I'd even be interested in her brother? "

Words that were traitors again. Yet Kylie actually meant what she said at this moment for somehow her pride stiffened at the thought of . . .

Well, the thought of what?

Hadn't she actually changed her mind about where she took a post because she had seen Brad Coulsell?

She blushed at her own deception and a little because she wondered at this sudden upsurge of pride that made her suddenly feel antagonistic towards Brad, instead of terribly attracted to him as she had been when he had come to the house in Mosman.

Men were said to believe they never understood girls. Did girls understand themselves?

Kylie clutched at an argument so that Tom would not notice the blush.

" But I only knew yesterday I was coming. I mean . . ."

" Yes, but Ray knew three weeks ago that *someone* would come. So she came back, pronto."

Tom pursed his lips in a silent whistle. Then oddly he changed his tone.

" Ray's all right," he said suddenly. " All the same, she'll be pleased to find you can wield the good old polishing cloth."

By this time Kylie was longing to ask Tom Flynn if he was married himself but judged that this question might bring another challenging rebuke. Instead she poured his tea for him and then poured some into the plastic cap of the Thermos for herself. They lapsed into silence, and Kylie watched the world of Rock Hill Station unfold itself under the first brilliance of the hot sun as it came up over the eastern skyline.

True, there were rocky outcrops, tufted with a grey spindly grass, and here and there a straggly tree stood crooked and lonely on the stony pile. She wondered which was the hill that had given the station its name.

Presently the track took them through light timber which gradually became more dense; the trees were higher and the undergrowth rich in foliage. The sky was colourless in the oncoming heat of the day.

They were running along a five-wire cattle fence now, and quarter of an hour later she could see the elevated tank of the station bore rising above a clump of buildings.

CHAPTER TWO

" Home, itself," said Tom Flynn. " Morning tea time. How's that for fast driving? "

" Do you ever kill anyone? " asked Kylie. She half listened for the answer for she was all curiosity as they swept up between a host of outbuildings to a wide gravel square on the far side of which was a lawn, a shrubbery and then the veranda of the homestead.

" Not yet," Tom Flynn said but Kylie did not hear him. Everything about the station was holding her half-nervous, half-fascinated attention.

A flutter of white dresses and black faces disappeared in a chorus of laughter and giggles as the lubras, several children amongst them, fled round the corner of the house, only to come back one at a time and peer at the new arrival.

The homestead veranda was partly obscured by a blaze of purple and orange bougainvillaea, but not so much so that Kylie did not see a young fair-haired girl in a lovely teal blue cotton frock leaning her hands on the balustrade and looking towards the car. On the three steps of the veranda that led to the pathway through the lawn was a small girl who was curious, but too shy to come forward.

Suddenly all around the homestead was commotion.

Tom Flynn got out of the car, was slamming the drive door shut, the lubras half round the corner of the house were shrieking with laughter at some joke of their own. Their white dresses fluttered and their white teeth flashed in their dark merry faces. Out of sight, fowls were fluttering. The vanes of the windmill spun round in a movement of air and the lift shaft clanked as water poured into the overhead tank.

A dog raced round the side of the house and two men on horseback came up between the outhouses.

Meantime the tall slim girl with the fair hair came along the veranda and down the steps towards the car. Kylie, with Tom Flynn's helping hand, was lifting herself somewhat stiffly from the front seat. She looked up, half anxious and half eager, as the girl came towards her. This would be Ray Coulsell.

"She's pretty," Kylie thought. "Oh, isn't she pretty!"

It was the fair hair, the smoothly sun-tanned skin, the simple yet charming dress and an air of poise as the girl came towards the car that made Kylie think this. At closer quarters she was a little older than she had seemed in the distance. There was a flicker of a smile in her face; then she held out her hand.

"How do you do?" she said. "I hope you have had a pleasant journey. Will you come in and meet my mother? Tea will be ready immediately."

"How do you do?" Kylie said with a smile that was just a little wintry because this girl's own smile was not yet friendly.

"I'm Ray Coulsell," the other girl was saying. "I'm sorry my brother is away at the moment. However, my mother is really your employer, you know."

"Yes, I did know that," Kylie said quietly as she followed the fair girl.

On the step the small child shaded her eyes with her hand and looked up at the newcomer.

"Hallo!" Kylie said with a smile.

The little girl, six or seven years old, had a sweet heart-shaped face, golden fair hair and tiny freckles on her nose.

Ray Coulsell looked down.

"Run away, Nonie," she said to the child. "If you stay there you'll be in the way."

The little girl's face lost its eager lighted look and became thoughtful. Then she stood up and smoothed her skirt down. She looked at Kylie and smiled again, but did not speak. She began to move away, her shy gaze still bound to the newcomer's face.

"Go along," Ray Coulsell said again quietly. "You don't have to take all day, Nonie."

Her voice was neither sharp nor kindly. It was disinterested with a kind of firm politeness. Kylie knew at once what it meant. Ray Coulsell had no feelings of sympathy for this small winsome freckle-faced child, but she was being polite about the way she showed this.

" Poor little girl," Kylie thought of Nonie.

Yet almost immediately Nonie herself rebuked Kylie for pity in her own way. She turned and waved, then went down the path and through the gate, every now and again giving a skip as she walked. She was small, untroubled, and bent on some adventure somewhere else.

Kylie found herself smiling.

" Does the little girl belong to the family? " she asked.

Ray Coulsell glanced at Kylie curiously, almost as if she had detected that momentary and unnecessary pity.

" Nonie Allen is the child of one of our former stockmen. He's now on Eagle Eye Station," she said. " Children near the territory border get sent away to other stations now and again for a change of air and diet. Otherwise they grow spindly, or anæmic, or something."

" What a splendid idea," Kylie said, her spirits already lifting. " I suppose it's quite a holiday for them."

" Nonie's life is one perpetual holiday," Ray said dryly. " Her father was once my brother's best stockman. In any case her parents are always out on the run and take Nonie with them. She's more at home with grown-ups than children. That's why she likes to come up to the homestead. She lives with Mrs. Craddock, the head stockman's wife, while she is here."

Ray held open the screen door of the house as she now dismissed the subject of Nonie, and Kylie could see into a wide hallway. Coming towards them was a middle-aged woman in an attractive grey and white dress of some heavy satin-finished cotton with soft white lace at the neckline. Kylie's immediate impression was that this woman was pleasant, more homely than smart, yet somehow looking well-groomed in that homeliness. Her hair, swept back in a roll, was shining and beautifully done. Her face was sensitive, with an edge of sadness to it. Also, for a startled moment, Kylie thought she had met or seen her, before.

As Mrs. Coulsell smiled and spoke Kylie knew this was not so but she could not help wondering where she had met someone like her.

" Good morning," Mrs. Coulsell said with a pleasant smile.

She shook hands with Kylie. " You are Miss Brown, of course. I'm glad you have arrived safely. Come in, won't you? We've tea and scones ready in the morning room and I'm sure you're in need of something refreshing."

This was a pleasant and generous greeting yet unexpectedly Kylie was aware of a distance. She did not feel as if she herself was being approved but rather as if Mrs. Coulsell was waiting to see if Kylie would approve *her*.

The " You are Miss Brown, of course," had caught her unawares because in spite of Tom Flynn's flippant greeting of " Listen, Miss Brown! " Kylie had not yet become accustomed to being anyone but Rosemary Bentley.

Unexpectedly she thought it was rather fun to be somebody else. A kind of dual personality. Also she was moved by that questing expression which she read in Mrs. Coulsell's face. This woman did indeed need someone around her, to reassure her and perhaps be a friend.

The attractive clothes, the delicate make-up, the beautifully arranged hair were not the adornments of a " smart " woman so much as an armour.

Kylie said " Good morning " in reply to Mrs. Coulsell's greeting and wished she could think of something bright to say so that both Ray and her mother would feel she was the right person to come and live among them. Instead, she followed them into the morning room—a lovely bright room, two sides of which were open and only shielded from the garden by wire screen walls.

It was very hot outside yet as soon as Kylie came into this room there was the refreshing scent of a newly watered garden and something unusual and aromatic which must come in through the wire screen from the shrubs outside.

" Tom Flynn will put your bags on the veranda near your room," Mrs. Coulsell was saying. " It's on the other side of the house. We have a veranda all round, you know. It keeps the homestead cool."

" I suppose you would like tea *first*," Ray said in her quiet, assured voice. " Most people do after that long drive. Sit over there, will you. . .?" With a nod of her head she indicated a comfortable chair with its back to the side wall.

" The light won't bother your eyes," Mrs. Coulsell said hastily. " It's very dazzling up here in the north." She was clearly telling Kylie, why Ray had told her to sit in that particular chair.

Kylie thought she might be going to like Mrs. Coulsell very much but she was uncertain about Ray. More because of Ray's attitude to the little girl perhaps than because of the cool withdrawn manner.

"Thank you," Kylie said and sat down. She crossed her ankles and put her hands in her lap.

A lubra in a snow-white cotton dress brought in a tea-tray and placed it on a small table by the side wall.

"Please pour out, Ray," her mother asked. "I want to talk to Miss Brown." She sat down and smiled at Kylie. "It's so difficult not being able to talk about your duties before you take up the post, isn't it? But then this always happens to station people. We're so dependent on the Pastoral Agency."

"They did explain that you personally needed some companionship and help, Mrs. Coulsell," Kylie said. How soon, she prayed earnestly to herself, will I learn to be Miss Brown?

Mrs. Coulsell looked pleased, as if the most difficult part of the interview had been got over in advance.

"I do like to have someone young around," she said as Ray brought her some tea and she helped herself to sugar.

"May I help?" Kylie said, getting up. She went across the room and brought the silver dish of hot scones to Mrs. Coulsell.

Ray did not appear to notice but Mrs. Coulsell, looking up after she had taken her scone, said:

"Thank you so much. That was kind of you. But we must remember it is your first day and . . ."

"Miss Brown would probably sooner make herself at home on her first day than not, Mother," Ray said. She turned to Kylie. "I'll bring you your tea. You've done your good deed for this session. Milk?"

Her voice was expressionless and Kylie could not tell whether Ray was being sarcastic and whether she herself should have stayed put until the formalities of a first meeting were over.

How does anyone ever know quite what to do in the first hour of a job?

The only advice she could give herself was to do for Mrs. Coulsell what she had done for Uncle Horace. She had not been a servant yet she had cared for him, always unobtrusively because he couldn't stand people fussing about. He had grown to accept all the care and attentions without even knowing he received them.

She would be more unobtrusive in her services another time. And did it matter very much what Ray meant, if Ray would be going away from the station again?

She was startled at the faint hope she felt that perhaps Ray would go away very soon. She had a feeling that she and Mrs. Coulsell were going to get on very well together . . . left alone.

*

Later she was shown to her room, a small but rather endearing annexe to the far side veranda, the outside wall of which, except for the wire screening, was open to the world of the station.

Here on this side the paddocks rolled right up to the house. All that lay between Kylie's outlook and that vast plain was a cement path and a wire fence with low shrubs below it.

In her room was a modern bed with a head-board for books and a reading lamp. There was a pretty blue candlewick cover on the bed. All very compact and modern. Kylie saw that by pulling a cord she was able to close heavy lined chintz curtains over the outside wall that was no more than screen wire, similar to the morning room.

She felt delighted with her small modern cubby-hole and the wonderful sense of space and fresh air that the open wall gave to it. The paddocks beyond, so brown and still in the hard bright light, were peace-giving.

*

A man's voice broke the stillness all around.

" Uh-huh! "

Kylie went to the screen wall and looked out. Tom Flynn was standing on the cement path, his hands in his pockets and Kylie's bags beside him.

" You can't see in from the outside through that screen wire," he said reassuringly. " But don't forget to pull your curtains when the light is on at night time . . . except when you go to sleep, of course. The whole idea is to give you the outdoor feeling."

He was grinning engagingly. Kylie leaned on the wooden ledge that ran the full width of the screen at waist height.

" Thank you very much for telling me," she said. " I was just working it all out."

" Slow motion, huh? "

Kylie smiled but realised her smile would be wasted if he couldn't see her. He bent down and picked up the bags.

" If you'd be obliging enough to open the wire door on to the veranda I'd be obliging enough to bring in your bags," he said.

This was quickly accomplished and Tom Flynn stood in Kylie's room, his hands once more in his pockets and smiling, half wickedly, half engagingly.

" Not a bad job, huh? " he asked, looking at her with those inviting and amusing eyes of his.

" What do you mean? You sound as if you had something to do with making the room."

" Did too. Built it, painted it, and by golly, furnished it."

Kylie looked around with puzzlement and then back to Tom Flynn.

" But I thought you were the book-keeper? "

" Sure. But a man has to have something to do with his week-ends and spare moments. I told you—stockman, rouseabout, manager and handyman too. That's me, Tom Flynn. Not forgetting being the chauffeur, and a dab at bacon and eggs in the small hours of the morning."

" But you didn't make that marvellous cupboard . . . and the bed. . . ."

" Clever chap, aren't I? "

" You certainly are. What does anyone else do round here when they've got Tom Flynn to do everything? "

" You'll have to go out on the run with the boss to find that out. Wait till he comes back and you'll see a few other blokes, including himself, find a thing or two to do—what's left over from Tom Flynn, of course."

He was standing in the middle of the room admiring his handiwork and showing no immediate concern about going. Kylie sat down on the edge of her bed. She was quite sure it wouldn't be the right thing to invite her guest to sit down. Except for the bed this little room was hardly a bedroom. All the same . . .

" I thought you advised me not to have anything to do with him," Kylie said, meaning Brad Coulsell, and making an effort to appear only half interested. " I thought he was untouchable, and it was dangerous for a young lady even to look at him."

Tom Flynn pursed up his lips and looked at Kylie with assumed severity. He was not going to tell her any more about the boss, that was clear.

"You know, Miss Brown, you've got a very nice voice and a cute habit of using long sentences. I bet you never wielded a straw broom in your life."

Kylie flushed.

"Straw brooms went out with the last war," she said. "We now use vacuum cleaners."

He looked at her closely for a minute, then laughed.

"Okay," he said. "You win." He turned and went to the door leading to the veranda. He pushed it open with one finger and then turned slowly round again. "People run away from something," he said, "when they come right outback. Something goes wrong with their world down south, so they run away. What was it? A broken heart?"

"I might have been running *to* something," said Kylie, with wry truth. Then she asked hastily: "What did you run away from, Tom Flynn?"

"Lack of money," he said with a grin. "In town I'm a spender and outback there's nothing to spend it on. How about you?" he insisted. "Going to tell?"

Kylie thought quickly.

"If you must know, then it was a broken heart."

Tom Flynn sighed.

"Now you know why you've got to beware of the boss," he said. "The last young lady came up here for the same reason and there was another a few years ago. As soon as they saw the boss they tried to mend their broken hearts with him. Don't do it, sweet Miss Brown. He can scent a phoney a paddock away."

"Thank you kindly for your advice. I promise I won't even look at him."

She had better not look at him, she told herself. She was only following in the pattern of other girls. How humiliating!

Tom Flynn went to the door, then put his head in again.

"See you later, Miss Brown," he said.

He jumped off the veranda and went along the cement path, whistling. It took Kylie one minute to realise the tune was, "If a lassie meets a laddie . . . comin' thro' the rye."

She went to the cupboard, opened the door and looked at herself in the long mirror.

"Is this really me?" she asked her image. "I never

talked to anyone like that before. I never met anyone like Tom Flynn. He is nice. I like him. Why did they say living on a station was lonely? I was lonely at home near a city. Here there are two nice men. And Ray. Even Ray is company of my own age. And the little girl. What did Ray call her? Nonie! "

Kylie fell to wondering where Nonie was and when she would see her again.

*

Kylie's first day at Rock Hill passed easily enough. Because of the early hour start from Two-way House Mrs. Coulsell insisted that Kylie have a long rest after lunch, although Ray said severely, " Don't *fuss*, Mother."

Lunch was served in the morning room. A lubra brought in the dishes of cold beef, mango, pineapple and paw-paw salads, then finished with ice-cream and black coffee served together after all the other dishes had been cleared away. Ray poured the coffee and served the ice-cream.

Mrs. Coulsell seemed a little nervous of displeasing Ray but she chatted pleasantly to Kylie.

" What was your last post like? " she asked. " Was it a nice home? "

This was a little hard for Kylie to answer. She did not ever want the Coulsells to know about her change of identity; of the lonely exacting life she had had to live with Horace Bentley. She didn't want them to know that Uncle Horace, as she had called him, the man who had had a share in this station, had left her penniless.

When she came to think of it she supposed that living with Horace Bentley, and keeping house for him, had been a kind of "post." If she thought of it that way she could talk about it more freely.

" I looked after an elderly widower," she said. " It was a lovely home, overlooking the Swan River. We did have a cook, and a cleaner who came once a week, but I gave him the things he liked. I made breakfast for him because then he always got his toast hot. And I knew how he liked his things to be kept. . . ."

" You've got the perfect companion, Mother," Ray said dryly. Then to Kylie, " Mother loves hot tea and hot toast in bed in the mornings. . . ."

" They have breakfast terribly early on stations," Mrs. Coulsell said, as if excusing this weakness. " Far too early when you get to my age. Morning tea at five o'clock and breakfast at six. The men are out on the run by half past six."

"By the way, Mother," Ray said, "did you get the transceiver message at twelve o'clock? Mrs. MacDougall said Sam and Brad flew in last night. Brad left for Rock Hill about ten o'clock this morning."

Mrs. Coulsell's face lit up.

"Why didn't someone tell me?" she exclaimed.

"You were too busy talking to Miss Brown," Ray said off-handedly.

Mrs. Coulsell immediately forgot Kylie and they went on talking about affairs that Brad had been attending to down south. He had been going to cattle sales, it seemed, and buying new equipment for the station. Kylie did not listen because her thoughts were again with that tall stranger who had come to the house in Mosman, and because of whom she had come now to Rock Hill.

How would she feel when she saw him again? Would he be nice, like Mrs. Coulsell? A little brash, like Tom Flynn?

Whatever he would be like, Kylie thought she must never, never let him know she had seen him before.

She also wondered how far away was MacDougalls' station. Would it be one of those places that took days to come from? Or only hours?

How would she feel when she saw him again? Disappointed? Embarrassed ... that was for sure. She would keep out of his way until she had got used to his presence in the homestead.

She mustn't give herself away.

*

It was nearly four o'clock when Kylie woke up from the afternoon siesta and, anxious for fear she had overslept, she hurriedly had a shower and put on a fresh cotton frock. It was still very hot and outside everything lay in a shimmering haze.

Kylie did her hair and put on a dash of lipstick.

When she went to the living-room she found that Ray had gone out riding, and this time she was able to pour the tea for Mrs. Coulsell.

When they had finished Mrs. Coulsell said to Kylie:

"Now dear, if you would just go out to the kitchen and find out what goes on you'll learn much quicker than if I fuss you. You know I've had girls here to help me before and that's one thing I have learned. If they're left alone, and are the helpful kind, it's much easier for them if I'm not there."

"Oh, thank you," Kylie said gratefully. "That is very thoughtful of you."

"I let the lubras do the cooking. They're very good plain cooks but they haven't any idea of serving things delicately. And I never let them loose in the pantry with the silver or good china. I can't bear to hear them laugh if something breaks. Everything is a joke to the natives, you know." She smiled happily because she could see that Kylie was feeling quite at home now. "Now you go and find your way about," she said, "while I try that transceiver set again and see if I can pick up news of Brad, and whether he is on his way or not."

*

At sundown there was an extra amount of laughing and screeching from the kitchen, the pitter-patter of bare feet on the linoleum floors, the banging of the back veranda screen doors, and outside the barking of two dogs.

Kylie was in the living-room, leafing through some magazines, looking for a knitting pattern for Mrs. Coulsell. She had had the feeling for quite a long time that out there in the kitchen something special was going on. The lubras had been working up to something.

Once Mrs. Coulsell, who was writing letters, lifted her head and said:

"Those girls hear something. I wonder if it is Brad coming home?"

Now a proper commotion had started. The kitchen was suddenly vacated and silence reigned there as giggles became the order of the day in the garden near the north corner of the house.

Mrs. Coulsell put her pen down and went into the short passage leading to the front door. Kylie, a magazine in her hand, walked quietly to the window overlooking the front veranda and garden.

The trees in the garden hung down their leaves as if tired of the sun but in their crowns that same sun shone red and gold. The earth of the great plain was dark against the backdrop of a sky so crimson Kylie could hardly believe her eyes.

Outside the low wire gate, silhouetted against that fiery

sky, somehow isolated in a small island of humanity in a world of sundown silence, stood a large dust-covered car and beside it stood a tall man, with his back to the homestead. At this moment he was rocking back on his heels, talking to Tom Flynn and Ray. Both men had their hats pushed to the backs of their heads.

The little girl Nonie came happily along the homestead fence and as she neared the car the tall man put out his right hand and took the child's hand in his own. He did not stop speaking, neither did he bend his head to look at her. He simply went on discussing something with Tom Flynn and his sister: the child's hand in his hand. Nonie stood still and happy, at peace with the world.

Kylie had an unexpected lump in her throat. It was because Nonie was a lonely child, she told herself. It was the natural way he had put out his hand and the natural way the child had put her hand in his.

He turned round and lifted his head to look up at the homestead as Mrs. Coulsell came on to the veranda.

Yes, it was just the same for Kylie as it had been that day he had come to Uncle Horace's house in Mosman. Her heart stood still.

There was something magical about him. She did not know why, except that he was like someone she had dreamed about in her loneliness, long long ago.

Brad Coulsell had come home.

CHAPTER THREE

BY THE TIME they all came to the living-room Kylie had made tea. Dinner was an hour and a half away and after that long drive anyone would want tea.

Brad hadn't seen her at Horace Bentley's house. She was certain of that. One can't see through lace curtains into a darkened house from the outside any more than one can see in through the screen mesh of her own veranda room. She was Miss Brown. He would never know she had been in that house. The caretaker had only known her as Miss Bentley and if he had mentioned her to Brad Coulsell it would have been as Miss Bentley.

Kylie's hands trembled a little as she plugged in the cord

for the electric tea-kettle. She could here the footsteps coming down the passage and through the dining-room to where she now stood. Mrs. Coulsell was speaking and then, as they came through the doorway, *he* spoke.

Yes, it was the same voice, firm, with the courtesy of quiet authority, that had said " Good afternoon " to the caretaker.

Kylie did not turn round. It wasn't necessary yet. The others were talking to one another.

" I had three sessions with the lawyer," he was saying. " We couldn't get anywhere. I couldn't stay down there for ever. They'll catch up with the whole business, given time. Meantime our option of purchase on the remaining shares in this place was established and the bank has taken that in train. . . ."

Ray's voice interrupted.

" Brad, do you have to start that business all over again? " Kylie knew from Ray's tone that she was not referring to what Brad was saying but to something he was *doing* this moment.

" What business? " he asked, breaking off his conversation with his mother. " Oh! Nonie? What's wrong with her? She doesn't eat much, and we can afford it." He laughed, a pleasant engaging sound. " Hey, Nonie? And she's certainly seen and not heard. Go on, young 'un, hop up on a chair over there and keep out of Ray's mind as well as sight."

Ray came across to the side table to help Kylie.

" By the way," she said over her shoulder, " you haven't met Miss Brown."

Kylie turned round and looked at Brad Coulsell.

She was glad she hadn't got a smile ready, for Tom Flynn was standing in the doorway. Over Brad's shoulder he raised his eyebrows and with them managed to signal the fact that, *Whack-ho! This was it.*

" I beg your pardon," Brad said formally. " I was talking to my mother. It was a minute before I realised we had a stranger with us. Now I remember. It's Miss Brown, of course."

He came forward and held out his hand. With determined gravity Kylie put her hand in his.

" Yes, Kylie Brown," she said quietly. She was afraid they would all notice the pulse she could feel beating in her throat.

The hand in which her hand lay was hard and the hand-shake was firm.

" I hope you like being with us, Miss Brown," Brad said. His eyes flicked over her but there was only a distant interest.

Kylie, looking quickly at him, saw the square brow and the searching eyes, which, though very perceptive, gave nothing away. He had a straight nose and firm chin. He would be six feet and very strong. He stood there in his brown tropical clothes, one hand actually holding her hand and the other—now that he was home—loosening his tie because it was very hot.

" Thank you. I'm very happy here already," Kylie said. She felt her smile was a pale effort, considering how she felt.

" Good," he said as she withdrew her hand. The smile reached his eyes for a moment before he turned away. " Don't let them work you too hard," he added, then went back to the table to join his mother. " Everything been all right while I've been away? " he asked.

Kylie felt dismissed, yet she was relieved now he had moved away. Now she could *breathe*.

Beyond Brad, Tom Flynn was making further facial grimaces and radioing some kind of psychic message to which Kylie was wilfully blind.

" Thank you very much," she managed to murmur to Brad Coulsell's back and immediately turned round to begin pouring the tea.

" Demure and self-effacing," she said to herself. " Just keep it that way, Rosemary Kylie. As for Tom Flynn—wait till I get him alone in the moonlight! "

This last decision eased the tension in her. Suddenly it was fun even to be *thinking* about getting a young man alone in the moonlight.

Ray, a cup and saucer in her hand, had gone back to the table in the centre of the room and once again they were all talking business concerning Brad's recent trip. Yet somehow Brad being there made it all different. He might have been alone in the room. Everyone else seemed to dwindle in the shadow of his personality.

Tea was served, and taken even by the others who had had tea earlier. It was a kind of homecoming ritual and an accompaniment to this talk about station affairs.

Kylie sat, withdrawn a little, and kept a watchful eye on the business of refilling cups. Brad had three cups of tea but he hardly seemed to notice who had brought them, or who had taken them away.

The Coulsells were all lost in their own world and though Tom Flynn rarely joined in he listened with acute attention to everything Brad had to say. It was about cattle and buyers and the Pastoral Company; the condition of cattle as Brad had found them after the overland trek; and new machinery being imported from abroad.

Presently Kylie stood up quietly and cleared away the tea things. With the last of the cups and saucers on a tray she went to the door, then looked across the room at Nonie, who indeed had been seen but not heard through the whole proceedings.

Kylie, balancing the tray on one arm, beckoned to the child. Nonie slipped off her chair and came towards her.

" I think we'd better leave them alone, dear," Kylie said kindly. " They're going to be very busy, I can see."

" I suppose they want to get ready for dinner in *peace*," Nonie said.

Kylie laughed.

" You and I like some peace too, don't we? " she said. " We'll have it to-morrow afternoon. Come and visit me in my room—siesta time—two o'clock. Remember and don't be a minute late. We have two whole hours then till afternoon tea."

" Okay," Nonie said agreeably, but Kylie's heart was a little sore to see the child walk away. Nonie was due home for her own dinner at six o'clock and that hour was near.

*

True to her word Mrs. Coulsell did not tell Kylie what to do nor improve the shining occasion by making suggestions when Kylie was already doing something.

No sooner had the tea things been put away than everyone in the homestead began scrambling for the bathroom or the shower house. Mrs. Coulsell, looking a little flowery, went first in a silk padded dressing-gown.

" So unspeakably hot, Mother," Ray said as she saw the dressing-gown. " Just because it's the fashion you don't have to wear it up here."

" But such a pretty fashion. It's worth it between the bedroom and the bathroom, isn't it? " Kylie said when Ray was out of earshot.

" Do you really think so? Then I shall wear it willy-nilly," said Mrs. Coulsell and went gaily on her way to the bathroom.

Kylie thought it was her place to go last so she busied herself setting the table with the silver one of the lubras gave her from the dining-room cabinet. She went out into the garden and picked some oleander flowers from the shrub by the front gate. They were for the dining-room table.

" They die at once," Ray called across the veranda from her own bedroom window. " They're really not worth picking."

" Oh, what a pity," Kylie said. " They're such a heavenly pink. Never mind. I'll put them in the vase just for to-night and then take them away after dinner."

They had oleanders down south too, but Kylie did not remind Ray of this.

When everyone came into dinner she wished she hadn't made the gesture. The oleanders in their bowl looked lovely on the table, but one after the other, Mrs. Coulsell, Brad and Tom Flynn looked at them as if they'd seen a sputnik—or something.

" Oh, they are lovely," Mrs. Coulsell said, determined to be happy in the face of everyone's silent consideration of those flowers. " I've never thought of putting oleanders there before. They're such a heavenly colour they make the whole room look pretty, don't they, Brad? "

" I beg your pardon? " he said as he took his place at the head of the table. " Oh, the flowers? Very charming." He looked directly at Kylie for the first time since he had shaken hands with her when he first came in. He had a way of looking at people intently—when he did look at them. " Your idea? A very pleasant one," he said formally.

He looked at Tom Flynn.

" What colour do you call that, Tom? " He made a gesture with his hand towards the flowers.

" Pink," said Ray crossly. " Don't be silly, Brad. You know one colour from another."

" Not necessarily the name of the colour," he said dryly.

He had drawn out his chair as he spoke. Everyone was sitting down now, Tom at the far end with Kylie on his right hand. Mrs. Coulsell and Ray were on either side of Brad.

Brad picked up the carvers on the table and with the knife in one hand and the fork in the other he looked down the table at Tom. Something seemed to pass between them that was nearly a smile, and Kylie knew that Brad was having a little joke—about colour—at Ray's expense.

Her heart warmed to him. He was human, after all.

He carved the joint of roast beef dexterously, looking at each person in turn as he served them as if he, at that moment, thought only of them. Yet Kylie had a feeling this was only his good manners. Really his mind was miles away again—with station affairs.

" Who did you see at MacDougalls', Brad? " Mrs. Coulsell asked when they had all been served and the vegetable dishes had been passed around.

Brad lost the thoughtful faraway expression in his eyes and came back to the people round the table. He smiled.

" Someone you'll be very interested in," he said. " Charmian Dane."

Speaking the name was like dropping a jewel in a still pond. When the eddies ceased the jewel lay sparkling in clear water.

Ray lifted up her head quickly and Mrs. Coulsell exclaimed with obvious pleasure.

" Charmian! " she said. " How lovely."

" And looking just that," said Brad.

" She always does," said Ray. " Did you invite her to come on to Rock Hill? "

" Of course he did," said Tom Flynn from the end of the table. " You don't suppose he would let an opportunity like that go by? "

" Did you, Brad? " Ray insisted, impatiently.

He gave his sister a smile.

" As Tom said—of course I did. I had to have some bribe in order to keep you home a little longer."

" There you are, Ray," her mother said. " Now you can't go back to the south. You wouldn't let Charmian come for a visit when you're away, would you? "

" I wasn't thinking of going until the Pastoralists' Ball date," Ray said coldly. " Certainly not until Miss Brown has settled down, anyway. In any case if I can't persuade Charmian to come before I go south for the ball I'm sure Brad can."

Tom Flynn winked at Kylie and Kylie wished she knew just who was Charmian Dane. Perhaps somebody would say in a minute.

Brad, however, changed the subject.

" The other personality of interest I met——" he said in his voice that drawled just a little when he was meaning to make an impact with his words.

" Old Jodrill, the fossicker," Tom Flynn finished for him.

" No. Someone just as interesting," said Brad. " The Whip Man."

Tom raised his eyebrows with interest.

" Heading this way? Still on that old bicycle? "

" Heading this way. Still on the bicycle; and still refusing a lift."

" The Whip Man spends his life walking round Australia, pushing his bike because it's loaded with his gear; making and selling stockwhips to every station that will give him a week's rations," Tom Flynn explained to Kylie.

" Pushing a bicycle? " asked Kylie, puzzled, and thinking of the hundreds of empty semi-desert miles she had flown over in the plane.

" On his *bicycle*," Ray said crossly. " Why the stockmen encourage him by buying his whips, I don't know."

" Because he makes whips better than they do," said Brad quietly. " He uses kangaroo skin and he does his own shooting and plaiting." He looked at his mother. " You can expect him here in a few days, I'm afraid. There'll be bargaining and whip-cracking down at the stockrails as long as the old chap stays."

Ray had been going to say something but Brad anticipated her and quietly cut her off. He looked at Kylie in that intent way that made his eyes seem darker than they were.

" We are not so very isolated here," he said. " What with the Whip Man and Charmian Dane we're bound to have a party. And a party means everyone coming from our neighbouring stations." His eyes, quite innocent of any expression now, turned back to Ray.

" Right? " he said.

Kylie laughed in her heart, as she knew that Tom Flynn was doing too. How clever Brad was! So quietly and dexterously he had presented Ray with someone she loved or admired in the form of Charmian Dane and a party too. Everything to keep her home a little longer and please her mother; and something to make her forget her intolerance of the Whip Man.

Oh, Brad, she thought. *But you're very nice to know.*

No wonder Tom Flynn had said he had " a kinda way with him."

" Lastly," said Brad, " and just to spoil this excellent dinner and take the colour out of those flowers in the middle of the table—we've a valuator coming. How and when I don't yet know but if he's as astute as most valuators are he'll hear about the party and arrange to be here in time."

" Oh blow! " said Ray. " That's because of the Bentley estate being wound up, I suppose."

" Now you tell me your news," said Brad, still barely smiling yet somehow conveying that a smile was meant.

" We haven't any news. Only Miss Brown, and you can see her for yourself. She arrived this morning."

Brad looked down the table again.

" Miss Brown? " he said mildly. " I thought her name was Kylie."

" Of course it is," said Mrs. Coulsell gladly. " We must call her Kylie. Miss Brown is too stupid. I mean calling her Miss Brown is too stupid. Not the name, of course."

Tom Flynn managed to get in another tantalising eyebrow dance in Kylie's direction but Brad was looking down the table at her quite steadily, that *meant* smile still at the back of his eyes.

" Is that all right, Kylie? " he asked.

" Of course," she said. " I'm so glad . . ."

" And you know all our Christian names? " Brad continued. " Good. Now which of you two girls is going to make the coffee? " He looked from Ray to Kylie and back again.

" Both of us," said Kylie, pushing back her chair and standing up. She smiled at Ray. " You boil and I'll mix," she said. " I found only instant coffee in the pantry before dinner."

It was a challenge Ray couldn't have refused. Somehow a request from her brother was an order and however wilful Ray might be on other occasions she was not wilful for long with Brad.

Kylie decided he was a genius as she went through the dining-room door in Ray's wake.

*

The next morning Kylie took the early morning tea to the men in the office.

It was five o'clock and the eastern skyline was an eerie grey, getting ready for the dawn. The light was on in the office and Brad, dressed in his khaki drill clothes and stock boots, was dictating names to Tom Flynn from a tally board.

Outside, below the veranda and in the shadowy garden, there were dark figures of men standing about. Kylie could see the glow of one or two cigarettes and the outline of one or two other men where the open office door threw a shaft of light on them, leaning against a tree. Not far away, probably at the homestead fence, she could hear horses stamping and occasionally the rattle of bridle and bit as a horse shook his head. It seemed to her as if there was a smell of leather in the early morning air.

Brad lifted up his head as Kylie came in the door.

"Good morning," he said. "Put the tea on the table, Kylie. Thank you. We'll pour for ourselves."

His attention went back to the tally board and when Kylie had put the tray on the table she turned to go away. At the door she could not help looking back—a last glance to see if all was well on that tea-tray. Brad's grey eyes met hers over the top of the tally board. He did not smile or speak, yet somehow Kylie knew that for that one moment he thought about her and not the name of the stockman he had just called to Tom Flynn.

What had he thought? she wondered as she went along the veranda, past the black shadowy men waiting below the veranda for the day's orders.

She couldn't possibly know but at that moment she made a resolve.

Coming to this station to work for the Coulsells was a much more serious thing than following a star. That had been impetuous of her, and perhaps a little *young*. This man, Brad Coulsell, was serious. He was courteous to everyone in the homestead and he expected courtesy from them. He would not countenance immature hero-worshipping from anyone. That look, over his tally board, had said to her, whether he meant it or not, *Grow up, Kylie Brown. We both have a job of work to do here and my standards are high. Shall we get on with it?*

Yes, that was how he handled Ray, too. He told her with his eyes what to do, and he softened it with mild words.

"He *is* a genius," Kylie thought soberly, as she went into the passage and towards the pantry to make tea for Mrs. Coulsell. "And I'd rather die than let him know how silly I've been."

Tom Flynn had told her Brad could "scent a phoney a paddock away"! Well, she wasn't going to be a phoney. She was going to be serious, too. Other girls had come and gone and now Kylie knew why.

But she was going to stay.

*

That afternoon, at siesta time, Kylie heard an intermittent bumping on the veranda outside her room. She went to the screen door and there, sitting on the edge of the veranda, kicking her heels against the woodwork, was the little girl Nonie. She had been sitting there indifferent to the heat, waiting to catch another glimpse of the newcomer to the homestead. She had not forgotten Kylie's invitation to come and see her.

" Hallo! " Kylie said, opening the screen door and looking down at the small fair untidy head.

The child looked up and smiled. Her foot went on bump-bumping but her eyes took in everything of interest about Kylie.

" Would you like to come in and see my room? " Kylie asked.

Nonie looked shyly away. Kylie held the door open.

" Come on," she cajoled.

Slowly the little girl stood up, pulled her dress down and stepped up on to the veranda.

" Inside? " she asked, as if to make certain of the invitation.

" Yes, inside. Would you like to see my things? I haven't much but you might like to see them. Then sometime you could show me your things."

" I'd like to see that," Nonie said shyly, pointing to Kylie's gold bracelet.

" It's hard to take off," Kylie said. " I usually have to put soap on the inside to get it to slide over my hand. It is meant to be unlocked with a little key, but that is such a bother. That is one of the reasons I wear it most of the time."

Nonie slipped into the room and Kylie let the door close quietly behind her.

" Come over here into the light and you can look at it on my wrist," Kylie said.

They stood together by the screen wall and Kylie held out her hand. Nonie put out a finger and touched the inch-wide gold bracelet.

" What's that on it? " she asked.

" It's called scroll work. It was made by a goldsmith in London a long time ago. A goldsmith is an artist who works with tools on gold."

" What's that writing inside it? "

" That's my name. See——"

Kylie held her hand in a way that the inscription on the inside of the bracelet might be read. Suddenly she dropped her arm. She had forgotten. The inscription inside the bracelet read—*Rosemary Kylie Bentley.*

" I must never do that again," she thought. " Never show anyone my bracelet."

For a long moment Kylie forgot the small girl beside her, still looking with delight at the bracelet. Should she take it off and hide it away with other mementoes of her past?

" Haven't you got a bracelet? " she said absently to the child as she twisted her own one uncertainly around her wrist.

" No."

" Then we must use some beads. They're old necklaces Mrs. Coulsell told me to do something useful with this morning —lots of them: and haven't been used for years. We'll make you a lovely bracelet."

" I want one that shines," Nonie said. " Like that. And like the things on Mrs. Coulsell's mantelpiece."

" Oh, you like Mrs. Coulsell's ornaments? " Kylie said, relieved that she could take the child's attention to something else.

" Yes. She lets me rub them sometimes. But not when Ray's there."

Kylie wondered why Ray was so cold to this attractive child but knew it was not wise to question Nonie about that.

" Come and look at my dresses and my shoes," Kylie said brightly. " I love looking at other people's things, don't you? And look, my brush and hand mirror have got pictures on the back of them."

Again her heart dropped. Her brush, mirror and comb set had been given to her by her aunt for a birthday long long ago. The backs were of sterling silver and embossed with cherubs, swinging carelessly about amongst silver leafery. The Coulsells might wonder how she had come to own anything so unusual.

Her circumstances were unusual, weren't they?

Like the bracelet, Kylie would not put them away. No, she must have something of her own! These, and the bracelet, were the only real possessions she had ever had, other than her inexpensive clothes in Horace Bentley's house. She had loved them.

Nonie was holding the brush with one hand and tracing the outline of the cherubs with her finger.

" Sort-of angels, aren't they? " she said brightly.

" Baby angels, I think," said Kylie. " Now I'll put them away safely inside my cupboard. Look, here are my dresses. Not many, I'm afraid, but they're quite nice, aren't they? I bought three new ones to come here. I hadn't had a new dress for years."

" I've got four dresses."

" Will you show me them sometime? "

" There's this one," said Nonie, holding out the skirt of her dress by the hem. She looked up anxiously into Kylie's face. Would the crumpled and somewhat faded gingham pass muster?

" That's a very nice dress for running round the homestead," Kylie said emphatically. " I like checks best of all for day-time. Next time I get a new dress I'm going to have a check. Just like that."

A loud clear sound echoed around and through the house.

" That's afternoon tea," said Nonie. She went reluctantly towards the door. " I have to go now."

" To have your afternoon tea? "

" Yes. Down at the storehouse. I'm not allowed to eat in the homestead. Except sometimes when Brad brings me up."

" Brad? "

" I'm going to marry him when I grow up," Nonie said, then blushed scarlet. She dashed through the screen door, off the veranda and away down the cement path, covered in confusion.

Ah, thought Kylie. So he stole all hearts. Even that of a small child!

*

A week passed and the atmosphere in the homestead was pleasant and homely. Ray was out on the run a good deal of the time. She seemed so much to love this side of station life that Kylie wondered at her other side which felt some kind of fascination for the south.

" It's the loneliness," Mrs. Coulsell said a little sadly. " She seems to think she's spending the best years of her life in a vacuum."

" A nice vacuum," thought Kylie. " It contains a modern homestead and much riding out on the run every day." To

Kylie it was a world full of people but she could not say this because it might imply a criticism of Ray.

Kylie liked best the nights when Tom Flynn came to dinner. He was kind, amusing, and made her feel truly part of the family circle.

His manner seemed to say:

"Don't forget my advice about the boss. One coy look too many and, much as Mrs. Coulsell likes you and needs you, you'll be out on your dear sweet pretty neck. They've been through the soup course before and know the flavour."

All this was conveyed with no more than a flick of his eyebrow, an occasional admonitory smile.

Yes, Tom Flynn alone made life on the station happy.

CHAPTER FOUR

IT WAS the day after Mrs. Coulsell had made her remark about Ray thinking she lived in a vacuum that Ray caught the heel of her riding boot in one of the tendrils of the trailing creeper by the front veranda step.

Kylie had discovered these green twining stems were stronger than rope. She had tried to pick some of them and when she couldn't break them had gone to the tool rack on the kitchen veranda for a pair of small secateurs.

Meantime Ray, running out of the front door and down the veranda steps, had caught her foot in the tendril Kylie had pulled loose.

Ray fell badly, and her scream could be heard all over the house. In a minute wire doors were banging everywhere. The lubras ran from the kitchen, Kylie ran the shortest way, into the garden and round the house. Mrs. Coulsell was coming through the front door as Kylie reached Ray, who was lying on her back on the path and crying out with the pain in her right foot.

While Kylie was trying to remove Ray's stockboot without hurting her, Mrs. Coulsell was scolding the lubras. Now, instead of perpetual smiles and laughter, they were all tears.

"Go and get the leather knife," she said. "Ray's only hurt her foot. . . ."

Ray stopped crying and lifted her shoulders from the ground.

" Only hurt my foot! " she raged. " My ankle's broken. Leave the boot alone, Kylie. You're too clumsy. . . ."

" We'll cut it off in a minute, Ray," her mother said sooth-ingly. " Be patient, dear. How on earth did you do it? "

" That damn' piece of creeper. Who pulled it down? "

Kylie straightened herself and looked with dismay at the trailing stems. She looked up and caught Mrs. Coulsell's eyes over Ray's head. Mrs. Coulsell shook her head beseechingly.

" Don't tell Ray *now*," that headshake said, quite clearly.

It was twenty minutes later that they got Ray inside, on to the lounge in the sitting-room, and the stock boot cut away.

The ankle had come up in a black and blue swelling. Mrs. Coulsell had not been a station wife most of her life without knowing something of first aid. While Kylie held the leg, she gently felt the injury with anxious searching fingers.

" Bowls . . . hot and cold water . . . separately," she told the lubras.

" What can I do? " asked Kylie.

" You'll have to fetch Brad, or Tom Flynn," said Mrs. Coulsell. " There may be a small ankle bone broken here. . . ."

" Oh no! " wailed Ray. " Get on to the transceiver, Mother. Ask the Flying Doctor . . ."

" Darling, I'm not going to bring him out here if it's no more than a sprain. I'm not sure, that's all. Brad or Tom will know. They've doctored hundreds of sprained ankles and broken bones. But don't worry, darling. I will ask the doctor but I must wait till it's his proper session time. It's not *urgent*, you see. . . ."

Ray turned her impatient head to Kylie.

" Well, go and get Brad," she said wildly. " Can't you hurry, Kylie? "

Kylie was standing mute and anxious.

Go and get Brad? The only way to get Brad was on a horse or in a car and she couldn't ride a horse or drive a car.

" Yes, there's a good girl," Mrs. Coulsell said to Kylie. Her head was still bent, her fingers still straying delicately over the ankle.

" You'd better take Goldie. She's always left in the saddling yard in case of emergencies. Even the jeep wouldn't be safe in the creek gully. Goldie will go anywhere."

The Coulsells were station people and it simply didn't

occur to them there was any grown person in the world who couldn't ride a horse.

"Mrs. Coulsell . . ." Kylie began lamely. "I don't think . . ."

"No, don't think, dear. Just go, or we'll have Ray making herself ill with worry. After all, a broken bone, even a small one—if it's that—can put her to bed for quite a while."

"I'm going down south for the Pastoralists' Ball," said Ray. If she'd been a small child, standing, and her foot not injured, she would have stamped both feet. "What are you waiting for, Kylie? *Go and get Brad.*"

Kylie went out on to the side veranda, the shortest way to the saddling yard.

What did she say? What did she do? It was all her fault. No wonder Mrs. Coulsell had cautioned her to say nothing just yet. Ray would have lifted the roof, if she had known her accident had been caused by someone else's carelessness. She would have to know in time, of course, but at the moment even Kylie wasn't worrying about that. She was worrying about how to ride a horse.

Mrs. Craddock with whom Nonie lived? Nonie herself? The day she had made a bead bangle with Kylie's help she had said she rode horses when she was three. The lubras?

Kylie tried them all.

The lubras could ride but none of them would go to the part of Creek Gully where Brad was mustering bullocks. It was forbidden ground because one of their tribe had died there.

Kylie ran madly down the station square to the Craddock cottage. It was empty, and then Kylie remembered Nonie had told her she was going with the stockmen's wives for a bush picnic.

Where?

Kylie hadn't any idea.

The blacksmith was old and lame; the windmill man was out at one of the bores miles from the homestead. There was not a native in sight.

"I'll ketch Goldie for you, miss," Smithy said. "An' saddle 'er up. She'll take you any place. Good as gold. That's why she got 'er name. Just git up and sit on her. She'll take you."

"But which way do I go?"

"Git up. Hitch on yer water-bag. Don't never go anywhere in the outback without yer water, miss. I'll put some tucker in the saddle-bag, an' Goldie's water-bag, too."

" How long will it take me to get there? " Kylie asked, feeling desperate. " I don't know the way."

" Way's easy. Straight down the run an' keep facin' north. At yore pace, sometimes walkin', sometimes canterin', ought to git there two o'clock. Stick to the canter, miss. 'S'easier thun trottin'.' "

" How do I know which is north? " Kylie asked. She looked up at the sky, colourless and directionless, in the haze of heat.

" Well, mos' people jes' say to theirselves they's goin' north, and goes thataway. I guess with you townies it's different. Well, what you better do is keep lookin' back. Git the homestead in line with thet bluff uv rocks way back there. That'd be about south. Then you jes' go the opposite way. See? "

Kylie nodded though she wasn't the least bit confident.

" Then when you sees trees in front keep goin' to the trees. Thet'll be Creek Gully. Then yer jes' keep goin' down the gully, an' sooner or later you'll git to where they're drivin' bullocks."

So easy to a station man, so frightening to Kylie!

" Well, now I'll jes' give you a shove up, miss. An' you'd better take this here hat. Belongs to Tom Flynn, I reckon. You can't go out there wivout a hat and seems like if yer goin' to hurry yer ain't got time to go back to the homestead."

" No, I haven't," thought Kylie. " I couldn't face Mrs. Coulsell and Ray after all the time I've wasted already."

*

It didn't take Kylie long to get used to riding Goldie. If her errand hadn't been caused by an accident she would have been thrilled. It was a little painful now and again but it was nothing to the sense of achievement in that she was actually riding a horse; had no fear of falling off and even if she was doing it badly she was more sorry for Goldie than herself. How the dear little mare must be regretting that townies ever came to Rock Hill!

Like swimming, riding a horse only took confidence. Goldie's kind of horse, anyway. Or so it seemed to Kylie in her innocence.

Nevertheless she was cautious enough not to try Goldie in a gallop. That way she *might* come off.

Kylie did not have a watch and it seemed hours before she saw the trees, then finally came to the gully.

The gully was two steep sides of rocky ground leading down to a red clay-like creek bed. There was no sign that water had ever been in that bed, except where there was earth between the rocks, smooth and water-marked. The trees had immensely tall slim trunks and the branches and leaves at the top reached only for light and air.

" Jes' keep goin' down the gully," Smithy had said.

Kylie let Goldie pick her way over smooth, water-rounded rocks; over small dried waterfalls and down again in dry pools and miniature billabongs which, when the Wet came, would fill up.

Kylie was pleased she had given Goldie her own judgment for it was quite clear the mare knew exactly where she was going. She had been here before, and often.

No wonder Brad always left Goldie in the saddling paddock against emergencies! The little horse would carry anyone faithfully—even a beginner. She probably knew the entire station run, the whole two hundred and fifty thousand acres of it.

The sun beat down relentlessly and when Kylie, shading her eyes, looked up towards it, she could see it in the western arc. It must be long past midday.

Rather pleased with herself, Kylie realised from the position of the sun she must now be travelling west. In a minute she would stop and have a drink. Her mouth had been parched for a long time but she had been reluctant to rein in Goldie for fear she mightn't know how to let the little horse get going again.

She had confidence now. She tugged both reins gently and Goldie instantly came to a stop. As Kylie twisted in her saddle and leaned over to release the water-bag, she felt Goldie start and rear back her head.

" Steady! " Kylie said, feeling very professional.

Goldie, however, would not steady. She shook her head. Her ears were pointed and Kylie could feel a shiver going through her muscles.

Uneasy, Kylie abandoned her attempt to loosen the water-bag, and loosened the reins. Goldie bent her head forward and down to tug against them and then, throwing back her head again, began to pick her way over the rocks. She was shivering.

Kylie was bewildered and a little alarmed. Even in her inexperience she knew the little horse was afraid.

Of what? Kylie wondered. Could this be the place where the lubras' tribal relation had died? And did horses have these superstitions too?

Goldie went on carefully, slipping on the stones as she had not done before, throwing up her head, her ears pointed all the time.

" At least she's going in the right direction," thought Kylie. She began to be as nervous as the horse. If only they could round the bend and see bullocks. If only Brad would hear them coming . . . and *come*.

At the thought of Brad a lump came in her throat. This was nothing to do with Brad the magical. It was to do with someone who would come and take this situation in hand.

Goldie was trembling so much now that Kylie was afraid she would miss a foothold. She herself dared not get off, either to give herself a drink—and thirst was really worrying her—or try to find out what was worrying Goldie.

Kylie closed her eyes and said a little prayer.

" *Brad!* If you can hear me the way natives can hear people coming, please come to me. Oh, not for me, but because of Ray's foot. I did it . . . so I must get help."

They had been approaching a big rock when Kylie closed her eyes and now, suddenly, Goldie stopped. She gave a shrill whinny.

Kylie opened her eyes.

For a moment she couldn't see why Goldie had stopped, then she saw the sun catching the shining edge of something beyond the rock.

It was the spokes of a bicycle that was lying on the ground! Kylie could see only the front wheel. The rest was obscured by the rock.

If she got off Goldie, would she ever get on again?

" Please, Goldie," she begged, patting her neck. " *Please*."

The little horse edged, step by step, around the rock, then stopped. Propped up against the rock was a very ancient man. His whiskers came down to his chest and his face was a pattern of red-brown skin between bushes of hair. On his head was an incredibly old hat, with a fly veil, weighed down by a fringe of corks hung from the brim. In spite of his age, his burnt-out scrub of a face, his eyes were the bluest Kylie had ever seen. He lifted one gnarled stained old hand and then let it fall beside him.

Kylie had to get down now. The old man was injured or ill. Clearly he could not speak.

Once again Kylie said a little prayer and then, grasping the pommel with both hands, she shook the stirrups free and eased herself over the saddle and slipped clumsily to the ground. She remembered to hold Goldie's reins. Whatever else happened she must hold on to Goldie.

She led the horse forward. At the back of her mind she registered that the little animal was no longer afraid. She was not shivering any more and she came readily with Kylie.

Kylie bent over the queer old man.

" Are you all right? " she asked.

He lifted his hand again and pointed to his half-open mouth. He closed his eyes and then opened them to watch her. He watched her as if he was looking at something far, far away and in which he had not very much interest.'

" Thirst," thought Kylie.

Now she began to move very quickly. She slipped Goldie's reins over a jutting spike of rock and unhooked her water-bag. She unscrewed the stopper and bent over the old man. She remembered out of her own folklore knowledge of Australia that you never let a thirsty man drink or eat freely. Little by little was the rule.

The stopper had a hollow centre so Kylie poured a few drops of water into it. Then making sure the bag was safe against a rock, she knelt down and lifted the old man's fly veil. His lips were as dry and parched as the dry sun-baked earth.

Kylie eased the few drops of water into his mouth. At first he could not swallow but then she saw the muscles of his creviced old throat move convulsively. He had swallowed. His eyes told her to give him more but she waited a few minutes.

Presently, after Kylie had given several of these tiny drinks, she remembered that she too was thirsty, and took a swig straight from the bag. She unhooked the wide-mouthed bag on the other saddle hook which Smithy had said was Goldie's drink bottle. She gave the mare about a third of it. It wasn't much but Goldie seemed satisfied to have her mouth wetted.

" How good she is," Kylie thought. " She knew he was

here. She was not afraid of the old man, only that he was injured."

She sat down beside the rock and every now and again gave the old man a few more drops of water. He was better now and his eyes were an even more vivid blue, and very alert. Presently, when he could be bothered, he would talk.

Kylie looked around.

In the place where there ought to be a seat on the bicycle was a pack. It was covered and strapped by a fine light brown skin. To the crossbar of the frame were attached billy-cans, a mug, leather bags and two guns strapped side by side. On the ground was a haversack such as hikers carried. Strapped across the top of the haversack and tied horizontally together were several leather-plaited stockwhips.

" The Whip Man," Kylie thought.

She turned and looked at the old man. Brad had said he walked from station to station all round the north, pushing that bicycle and selling whips. How could he have come to such a pass?

She got up and went to the bicycle and looked it over. There was an empty water-bottle lying on the ground and another that looked as if it still had quite a lot of water in it. The stopper was wedged in tightly. She lifted it up.

The old man suddenly made a croaking noise in his throat.

" Poison," he said.

Kylie put the water-bottle down as if she had been stung. She went back to her seat by the rock.

" You're the Whip Man, aren't you? " she said. " How do you know the water is poisoned? "

He found it painful to speak so Kylie gave him a few more drops of water.

" Took a swig. Knocked me sick. 'S why I'm sittin' here. Could have got to homestead . . . only sick."

" Why didn't you throw the water away, if it is poisoned?"

" Want to see what's in it. Knew someone'd find me. Natives must be right outback of run. They'd uv known."

Kylie nodded.

" Is it safe for me to give you something to eat? "

He shook his head, and pressed his hand to his stomach.

" Sick," he said.

Kylie was about to give him a little more water but he shook his head.

" 'S'nough," he said. " More later."

He was a bushman and he knew best, much as he must have wanted to drink the whole bag, Kylie thought.

He closed his eyes and dropped his head a little on one side but Kylie could see he was only going to sleep. She got up and made him comfortable, putting his swag near his head and helping him to ease over sideways so he could rest his head on it. Presently he was quite sound asleep.

What did she do now?

She looked at Goldie but Goldie, like the Whip Man, knew the law of the country. She had dropped her head and was having a doze, too. " We stay here," that restful attitude quite clearly said.

Kylie leaned against the rock as the old man had done and like the old man pulled Tom Flynn's felt hat forward on her head so that it would shade her eyes from the glare. All she could see before her was the rocky upland of the creek bank with its spindly spikes of grass sprouting between rocks and thin burnt-out stems of ancient and tired bushes.

There wasn't any choice really, she thought. Nevertheless she felt a little sick herself when she thought of Ray.

It had been her fault. How had she ever come to leave that stem of creeper lying by the step? If Ray had a broken bone in her foot and couldn't go south for that ball she would never forgive Kylie. Up there at the homestead they would be waiting for Brad or Tom Flynn to come home and do some doctoring. Ray was in great pain, too.

Of course Mrs. Coulsell would give her aspirin or something. . . .

Kylie thought of Ray lying on that lounge, waiting and suffering and suffering and waiting.

" But I haven't any choice," she thought, turning her head and looking at the Whip Man. " Ray's pain is less than this old man's need."

Oddly enough she wasn't afraid of the eerie loneliness for she believed what had been told her about the natives. They would know, and they would bring help.

She thought of tying Goldie's rein to her saddle and seeing if the little mare would go home for help but she decided against that. Goldie was her own only lifeline, if the old man became desperately ill, or worse, died.

She glanced at him again. He was asleep, and peacefully.

*

All through the long afternoon Kylie sat there, her back to

the rock, and waited. She thought she might fry up, like bacon, on a stone but fortunately the westering sun edged round the rock and presently they were sitting in shade. The old man, even in his extremity, had not forgotten his bushcraft. He had sat himself where presently there would be shade.

Now and again Kylie gave him some water but after each dose he went to sleep again.

There was nothing to do but wait. If only she had known how far that bullock muster was! If only she had any idea of distance as she rode a horse!

"If the muster turns out to be only a mile or two away I shall die of shame," she thought. "And of course Ray will not only hate me, she will laugh at me."

It was Goldie's instinct to stay. So Kylie stayed.

The sun went down with a fantastic blaze of glory in the western sky and with its going down came the silence of sundown. Everything stood still, all the small creatures were silent. The lizards on the rocks went back to their cubbyholes and not even a grass rustled or a leaf turned over.

Kylie thought she had never known real silence before. Or such emptiness in the world. She was alone in it with Goldie and the Whip Man.

The sky went black and the stars came out in it like brilliant lamps.

Somewhere up there the spacemen had gone. Kylie wondered what it would be like to swing about up there among the stars.

And she wondered if, perhaps, no one was coming after all. Then she too fell asleep.

*

It was Goldie whinnying that woke her. Suddenly there was no more of that vast silence. Another horse was stumbling and clattering amongst the foot rocks. The shape of a man on horseback came round the far edge of the rock. He was a black silhouette against a blue-black sky as he swung himself from his saddle. His boots clattered and slipped on the rocks as he came towards Kylie and the Whip Man.

Kylie was too stiff and dazed to move; afraid now that she had done the wrong thing and so was afraid to speak.

The man leaned over her and flashed on a torch. The beam of light swung from the Whip Man to Kylie, then rested dazzlingly on her face. She could see nothing but its blinding light.

She knew it was Brad. Half of her heart cried with relief that it had been he who had found them. The other half waited.

If she had done wrong in staying instead of going for help, she hoped he would say so now. Then it would be over.

He didn't speak at once. Instead he leaned forward and took Kylie's chin in his hand and tilted up her face. There was no torch now and only the stars made a light in the darkness. She could see an edge of light in Brad's eyes, and they were puzzled, but kind.

"Good heavens!" he said. "And Smithy told me you couldn't even ride a horse!"

Kylie felt the tears of relief smarting in her eyes.

"The Whip Man?" she managed to gulp. Had she or hadn't she done the right thing?

"Right as rain," came a gruff voice beside her. "Jes' been sleepin'. Brad, git that girl up on yer horse and git her away to the homestead. I'll walk same as I've ever done."

Brad flashed the torch at him again.

"For once, old chap, I've got you down on the ground," he said. "This time you'll do as you're told. The men are coming down the gully now. They'll make a litter and that's how you'll ride."

The old man tried to rise but found himself too weak.

"Guess I'm gettin' old," he said. "This time you win, Brad."

Brad's laugh in the darkness was kind.

"Not old," he said. "Just cantankerous. Anyhow, why not ride like royalty? After your long reign alone in the bush you've earned it."

"Git that girl up so she won't hear me bones creak," said the Whip Man.

Brad had straightened up now. He put out his hand to help Kylie get up.

"Coming?" he said.

"But Goldie . . ."

"They'll need Goldie to hump the Whip Man's gear. You'll be safe up on Joachim with me."

Kylie gave Brad her hand and then she was standing beside him. He drew his horse forward by the reins and swung himself up. Then once more he gave Kylie his hand and a minute later she was up in front of him. He put one arm round her to hold her firm and the other arm round her to take the reins in his hand.

Kylie shivered a moment and then leaned back because Brad's arm seemed to tell her with its pressure that this was the way to ride home when a man was carrying you on his horse.

"Home, Joachim!" Brad's voice said.

Kylie closed her eyes.

"When I wake up I'll know I've been dreaming," she thought.

CHAPTER FIVE

IN THE MORNING Kylie got up earlier than usual. She felt she needed that little extra bonus of time to " ease " herself; to become natural when she took in that early morning cup of tea to Brad and Tom Flynn in the office.

The return to the homestead had been quite dramatic in its way. On the long ride home Brad had not talked at all except to say once, " Sleepy? " and when she had nodded, replied: " Then lean back and go to sleep." With a natural ease and lack of self-consciousness he had helped her turn a little and rest her head more comfortably against his shoulder.

Funny, how all one's life one had wanted a shoulder to lean against; and not really known it. That ride home, to Kylie, was a moment of complete peace and happiness. She knew it would be short-lived but while it did live she gave herself up to it.

In the stables he had lifted her gently, but quite impersonally, from the saddle. Smithy and two of the stockmen were waiting with all lights full blaze in the stable.

" How's things, Brad? " one of the stockmen asked casually as if nothing momentous had happened.

" The Whip Man," Brad answered equally casually. " Down on his uppers for once. Tom Flynn and the boys are bringing him in." He turned to the blacksmith. " Take Miss Brown up to the homestead, Smithy, will you? She's had quite a day of it."

" Thank you, Brad," Kylie said, trying to be as casual as he was. Evidently, on a station, it was the thing to handle matters of life and death this way. One just didn't let anyone know how one felt.

Brad had turned away, helping unsaddle Joachim. He

glanced round at Kylie as she thanked him. His brief smile flashed, but it was strictly impersonal.

"That's okay," he said. "Hope the ride home wasn't too rough."

Kylie patted the horse's neck and said, "Thank you too, Joachim," and then went up towards the homestead with the blacksmith. The yard light was on and the two white cockatoos in their cages by the back door woke, lifted their heads, made the kind of screeching noise that said they had no patience with people who left lights on in the night and tramped across the gravel square with heavy boots, keeping them awake.

"How'd she go? Meanin' Goldie?" was all Smithy asked.

"She's a darling," said Kylie briefly. "She did all you said she'd do, and more."

"Sure. She would." They had reached the screen door and he opened it for her. "Put some salts in yer bath, miss. Thet way you won't be stiff in the mornin'. G'night."

"Good night, Smithy," Kylie said. "And thank you."

Lights were on in the homestead and Mrs. Coulsell came hurrying to the passage door and on to the back veranda.

"There you are, Kylie. My goodness me, what a fright you gave us. Where have you been, child?" The little nervous puckering of Mrs. Coulsell's mouth showed how anxious she had been.

Kylie touched her arm to reassure her and explained as briefly as possible.

"Was Ray in great pain?" she asked anxiously. "I didn't know quite what to do. It seemed as if the Whip Man might be worse than Ray. I thought I ought to stay."

Mrs. Coulsell led Kylie in. She had her hand on the girl's arm and seemed full of kindly, solicitous care.

"Well," she said, shaking her head judiciously, "a sprained ankle is painful, you know. Don't worry, Kylie." She dropped her voice. "I sometimes think a little adversity is good for all of us. Anyhow, there was no broken bone, though Ray did have to wait till the men came in at sundown. She's very cross with me because I wouldn't call the Flying Doctor out. He can't land here, you know. He would have had to drop down at Harveys' and overland by car. I did talk to him on the air, of course."

They had reached the living-room and Mrs. Coulsell took the old felt hat from Kylie.

"My goodness me," she smiled. "If that isn't Tom Flynn's worst piece of headgear! Whatever would the Whip Man have thought of you?"

"You ought to see his own headgear," said Kylie. She sank thankfully down on the lounge. Yes, indeed, she must put salts in her bath to-night. Every muscle in her body ached. Meantime she was wondering what Brad, not the Whip Man, thought of that hat.

"Ray's in bed," Mrs. Coulsell said. "But she's got her lights on. Perhaps you'd better go and see her when you've had some tea, dear. Tom fixed her ankle for her. He came in half an hour before Brad."

"I'll go now," Kylie said, getting up awkwardly, then had to steady herself against the arm of the lounge. Oh, those aching bones! "I must go and see Ray," she said gravely as Mrs. Coulsell demurred. "I pulled those creeper stems down. I've got to own up now, or she'll think I'm not very honest."

"Don't let her upset you, dear. These things happen, and I'm afraid Ray is not a very good patient. . . . But she has been in pain, poor child."

"And you too have felt the nervous tension," Kylie thought regretfully.

She went to Ray's room and tapped on the half-open door. "Come in."

Ray was sitting up in bed; a bedside lamp, through a very pretty pink shade, was casting a warm glow over Ray's face. She had on an attractive nylon bed-jacket. Her hair was gleaming like a halo because the light from the lamp was shining through it. She had a book open on her lap and she looked up as Kylie came in. Her eyes were bright and full of an angry kind of curiosity.

"Just where have you been?" she said. "Half the homestead has been out looking for you."

There was not a word about how hard it might be for a stranger to find her way around a cattle run. Kylie took it for granted Ray did not know she, Kylie, had never before ridden a horse.

"I didn't quite get lost," Kylie explained. "I found the Whip Man. He was sick. So I had to stay with him."

Ray shut her book with a snap.

"You stayed with the Whip Man when you knew I had sprained my ankle? Possibly broken it?" There was a childish rage in her voice. " I suppose you were dramatically taking care of him so that Brad or Tom would ride out for you? They've got other things to do, Kylie, and there have been other girls here who go in for stunts."

Kylie flushed and bit her lip. She was dusty and dishevelled and standing there at the foot of Ray's bed felt exactly the same as she had once felt when Uncle Horace had sent for her to demand why she had dared to want to go out to the cinema. " Isn't this home good enough that you have to run away from it? " he had asked. " Who's been putting ideas in your head? The servants? I shall dismiss them."

The sheer injustice of it rendered Kylie silent; then as now.

She would never dare tell Ray, Brad had brought her home on his horse. She hoped no one else would say anything.

" I'm terribly sorry, Ray," she said. " I just didn't know what to do. I had to stay with the Whip Man. He was really ill."

" Nuisance that he is! " said Ray angrily. " These eccentrics who walk or ride round the outback are a hazard to the station owners. Somebody is always having to rescue them from *something*. . . ."

" Is your foot easier? " Kylie asked, trying to change the subject and because she was really anxious. How much had her failure to return with help handicapped Ray against a quick recovery?

" Sore, if you want to know," Ray answered ungraciously. " But not as bad as it was."

" I'm afraid I have another confession to make," said Kylie. " I'll be well and truly in your bad books to-night. I had been trying to pick that creeper so the fact that some of it was trailing on the ground was my fault."

Ray stared at her.

" I guessed as much," she said. " I saw the secateurs in your hand. Well, just take a look at my foot and see what you're responsible for." She threw off the sheet, the only covering on the bed, and showed her foot, resting on a small rounded pillow.

" What a beautiful piece of bandaging," Kylie exclaimed, looking at the professional job Tom Flynn had made of it. " Are they all as good at first aid as that? "

Ray looked at Kylie, speechless. She had expected pity and remorse.

Later Kylie was a little ashamed of herself, yet somehow she felt Ray had deserved that small punishment. Not for the world would Kylie have wanted Ray to injure her foot but if it had to be so she thought Ray might have been a little more gracious about an apology and definitely a little more patient as a sufferer.

Besides, she herself was smarting from that suggestion that staying out in Creek Gully with the Whip Man had been a " stunt." One to attract the attention of the men.

*

Kylie had had her tea, a bath loaded with salts; and gone to bed weary but not unhappy. In spite of Ray's anger she had something more to occupy her mind. She wanted to live again, alone in her room, the moment Brad had found her and ridden her home on Joachim.

*

The next morning she had to get back to normal. The " stunt " had to be forgotten, just as the ride home on Joachim had to be forgotten.

Kylie dressed herself and went to the kitchen to make the early morning tea. She could hear Brad's booted footsteps and later those of Tom Flynn going to the office so she knew just when to pour the boiling water into the teapot.

She made sure everything was right on the tray. The two big cups, the teapot and milk. Some hot water, sugar and the thinly sliced bread and butter.

" Now behave as if nothing happened, Kylie," she told herself.

She lifted the tray, straightened her shoulders and went out on to the veranda, around the corner to the office door. She tapped and Tom Flynn came across the room and held the screen door open for her.

Brad was bending over the table, jotting a note on the table calendar. He looked up, delivered himself of that brief smile, said " Good morning " and went on writing notes on the page before him.

Kylie expected a punctilious return to normal but not quite this anti-climax. Perhaps Brad *had* to do this sort of thing to bring girls back to normal when he had had to go out of his way to help them. Perhaps it was a technique. Whatever it was, Kylie felt the keen edge of disappointment. Suddenly in her heart there spurted a tiny flame of anger.

What with Ray reminding her of other girls and their stunts and Brad appearing to be completely disinterested in how she felt after being out in the gully for hours and hours, Kylie decided that *all* Coulsells were spoilt. It hurt her pride to think Brad had to use a studied preoccupation to protect himself from some claim she might now make on his attention.

She actually felt like the proverbial " woman scorned " and was angry because she was humiliated.

She said " Good morning " without looking at him again but gave Tom Flynn a flashing smile. After all, Tom was never unkind.

" How's the aches and pains? " asked Tom. His blue eyes laughed at her because he guessed she was hurt by Brad's lack of attention. She thought she'd die rather than let Tom know just exactly how she did feel.

She tilted her chin gaily.

" Plenty of salts in the bath," she said. " Besides, I'm tougher than you think. How is the Whip Man, Tom? "

" Fighting fit. You can't keep those old swaggies down for long. Couple of us are going out this morning to find what kind of dead animal's floating in the water-hole the Whip Man filled his bag from. Can't have any more poison casualties on our hands."

The tray was on the table and Tom was once again holding the door open for Kylie. She smiled at him again as she went through.

" See you later," she said a little perkily. She wasn't sure, because she wasn't looking, but she thought Brad jerked up his head as if something had surprised him.

Well, if Kylie being perky surprised him—not to worry. It was wonderful that he noticed Kylie at all.

Nevertheless as she walked down the veranda, she had to swallow a lump in her throat and at the same time felt a little ashamed of the smile she had given Tom and that " See you later " which might be all right for station people because to them it was just a figure of speech. A kind of salutation. They would have known, however, that to Kylie it was foreign language.

Now tea for Mrs. Coulsell and Ray.

She would be specially careful and remorseful with Ray. After all, the girl was *hurt* and was bitterly disappointed because she might not be able to go back to the south as early as she had planned.

Working round the homestead all day—a little bit at Mrs. Coulsell's beck and call over tiny things because Mrs.

Coulsell too was having something of a reaction to yesterday's events, Kylie managed to exercise her muscles so much that the stiffness wore out.

"It's like working in a heat wave," she thought. "So long as you keep going you can stand it. As soon as you lie down you can't bear it."

She did everything she could to make Ray comfortable. Fixed her pillows; brought her the magazines from the living-room; made extra tea for her; talked to her as winningly as possible, for she felt there were some nice things about Ray and if she could only win her over life in the homestead might be different.

It was a relief to have an hour with Nonie after lunch.

"I wish I could have been with you," Nonie said, sitting on the end of Kylie's bed while Kylie leaned back against her own pillows and tried to cool off with the electric fan whirring top speed on the table beside her.

"I want to see the Whip Man," Nonie said. "Daddy's told me all about him ages ago. Daddy has a stockwhip he made. It's different because it has plaits on the handle and there's two whips, one plaited on top of the other. Daddy says it's a work of art. Brad gave Mummy one when she left Rock Hill and went to Eagle Eye."

"So Mummy lived on Rock Hill once, did she?" Kylie asked casually. She thought it made Nonie happy to talk about her parents.

"She used to help Mrs. Coulsell like you do," said Nonie, smiling and swinging her legs as she sat on the end of the bed.

Something jolted Kylie's memory. On the drive from Two-way House to Rock Hill Tom Flynn had told her some joke about the girls coming to Rock Hill who fell in love with the boss being married off or sent home by Mrs. Coulsell. Could Nonie's mother be one of these?

Kylie made an attempt to banish the thought.

She was silent so long that Nonie thought she might be going to sleep.

"I'm going now," she said, slipping off the bed. "I guess you want to sleep, Kylie."

"Darling," Kylie said apologetically, "I'm so sorry."

"It's all right," said Nonie. "Next time you ride a horse I'll take you, Kylie. I'll show you how to ride so you don't get sore." She went over to the veranda door, then looked back with a conspiratorial expression on her small piquant face.

" They've locked up the Whip Man. That's why I couldn't see him yet. They locked him up so he wouldn't get up and walk around. They said he's got to rest. When they unlock him I'll come and tell you."

" Thank you, dear. I'm longing to see him, too."

" It's only so he doesn't wander round in the sun and get sick again," Nonie said by way of further explanation.

" How odd," Kylie thought as Nonie went through the door. " It isn't prisoners they lock up for their own good in this world. It's poor dilapidated brave old sundowners who want to die with their boots on."

She listened to Nonie's feet skipping along the cement path past the veranda. Suddenly she turned over and, putting her arm on the pillow, rested her forehead on it.

Charmian Dane, the beautiful girl Brad had seen at the MacDougalls' station; and now Nonie's mother! Did she, Kylie, have to put every girl known to Brad on a *list*?

" How badly I've got it," she thought unhappily. " Now I'm on the list too. If I sort-of start listing people, no wonder the Coulsells and Tom Flynn do that. It's an *awful* thing to do."

Then she told herself that of course it made Brad conceited and was the reason he put up that protective wall of disinterestedness. She wondered what he would really be like if he ever *was* interested in somebody.

Just before she dozed off she decided that the anger of the " woman scorned " was the safest role. Even safer than being good at a distance. This way she could kill her own interest. This way lay safety.

What on earth had made her follow that star?

The serpent, she decided. It was he who had started offering apples around. Not Eve, who had been blamed for everything.

Kylie was too tired and too near sleep to realise she had mixed up stars and apples in a very unmetaphorical way.

*

Brad didn't come in for dinner that night. He sent a message to the homestead to say he was having dinner with the stockmen down at the quarters.

" What he means is he's having dinner with that old swaggie of a Whip Man," Ray said crossly when Kylie told her. " He doesn't say so, of course. Brad never says what he's doing unless it suits him."

Kylie, as she put a nicely set tray on Ray's knees, decided that Ray was really very fond of her brother. Fond enough to be unwilling to share him. Hence her distrust of lovelorn girls, and her dislike of the Whip Man. She knew Brad liked him. That was enough. She was often sharp and difficult with Tom Flynn too. Perhaps this was the reason for that.

Her seasonal returns to Rock Hill from the south were more from love for Brad than for her mother. Her mother she was willing to leave to " companions," provided, of course, they didn't fall in love with Brad.

Just as they were sitting down to dinner Tom Flynn whispered an aside to Kylie.

" You know that *See you later* crack you gave me this morning? I'm taking you up on that. Come down to the workshop after dinner and I'll show you what Tom Flynn does in his spare time." There was a joke in his smile so Kylie accepted his invitation.

While they were having coffee Brad came in. He was dressed in clean clothes so whatever his dinner had been with the Whip Man he had showered and changed down at the quarters in honour of it.

" I wonder if you could spare me a few minutes in the office when we have finished coffee? " he said to Kylie. " I think we ought to go into that most awkward of all topics, the Rock Hill pay way. And there are one or two other things I would like to speak to you about."

" Yes, certainly," Kylie said, not looking at him as she stirred her coffee.

This situation of not looking at Brad, of not drawing his attention to herself, was going to be quite an exercise.

Brad signalled to Tom Flynn and the two men left the room.

" I'll see you presently, Kylie," he said as he passed her.

CHAPTER SIX

It was half an hour later, and the coffee cups had been cleared away, when Tom Flynn put his head in the door.

" You're on the carpet next," he said to Kylie. " Don't stay too long. I'll think the worst. Besides, I've a date with you myself. Come down to the workshop later. I'm in a talkative mood. *See you later.*" He laughed, pleased with himself at this last quip.

Kylie went down the long passage to the office. She did not have to knock because the door was wide open to allow a passage of cool air; and Brad heard her coming. He had risen from his seat, come round the side of the table and now offered Kylie a chair.

It was clear from his manner he was going to make no reference to what happened yesterday. This was strictly business and Brad both looked and sounded it. His manners were natural. His smile was designed to put her at ease.

" I won't keep you a moment," he said. Instead of going back to his chair, he half sat, half leaned against the edge of the table and lit himself a cigarette.

He looked at the tip of his cigarette, then at Kylie.

" Getting paid is tiresome," he said with that impersonal put-you-at-your-ease smile. " But nothing like as tiresome as not being paid." The real smile came through for a minute but Kylie had hardened her heart against it. She too had to have her defences.

He explained to her the methods of remuneration on a station. An entry would be made in her account on the station books, monthly. She could draw against it from the book-keeper, Tom Flynn, or charge any purchases she might want to make from the station stores or through Rock Hill's account with the Pastoral Agency in Perth.

" We have a balancing of books every three months," Brad said. " And the difference in your favour can be paid into a bank account if you wish it." Once again he smiled. " Meantime anything you purchase at the store or through Rock Hill account is at wholesale prices. So if you want to buy a motor-car any time just buy it through Rock Hill. You'll save twenty per cent on the deal."

" Oh no," said Kylie quickly. " I could never afford to buy anything like that."

" Never mind, we'll lend you one on the station occasionally. It's a useful thing to be able to drive a car."

He straightened himself, then walked round the table and sat down behind it.

His next question was a much tougher one. He put his right elbow on the desk and rubbed the line of his jaw with his forefinger.

" I wonder if you could help me," he said thoughtfully. He was looking beyond her and not at her now. " I am trying to trace someone and it is just possible you could help me."

His eyes came back to her. Kylie nodded her head.

" I hope I can help you," she said.

He reached forward and took another cigarette from the box and lit it.

" It's odd," he said as he flicked out the match and inhaled the cigarette smoke, " but you went to the Pastoral Agency, inquiring for a post on the day they were expecting another young lady. A firm of lawyers I have occasion to deal with referred a young woman to that agency for advice. The lawyer even rang the agency and asked them to do what they could to help this particular person. She never arrived there."

Kylie could think of nothing to say but " Oh? " She was not panicking. Something about Brad's thoughtful manner told her he did not suspect *she* was that young woman.

He shook ash into the ash-tray.

" It is purely coincidence, of course," he went on. " But you happened to apply to the agency on the same day they were expecting the other young woman to call. I can't help wondering if by any chance she recommended it to you, and therefore you know her. Or her whereabouts. Her name is Rosemary Bentley."

I haven't moved a muscle, Kylie thought. *How dead is poor Rosemary Bentley.* She was so busy contemplating this sad fact and wondering how to reply that she did not, for a moment, wonder why Brad Coulsell should be wanting to know the whereabouts of Rosemary Bentley. Perhaps the caretaker at Horace Bentley's house had spoken of her.

Perhaps someone having entry to Uncle Horace's house after she herself had left had gone off with some booty? She wondered what it would have to do with Brad, anyway. He was the manager and part-owner of a station in which Uncle Horace had had a financial interest, that was all.

Kylie simply shook her head.

" The agency advertises its posts as a rule," she said. This was better than a guess because after she had made that call she had read the newspapers, looking for alternative posts offering, and had seen the agency's advertisement.

" I thought it would be more than good luck if you happened to be a contact," Brad said with a half smile. " But I had to try."

He stood up, a sign of terminating the interview. Kylie too stood up.

" Is it—er—is it serious? " The question was out before she had time to swallow it.

" For Miss Bentley? I would say yes," he said quite coolly.

So someone had perhaps taken something from that house! Or all was not well with the way the house was left. It was big and empty a good deal of the time. The caretaker was often away, keeping an eye on Horace Bentley's other properties.

What did she do now? Confess in order to clear the ghost of her past self and put a period to vain searchings on the part of lawyers?

No. She had a clear conscience. Poor Rosemary Bentley was dead. No ignominy could touch her now. She was beyond reach, buried in the identity of Kylie Brown.

" I'm sorry I can't help you," Kylie said lamely as she went to the door.

Funny, but since she'd arrived at Rock Hill, she'd almost forgotten she had been someone else once—with a different name. She had entered a new life and it was a shock to her to realise how easily she had stepped into another role. She thought if only Uncle Horace had let her have friends, or go out and join clubs—or something—she might always have been like she was now. She never wanted to be Rosemary Bentley again.

From the door she heard Brad's last remark.

" I also am sorry you can't help me." He spoke so quietly Kylie turned round. Across the room their eyes met. His conveyed nothing. Even the searching look had gone. His face was expressionless.

Did he guess, after all?

Supposing he did, then he would think she, Kylie Brown, had left something undone about that house—or worse, taken something from it.

A bitter little smile curved the corners of her mouth. There was a great deal more than mere " booty " she could have taken from Uncle Horace's house and estate, had she wanted. There had been treasures in that house no one had known of until the valuators came in and she herself had shown them. There had been her aunt's jewellery. No one had known what, or how much, of that existed!

She twisted the bracelet on her wrist. Then, realising what she did, her eyelids lowered and she looked down at its gleaming gold.

This bracelet—and my clothes—so few of them too. That was all I brought away with me.

Let him, or the lawyers, or the agency—or even the police, if they were in it, think what they would. She would never tell anyone, voluntarily, what had happened to Rosemary Bentley.

" I'm sorry," she said again.

" Don't be sorry, *Kylie*," he said. " I am sure you would have helped me if you could."

Had he underlined that " Kylie " or was it her imagination?

" Good night," she said quietly.

Unexpectedly his last words were kind.

" Thank you, Kylie, for helping the Whip Man," he said. " It was very brave of you."

Suddenly as she went through the door tears smarted in her eyes. For some stupid beastly reason she would have liked to tell him the truth. Not the others, but Brad. He was quite kind behind that barrier of reserve. Why did she have to turn away from him as from an enemy? Why did she have to be on guard against him when it would have been so wonderful to be allowed to tell him of her past?

Or was she only being on guard against herself?

*

She went down the veranda steps through the moonlight towards Tom Flynn's workshop.

On the other side of the gravel square outside the garden fence was a series of outhouses. It was easy to find where Tom Flynn worked because, the light being on, Kylie could see him through the wire screen. He was standing by a bench, carving something small and fragile with a fine-bladed knife.

" Ha! " he said, looking up as Kylie pushed open the screen door. " Why so sad? You didn't get the sack, did you? "

Kylie made an attempt to recover her usual brightness.

" No, I didn't get the sack. I was told to refer to you about my finances."

"That would sadden anyone," said Tom, going on with his carving. "The subject of finance, I mean. Not the fact of being referred to me."

Kylie drew out a wooden chair and sat down by the bench and watched Tom Flynn's hands. They were long slim hands and handled the knife and tiny piece of woodwork with great dexterity.

"Why does finance sadden you, Tom?"

"Not enough of it. Like I told you."

Kylie sighed.

"We all suffer from that, I suppose."

Tom looked up, then pointed with the blade of his knife to Kylie's bracelet.

"You could always hock that. Where did you get it, young 'un? From the man who broke your heart?"

Kylie had forgotten that silly story she had told Tom Flynn.

"Really, Tom, the way you put two and two together and get five amazes me. I've had this bracelet years and years; before I met anyone capable of breaking my heart. Since childhood, in fact."

"Someone must have been awful rich in your childhood."

"Someone was," said Kylie gravely. "And gave me that bracelet. That someone is dead now."

Tom looked up again, his eyebrows flexed.

"Sorry," he said. "I didn't mean to hurt your feelings. Am I forgiven?"

Kylie nodded.

"It doesn't matter, Tom, except that my past history is dotted with deaths. The memory of them kind-of hurts."

"Sorry again, and then again. Will not offend in the future."

Tom leaned over the bench and pushed a packet of cigarettes towards Kylie.

"Light two," he said. "One for you and one for me."

Kylie took two cigarettes from the packet, lit one and as she held it towards Tom he leaned forward as if to take it. Kylie too leaned forward, without thought but as a moth is drawn to the warming light of a candle, and Tom kissed her gently. It was a sweet kiss, tender and kind, and Kylie's heart suddenly went out to Tom. No one had ever kissed her before but she did not think of this. It was as if both of them, for some indescribable reason a little sad, comforted one another with a kiss. Why Tom, with all his brash manner should be a little sad Kylie did not know. Nevertheless she knew at this moment that that was how he felt.

Tom took the cigarette in his mouth and as he inhaled the smoke he looked sideways and comically at Kylie.

" No tears about broken hearts? " he said.

" No tears," said Kylie.

As they spoke both seemed to know intuitively that someone was standing in the open doorway of the workshop. They turned their heads. It was Brad.

He took out a cigarette as he came across the floor towards them. He picked up the piece of miniature furniture Tom had been carving.

" Nonie again? " he asked, smiling slightly, making an effort to ease the unexpected tension.

" Sure," said Tom. " That's only one chair. There's six more to come. Next thing she'll want the whole darn' dolls' house furnished."

" I'm afraid I came to impose another one on you, Tom." Brad looked at the other man through his clear cold grey eyes. " We'd better put up a solid notice by that water-hole where the Whip Man filled his bag. The boys have cleaned it out of that poison weed but it won't be safe till the Wet gives it a proper sluicing." ·

" Warning to thirsty travellers," said Tom wryly. " Six foot by four and with iron stakes four feet underground. Shall do."

" I'd be grateful if you would," Brad said. " We don't want any more heroics for quite awhile."

Kylie flushed. The deep red dye stained her throat and face and when it receded it left her pale. Tom looked at her in surprise but Brad, not noticing, turned away towards the door.

" Good night to you both," he said and went out.

There was silence in the workshop as Kylie and Tom listened to those firm receding footsteps as Brad went back to the homestead.

Tom looked at Kylie with raised eyebrows as if he wanted an explanation for that overwhelming blush. The time for Kylie to have blushed would have been when Brad came in. The odds were ten to one on ... in Tom's parlance ... that Brad saw that gentle and unhurried kiss.

Kylie shook her head mutely. Neither Tom nor Brad

would have known that other cutting remark . . . so closely related in meaning.

There have been other girls here who go in for stunts.

They had been Ray's words but evidently this was the way of thinking of all members of the family.

It was hard to reconcile this wish of Brad's about "heroics" with his last words to Kylie in the office. Then he had thanked her for looking after the Whip Man. He had probably been sarcastic and she had been too naïve to know it.

Tom thought now was the right time to change the subject and take everyone's mind off kisses, if that was what was troubling Kylie and causing wrongly-timed blushes.

"To-morrow I'll take you out to the water-hole," he said. "You're due for a day off, you know, and Mrs. C. likes days off to be passed miles away from the homestead. That way she doesn't think she's a domestic tyrant."

"Oh, Tom," Kylie protested. "I don't think Mrs. Coulsell could be tyrannical if she tried. Actually, and a little sadly, she herself is always trying to please. She is so grateful for any little personal thing done for her."

"I didn't suggest she was tyrannical. What she is afraid of is that image of herself." He stubbed out his cigarette and picked up the fine-bladed knife, and went to work on his piece of carving again. "So what about the water-hole?"

"I'd love to go. Do we ride? I'm dying to improve my style on horseback."

Tom shook his head, slitted his eyes as he held his fragile doll's chair to the light and then bent over the work again.

"Too far," he said. "And don't forget we've got to take the notice warning all travellers. It'll be the jeep to-morrow, I'm afraid. Leave all to Tom Flynn and don't be surprised if I turn up with a few surprises myself." He looked up and catching Kylie's eyes grinned affably. "Go and get some beauty sleep and don't worry about Tom's comments re the Coulsell family. Sometimes they're double dutch to Tom himself."

Kylie stubbed out her cigarette and stood up.

"I think so too," she said with a smile.

Tom walked with her to the door.

"Good night, Kylie," he said. "And don't forget I love you."

She laughed back at him.

" I love you too, Tom," she said. " I'll dream on it."

" Mind you do," he called as she went out into the night.

*

Tom's surprises for the jeep ride the next day consisted of Nonie with a picnic basket from Mrs. Craddock, and the Whip Man, clean but not shaved or dewhiskered, who wanted to find out for himself how, with his lifetime of bushcraft, a new kind of poison weed could find its way into a water-hole and he not detect it.

" It's these here birds flyin' over," he explained to Kylie. " They shake their feathers in the air, worse than airyplanes. Seeds they've picked up when roostin' drop. Most times there's a dead snake or two, birds theirselves an' rabbits and such, lyin' round a water-hole that tells a tale of itself. Now there was nothin'. . . ."

" Except the Whip Man," said Tom Flynn. " Somebody's got to be first. Why not a human being? "

" Well, come to think of it, you're right there," said the Whip Man, scratching his whiskers with a hand so horny it was nearly a claw.

Kylie had a lovely day in spite of the long hot drive over bush scrub and tracks that only bushmen like Tom and the Whip Man could discern as tracks at all. Nonie bounced about with delight and Kylie saw, with astonishment, that when Nonie was handed a gun by the Whip Man she knew all about loading, cocking and firing it even though it was so heavy she had to rest it on a stump to get a sight. They brought home half a dozen rabbits and a kangaroo . . . shot by the Whip Man . . . for the stockpot.

In the homestead only Ray was angry about this outing.

" You really do go after the men, Kylie," she said. " I must say you're a fast worker."

Kylie was so surprised she nearly dropped the dinner tray she was carrying in to Ray.

Tom Flynn and the Whip Man. Well!

" Come to think of it," Kylie said to herself, " one could see the Whip Man and Nonie as chaperons. Funny, but I never thought of that myself."

" Tom would be very shrewd about being run after," she said lightly as she put the tray on Ray's lap. " And of course the Whip Man was there to look after Tom and Nonie was there to look after the Whip Man. . . ."

Ray was not looking at her tray but at Kylie.

"And who were you looking after?" she asked, still un-smiling.

Kylie laughed, trying to make a joke of it all.

"I wasn't looking-after. I was running-after," she said. "Like you said. Tom Flynn, I suppose. You wouldn't expect me to marry the Whip Man, would you?"

Ray's set face told Kylie she did not appreciate the joke. Kylie wished she hadn't made it. Naturally Ray didn't like being laid up while others were enjoying themselves. And it was all her own, Kylie's, fault.

"Ray . . . please . . ." she said. "Do let me massage your ankle a little for you after dinner. If we do that two or three times a day I'm sure we'll hurry down the swelling. I'd love to help you, you know. I'll be ever so gentle."

For a minute Ray struggled with the inclination to say "No" but her good sense prevailed. She gave Kylie a watered-down smile and said ungraciously:

"Well, if you must. I'm sure you don't want to be carrying three meals a day in to me for ever."

Kylie did more than gently massage the ankle. Her feather strokes with the lightest of fingertips seemed to soothe Ray's nerves and that reminded Kylie that people having their hair brushed and their faces and hands gently massaged felt soothed. She would give Ray a beauty treatment; the whole box and dice.

Ray was so pleased with the little bit of movement she could now get into her foot that she acquiesced to the facial. When Kylie had finished she not only looked a lot happier, she looked very pretty.

They had quite a lot of fun trying out different shades of cosmetics for the final make-up and when at last Ray was sitting up in a fresh lacy nylon bed-jacket, her make-up expert and her hair shining, Mrs. Coulsell came in and exclaimed with pleasure. She called to Brad and Tom Flynn, who were having some coffee together in the lounge, to "come and see how beautiful Ray looks."

When the two men came into the doorway, Ray, looking a dream, smiled. Her anger with Kylie was forgotten.

Tom Flynn swept his right hand across himself as he made an imitation of a courtly bow, but Brad just stood, his back to the door jamb, and smiled.

"You look marvellous, Ray," he said. "We'll have you up and out on the run in ten days. I've got news for you but

I was wondering when to break it." His smile said it was good news.

"Come clean," said Ray eagerly. "Did you hear from Charmian?"

Brad nodded.

"She's coming. She has to go on to Rathna-moor but will be here in time for the party."

"Oh, *gorgeous!*" said Ray. "When did you hear, and why didn't you tell me?"

Mrs. Coulsell was tidying up the beauty-tray and Kylie went to help her, picking up the bowl of water she had used. She liked being in Ray's room in the middle of what was suddenly a happy family scene but having the bowl in her hand there was only one thing to do . . . take it away.

She said "Excuse me" to Brad who moved forward out of her way but otherwise did not appear to see her. He was looking at Ray. Tom stood back so she could go through the door.

"Promise me you'll be sweet to her," Ray was saying to Brad as Kylie went into the passage. "Last time it was spoilt by having that wretched Sara Allen here."

Sara Allen! Nonie Allen's mother, Kylie thought.

Even though Sara had married and gone away to another station she sometimes came back then? And was still attracted to Brad?

Funny how you can be jealous about people you've never seen.

This sudden low feeling must be jealousy, Kylie thought. Yet she wasn't sure. She longed to know what Sara Allen and Charmian Dane—Brad's list—looked like. Yet she couldn't ask even darling Tom Flynn who was this minute thundering down the passage after her. Tom was very perspicacious and he would want to know why a young person such as herself was curious about two other persons who were probably young and certainly attractive.

Anyhow, as if Brad wouldn't have had love affairs! A man like Brad wouldn't have reached thirty without having some skirmishes with love, surely?

And how did he "hear" from Charmian? A letter surely. Although there was the transceiver, of course. Perhaps the mailman had been.

"Why so pensive?" Tom asked, holding open the screen door to the kitchen for her.

Kylie shook her head to shake away the thoughts. She looked up at Tom. His blue eyes weren't laughing, they were inquiring.

"Why don't I fall in love with Tom?" she asked herself. "It would be so much easier. And such heaven. He's *fun. . . .*"

"Next time we have a day out together we'll go to the Wirradonga Dam," Tom said when Kylie did not answer him. "How about it?"

Kylie smiled.

"I'd love it," she said.

CHAPTER SEVEN

THE DAY OFF, to the Wirradonga Dam, seemed faraway, and so much happened round the station the next day or two that Kylie forgot Tom's invitation. There were other things she had on her mind.

Kylie had thought the life on a cattle station might be lonely but she was fast learning that remoteness from towns had nothing to do with being busy, and having lots of people around. Things began to happen that made her think she might as well be living in the middle of a great city like Sydney, or London.

That night, after the drive to the water-hole with Tom Flynn, Nonie and the Whip Man, Kylie ought to have been tired enough to drop straight off to sleep.

But it seemed hours before sleep came.

She had lain in her bed, making more resolves not to look at Brad; not to wonder if he approved or disapproved of something she had done—like waiting with the Whip Man in the creek gully. Mostly she was trying not to think about Brad's "list" and not to keep on wondering what Charmian Dane and Sara Allen were like . . . and feeling very low every time she did think about them.

Meantime she could not help loving Nonie. If Sara was like her daughter Nonie then of course Brad would have loved her.

Kylie was woken very early the next morning by the sound of intermittent bumping outside her window. It was Sunday and to-day there was no early five o'clock tea. Anyone who wanted early morning tea got up and got it for themselves on Sundays.

The bumping went on and as it was barely dawn Kylie slipped out of bed and switched on her light so that it streamed out through the wire screen wall.

There was Nonie, very diminutive, sitting on the edge of the veranda, dressed in a shirt blouse and jeans, kicking one foot against the foundation boards.

" Nonie! " said Kylie. " Whatever are you doing at this time of the morning? "

" I've come to take you riding, Kylie. I was waiting for you to wake up. I'm going to teach you."

The little girl stood up. She was seven and didn't look a day more than that.

" Oh, Nonie! " Kylie said. " Wait till I get dressed, dear," she added. " Of course you couldn't possibly take me riding but I'd love to come and watch you."

" You can have Goldie," Nonie said. " No one falls off Goldie. She won't let you."

It had been a hot night and Kylie's pyjamas had stuck to her most of the time so she had to have a quick shower before she pulled on some clothes. The portents were for a heat-wave day.

Horace Bentley had always been away from the house in Mosman during the day-time so he had never known Kylie had a pair of slacks for gardening. They had been her precious and well-loved secret. Horace Bentley couldn't abide " women dressed up like men." He couldn't stand the younger generation at all, which was one of the reasons he wouldn't let Kylie go out, join a club, or bring anyone to the house.

As she pulled her slacks on now she thought again of those lonely days, now past.

" Goodness, I'm so busy here," she thought, " there isn't really time to *wallow*."

In this last reflection she was thinking of the sleeplessness of the first hours when she had gone to bed last night. She had tried to banish Brad from her thoughts, and think only of Tom Flynn. Tom's friendship meant a lot to her. In him, she thought, lay her salvation.

" Work is the only antidote to sorrows," she now decided in the eerie light of dawn. " Though I can hardly call going riding with Nonie *work*."

Even saying that to herself she still didn't believe that seven-year-old Nonie could teach her to ride.

How wrong she was! When they got to the stable Nonie had Goldie and another horse saddled. They were both well trained riding hacks but Kylie was astonished to see Nonie climb on to the middle rail of the stable stall and from there slip into the saddle of the bigger horse. The stirrups were so shortened the irons were nearly on the saddle themselves.

Nonie who couldn't herself reach the stirrup to mount a horse from the ground was able to tell Kylie what to do about it. This morning there was no Smithy to give her a "shove" on to Goldie and no Brad to put out his hand and swing her up on to Joachim.

"Put *that* foot in *there*," Nonie called. "And put your hand up there on the pommel. That's right. Now pull with your hand as you give a sort of jump off your other foot. Then up! Gee, Kylie, you did that awfully right. You must be light. My Daddy says that if you're light off your foot the horse loves you first go."

Kylie wondered if she was mad going with Nonie like this. Suppose something happened to the child? More "heroics" or "stunts" as Brad and Ray had called her adventure with the Whip Man.

Yet for the life of her she couldn't stop herself. She wanted so badly to ride and Nonie was so much the assured teacher, and she herself was now the child, that somehow she was simply obeying Nonie as if she was under a spell.

"How am I doing?" she called, as they cantered down the slope.

"Aw gee, Kylie, you can ride. Stop asking how are you doing," Nonie said in a grown-up voice.

That was the first of many riding lessons. True, they consisted more of copying Nonie and letting Goldie, under her, teach her than "taking lessons." Also Kylie, because she too had youth, had the certain fearlessness of youth. Riding, especially on a mount like Goldie, came easily to her so she had no fear.

When she got back to the homestead that morning nobody seemed surprised that she had gone riding, let alone with Nonie. They simply took it for granted. Kylie discovered for the second time that station people took riding and horses as a matter of course. To them there was nothing the least bit adventurous or unusual in a pre-dawn ride.

That was the beginning of Sunday, the " rest day."

*

They were all having tea behind the wire screen on the front veranda when Brad put down the pastoral magazine he was reading and looked up. Kylie from the other side of the tea table could tell by the sudden lift of his head and its slight tilt, as if he were listening, that something had happened to attract his attention. He sat quite still, gazing through slitted eyes out through the garden trees to the paddock and at the same time listening carefully.

Ray too, stretched out on a cane lounge, her injured foot resting on a pillow, looked up.

" What is it, Brad? " Mrs. Coulsell said. There was that little edge of anxiety in her voice that always betokened her nervous reaction to something unusual.

" Someone coming," he said.

" The stockmen," Ray said. It wasn't a statement but a possible explanation.

Kylie could hear all sorts of small noises, like the intermittent rush of water into the overhead tank from the bore, the distant thrumming of the engine house. Yet oddly enough it was the silence down at the men's quarters that was more noticeable.

Brad put down his magazine and stood up. He went to the edge of the veranda and stood above the steps looking out over the station run.

After a minute or two he turned and spoke to his mother.

" The men all went out last night to the boundary camp for some kind of party. They'd be whacking it up out there and not one of them likely to come in. The natives have got themselves tied up in a corroboree the other side of Black Range."

" Tom Flynn? " said Mrs. Coulsell, still with thát touch of nervous tension.

Brad had turned and was once again looking out past the stables and outhouses to the far distances.

He remained with his back to them as he said:

" Something annoyed Tom Flynn last night so he went out to join the men."

Kylie and Ray both seemed, simultaneously, to steal a glance at one another.

" Funny," Kylie thought. " Ray thinks I have said something to Tom . . . or done something. . . ."

She looked at Brad's back. That last remark of his hung in the air as if he had intended it that way. Did he too think something had happened between herself and Tom last night? Just because he had opened doors for her? And asked her to the Wirradonga Dam?

For a moment her thoughts were taken off whatever it was Brad was listening to.

Suddenly Brad broke the silence.

"That's it," he said, confirming his own thoughts. "A man coming. And on foot."

He swung round and picked up his hat which was lying on the floor beside his chair. His hat was never more than a few yards away from him. He clapped it on his head, went down the three steps and strode away across the garden at an angle. Kylie half saw and wholly heard him vault the garden fence.

"Goodness," Mrs. Coulsell said. "*On foot?* It must be one of the stockmen."

"Don't be silly, Mother," Ray said. "One of the stockmen wouldn't be coming in by himself on *foot*."

"No, of course not," Mrs. Coulsell said. She got up and went to the edge of the veranda where Brad had been standing. "Kylie, come and see if you can see anything."

Kylie joined Mrs. Coulsell and peered in the direction Brad had gone. He wasn't much more than a brown man in a dust cloud, striding at a great pace down the track away from the homestead that Kylie had heard the others call the Inland Track. She had never seen the stockmen using it. Whenever the men came or went on the run they seemed to go either west or north.

Yes, she knew her directions now, thanks to Smithy and the Whip Man. Brad was going in the direction of the rock bluff. This was the one Smithy had told her to take a line on with the homestead to find due south so that she could then make her way north. That was when she had gone down to Creek Gully and found the Whip Man.

The Whip Man had doubtless been taken out last night with the stockmen to "whack it up" at the boundary camp. Except for Brad they were all alone in the homestead area of the station.

Kylie remembered Nonie saying the few stockmen's wives who were on the station had gone to a party too. There was only herself and Mrs. Craddock at home to-day.

Four hundred square miles of empty station run . . . and they had somewhere to go to a party! Sometimes things about the station made Kylie shake her head in bewilderment.

"Well, what is it, Kylie?" Ray said irritably from her lounge. "Can't you see anything?"

Kylie shook her head.

"Nothing, except Brad disappearing into the distance." She turned round. "How could Brad hear and see anything so far away?"

"Of course he could," Ray said, going back to her book. "When you've lived all your life on a station you can hear anything that's unusual. All the noises are the same . . . and there aren't many of them." She lifted her eyes and said with a touch of scorn for the "townie," "Of course he can hear anything *different*."

"If it's a man on foot then there's been trouble," said Mrs. Coulsell. "Kylie, do you think we ought to put the kettle on . . . ready?"

"The bottle of brandy and a hot bath is more like it," said Ray, immersed in her book again.

It was twenty minutes before Brad came back. He stamped up the veranda steps, pushing his hat to the back of his head as he came.

"It's a chap whose car's blown out on the back track," he said to his mother. "I've left him to walk in slowly because someone will have to go back for his wife. He says he's left the car back about twelve miles. His wife came with him but after four miles he had to leave her under a bush on the side of the track. He thinks she's all right. They were out of water except for the bag he's left with his wife. He's about done in."

"I should think so," said Mrs. Coulsell, shocked. "Twelve miles in this heat . . . and no water. Why, it was a hundred and five, veranda shade, at nine o'clock this morning. Must be a hundred and ten now."

"Do you mean to say he didn't have any water in the car?" demanded Ray.

"He didn't," said Brad shortly. He turned to Mrs. Coulsell and Kylie. "Someone's got to go back for the wife. The jeep will take that track. Kylie? No. I think you said you can't drive."

Couldn't drive and couldn't ride a horse! What good was she in emergencies, Kylie wondered, on a station?

Brad thought a minute, looking at his mother more than at Kylie yet not really seeing anything but his thoughts.

"I'll get the jeep out and pull it round," he said. "I'll bring the fellow in from this last lap." He looked directly at his mother now. "Can you and Kylie get something for him? Hot tea first, then a shower. I'll wait to see how he goes. . . ."

"Are you going out to get the wife, Brad?" his mother asked. "The man only *thinks* she's all right. She may have collapsed. You'd better take Kylie. . . ."

"Yes, I'll come," Kylie said quickly. She had to have a chauffeur, it was true, but she still could be of some use.

"Yes, you'd better come, Kylie, in case she's ill," Brad said shortly. "Get a hat, the first-aid chest and some food. A Thermos of tea is the best thing."

"See there's water in the jeep storage tank, Brad," cautioned Mrs. Coulsell as he went down the veranda steps again.

"There's *always* fresh water in the jeep tank," he said.

"That's one for the man and his wife travelling without storage water," Ray said, nodding her head at Brad's receding back. Her eyes moved round to Kylie.

"Don't say it, Ray," Kylie said. "I know. Out on another *stunt*. But you will run stations in the middle of a desert." She laughed so as not to annoy Ray with her words, and went inside to put on the kettle to make tea for the man coming in; and to fill the Thermos.

She felt elated she could do something man-sized to help. If Nonie could teach her to ride a horse then, by hook or by crook, she would find someone to teach her to drive a car or jeep. She would not be caught out as useless again. She would watch everything that Brad did. . . .

She had her hat on, the Thermos of tea, the smaller first-aid chest, a flask of water and medicine bottle of brandy in a basket, together with some biscuits and scones, by the time Brad came out of the shower house. He had been helping the man he had just brought in to undress.

"He's okay," Brad said to his mother. "Let him sit down as soon as he comes out but don't ply him with questions. He's not a bushman and that walk has cost him something. Ready, Kylie?"

She nodded.

The jeep was waiting on the gravel beside the back veranda

where Brad had brought the man. She put the basket on the back seat and got in while Brad was giving his mother last instructions.

"He must have had a terrible time," Kylie said to Brad as he clambered in the drive seat and slammed the door beside him. "Imagine walking one mile in this heat. It's so *treeless*."

"Don't use your imagination when you're walking in the bush," Brad said without smiling as he switched on the ignition and started the engine. "Imagination is worse than reality."

This was a little hard, Kylie thought, and she was surprised that Brad did not show more compassion.

"Aren't you ever afraid of the bush . . . in this heat ?" Kylie asked.

He had thrown the jeep into top gear and was swinging it round on full lock in the gravel square. He glanced at her.

"No," he said, and did not follow it with any explanation.

"Of course you *know* the bush," Kylie said, trying to make civil conversation.

Brad did not answer. He appeared to be concentrating on where he was driving. That reminded Kylie that she intended to learn by watching him. She too fell silent, watching what he did with his hands and feet when he changed gear. He did this from time to time as they went up and down rocky inclines and over a track that sometimes twisted and turned at right angles between the low thick bush that grew along its route. Away from the homestead there was not a tree in sight and Kylie wondered what the woman would be sheltering under.

Maybe this thought was in Brad's mind and it was the reason for his silence. He had urgent things to think about.

Kylie began to think Brad would remain uncommunicative all the way and she was beginning to feel unhappy about it.

Unexpectedly he broke the silence just as Kylie was trying to reconcile herself to it. He did not turn his head or look at her as he spoke.

"Well, how's the great friendship ?" he asked.

Kylie was puzzled.

"Friendship ?"

Brad changed gear to negotiate a sharp turn.

"You and Tom Flynn," he said.

"Oh," said Kylie. "He is a darling, isn't he ?"

They were on the straight now and Brad turned his head. His eyes were light grey, probably because the harsh sunlight drained them of any other colour.

"You obviously think so," he said.

In an obscure way, his eyes were challenging her.

Kylie looked straight ahead through the windscreen. A small frown knit her brows together.

"I do like him," she said. "I didn't know it was obvious. But . . . well, why not?"

Kylie did not know that it was possible, even probable, that Brad had seen the kindly kiss that had passed between Tom Flynn and herself the night she had visited Tom in his workshop. So she was puzzled that her feelings for Tom Flynn were so very obvious to Brad.

"Quite," said Brad after a pause. "Why not?"

It was more a statement than a question. Kylie glanced at him and for the first time since he had lifted his head on the veranda, because he heard something that told him someone was coming, she saw expression on his face. It was hard to define. He looked as if care sometimes weighed a little heavily with him and that care—probably for the well-being of everyone on Rock Hill—was weighing with him just now.

"Don't worry," she said lightly. "It's only *fun*."

"As long as it stops at that," Brad said unexpectedly.

Stops at that! Kylie thought, puzzled. She wondered if he was afraid that one of them would make the other unhappy. How absurd!

But was it absurd?

Silence settled on them again and Kylie filled in the time by worrying just what Brad meant, and why he had had that look of care on his face.

Presently she forgot about herself and Brad because she had begun to wonder what were the chances of finding the woman they were looking for, conscious. She was sure she wouldn't be conscious herself, alone in the bush in the heat. The veranda temperature as she had left to get into the jeep had been one hundred and twelve. The sun heat, registering on the thermometer hanging on the tankstand, had been a hundred and twenty-seven. And that thermometer was shaded, too.

Because of the rough nature of the track it took them more than half an hour to travel the eight miles before they found the woman.

She was lying full length under a small bush that had very sparse shade, but she was quite conscious. As soon as the jeep stopped and Kylie and Brad got out she began to cry.

" I'm all right," she said chokingly. " I had water. I was afraid Jim mightn't find his way. He didn't have any water. He's all right? "

" Bathed and fed," Brad said. " Have you any injuries ? I'm afraid I forgot to ask your husband his name."

" Smith," she said. " Just Smith." She looked from Brad back to Kylie and something of the sympathy and kindness in Kylie's face made her tears flow again.

" Just lie there," Kylie said gently as she knelt beside her and, turning, lifted the cover off the basket and began to bring out the Thermos of tea and a cup.

" I'm not hurt," the woman gulped, shaking her head as much to brush away the tears as to give the negative to Brad.

It was Kylie's turn to take charge now. She looked up at Brad looming overhead.

" I'll look after her," she said.

" Yes, make her comfortable," Brad said and he walked back to the jeep, unscrewed the cap of the radiator and measured the water content.

How aloof he was! Kylie was perplexed. He did everything that was right yet he showed no feelings. He does have them, she thought, remembering his comments about the " great friendship " between herself and Tom Flynn.

For the moment she had to put Brad out of her mind and help Mrs. Smith to some tea. Kylie had had the foresight to bring a flannel and soap as well as a small bowl in the first-aid kit. She poured out some water when Mrs. Smith had finished her tea and gently sponged her face and hands. She dried them on a small hand towel.

" Better? " she asked.

Mrs. Smith nodded and Kylie helped her to stand up. Brad had walked down the track and came back smoking a cigarette.

" Do you feel able to make the further trip to the place where your car is stranded? " he asked Mrs. Smith with a sort of grave politeness.

Again she nodded. She was not injured and was suffering only the effects of fear and the long wait in the heat. Yet these things had taken a toll of her and Kylie helped her into

the back seat.   After Kylie had repacked the basket she stowed
it away and got into the back seat with Mrs. Smith.

Without ado Brad started up the jeep and they went on
down the track the further four miles to the stranded car.

Every now and again Kylie patted the woman's hand but
she did not try to engage her in talk.   Clearly Mrs. Smith
was still too upset to do anything but lean back in her corner,
occasionally wipe her eyes, and rest.

This part of the track was less rough and in a short while
they came to the car.

Kylie was shocked when she saw it.

It was a dilapidated old tourer and the right rear tyre was
cut to pieces, the wheel rim was distorted in shape.   It was
a complete blow-out.   The spare wheel on the back was
worn and shabby.   It, too, had been punctured.

Brad pulled the jeep on to the side of the road and got out.
He said nothing but went to work.   He took a new wheel
and tyre from the top of the jeep and, jacking up the tourer,
replaced the back right wheel.   He'd brought the second wheel
from the top of the jeep and put it on the back of the tourer
in place of the spare.

The cap of the radiator was off, showing that the couple
had not only gone through their tyres but the radiator had
run dry.

Brad had filled the radiator with water from the jeep water
tank; put a water container, which he had brought with
him, on the back seat of the car.   He opened the tool-box,
examined the tools and added some from the jeep to them.
He put oil in the engine and petrol from the jeep petrol
storage tank in the car's petrol tank.   He then got in and
started it up; drove it a hundred yards, then backed it to
where the jeep was waiting.

He got out, shut the door and came back to the jeep.

" It's okay now," he said.

Brad had worked in silence but with a speed, strength and
efficiency that amazed Kylie.   What amazed her even more
was that a car like the stranded one, in that condition, was
overlanding in this territory.

What Brad thought she had no idea because he said
nothing, not even when he got back into the jeep, swung it
round on full lock and drove home.

Every now and again Mrs. Smith gave another little sob

and Kylie patted her hand. When they got back to the homestead Brad punctiliously held the door open for them, then took the basket from Kylie's hand.

Their eyes met for a minute but he still gave none of his thoughts away.

"Thank you, Kylie," he said briefly and went round the side of the house with the basket.

CHAPTER EIGHT

KYLIE TOOK Mrs. Smith up on to the veranda where she helped her into a comfortable chair. Ray had gone inside, probably because of the heat.

Mrs. Coulsell came to the door.

"Oh, there you are!" she said kindly. "Mrs. Smith? Is that right? Will you come inside. You'd like to have a bath, wouldn't you? There are towels and bath salts in the bathroom. Then when you're ready we'll have some lunch."

"My husband . . . ?"

"He's all right. He's asleep on the lounge under the pepper trees at the back. I think we'll leave him there till you've had your bath."

This, Kylie thought, was kinder than it sounded, for poor Mrs. Smith did indeed look a wreck. Her dark cotton dress was dusty from where she had been lying down under the bush. The dust, together with the tears and heat, had left grubby stains on her face, in spite of Kylie's earlier sponging. Her hair was bedraggled.

Kylie herself was dusty and hot and Mrs. Coulsell, suddenly no longer anxious or nervous but rising calmly to the situation, made her go and "freshen up."

Kylie would have liked a shower but thought she should hurry to help Mrs. Coulsell with the lunch.

However, when she came out all was ready. On the green formica-topped table on the side veranda was set a lovely delicate meal of cold meats, fresh salads, scones and iced fruit drinks, all set about on gaily coloured mats. A tray was ready to be taken to Ray who had gone back to her room.

"Cooler," Ray had said non-committally when Kylie had put her head in. "Was the wife all right?"

Kylie nodded.

" Suffering a bit from the ordeal of waiting and fearing,
I think," she said.

" She'll get over it," said Ray. " They always do."

Kylie was puzzled at what she thought was lack of sympathy.
Yet sympathy and help had not really been wanting. Mrs.
Coulsell and Brad had done everything humanly possible to
help the Smiths.

The lunch was a formal, not very conversational, meal.
Mr. and Mrs. Smith were perhaps a little shamefaced that
they had put the Coulsells to so much trouble, Kylie thought.
Brad was polite, aloof, briefly conversational about the state
of the tracks, the price of beef—about which Mr. Smith knew
nothing—and the prospects of an early Wet. Mrs. Coulsell
was kindly and patient with Mrs. Smith who was not only
reluctant to talk but reluctant to eat.

Kylie did the serving and the going backwards and forwards
to the kitchen. She brought ice-cream and paw-paws for
the dessert and contrived to give Mrs. Smith the nicest
helping. Out of her own warm-hearted pity she gave her an
extra dob of cream and an extra spoonful of passionfruit on
the ice-cream. In this very formal atmosphere she found these
attentions a good substitute for words.

Brad, she noticed, did not produce the usual bottle of beer
for lunch.

Yet it was a beautiful lunch, so appetising and so beautifully
served. In his curious, restrained manner Brad was the
perfect host. But Kylie herself felt there was a barricade of
aloofness which even his mother made no attempt to penetrate
and she herself did not dare to do so.

After lunch the Smiths had a rest and then Brad drove them
back to their car. They very emphatically expressed the
wish to go on and declined the invitation to stay the night
on the station and continue the following day.

Kylie did not see Brad again until late afternoon, when he
came back to the veranda for the usual Sunday " sundowner."

Once again they were all there, only Tom Flynn was
missing because neither he nor the stockmen had come back
from " whacking it up " at the boundary muster camp.

Ray, bathed and more vivacious than she had been since
she had injured her foot, was looking very fresh and pretty
as she lay stretched on her lounge. For the first time she was
in a dress and did not look so much like an invalid. Kylie

had massaged her foot again; there was much more movement in it and Ray was beginning to decide that an invalid's life was dull. She hobbled, with the use of a stick, on to the veranda by herself.

" Well, that's that," she said as she accepted a frosted drink from Brad. " How on earth did those people come to be travelling in such a condition? "

Brad shook his head because he had no answer to that himself. He had given a drink to Mrs. Coulsell and he now looked at Kylie.

" What can I give you? " he asked. " Still a lemon drink? "

" This time I think I'll have some gin in it," Kylie said. " A day like to-day makes me think I'm growing up." She looked at Mrs. Coulsell. " Does this often happen? " She meant the rescuing of the Smiths.

" Every now and again," said Mrs. Coulsell. " Generally people aren't quite so broken down as the Smiths were. *Everything* wrong you said, didn't you, Brad? "

He gave Kylie her drink and then poured one for himself. " Well, the engine was all right," he said. " After I put oil in it."

" You didn't seem very pleased with them, Brad," Mrs. Coulsell said in a puzzled manner. " I've never known you quite so silent. When you get that way I even feel frightened of you myself."

Brad did not say anything and suddenly even Kylie was impatient with him. What was going on behind that mask?

" The Smiths had everything done for them that could possibly be done," Ray said. " We even asked them to stay the night."

" Yes, *but* . . ." said Mrs. Coulsell.

" They got two new wheels . . . not tyres, Mother . . . wheels," Brad said quietly. " They cost roughly thirty pounds each. Two pints of oil, eight gallons of petrol, a hamper of food to last them several days, not to mention water. . . ."

" Yes, dear, but that often happens," Mrs. Coulsell persisted. " People always return things like wheels, or pay for them or something. They always do in the outback. They're so glad to be rescued. After all, they could have died of thirst if Mr. Smith had taken the wrong track and not found the homestead."

"Quite," said Brad.

"And Kylie was so kind . . ." Mrs. Coulsell added.

"Kylie is always kind," said Ray. No expression in her voice this time. Well, that was better than suggesting she had been in for another "stunt."

"What was wrong with you, Brad?" his mother persisted.

"I occasionally listen to the transceiver," he said. He took a sip of his drink and remained sitting, looking out over the garden to where the sun, having gone down, left a path of reflected glory across the western sky.

Mrs. Coulsell wrinkled her brow.

"The transceiver? *Oh, Brad!* You mean what the Harveys were saying yesterday? You mean the people who could only pay for their night at Senior's Crossing with an I O U? And drove off after the Harveys filled their car with petrol from the bowser without paying? Were *they* the Smiths?"

There was a little silence on the veranda and Brad made no comment.

Kylie digested what Mrs. Coulsell had just said. The Smiths hadn't any money . . . they weren't terribly honest . . . they were incredibly careless about how they travelled across the outback. That was what her words meant.

Yet Brad had gone to their aid; given them two new wheels complete with tyres, serviced their car, fed them hospitably in the homestead and seen them, well victualled, on their way.

All the time he knew he would never see his car wheels again. Moreover, that had been hard work, changing wheels in a temperature of over a hundred and thirty—for that was what it must have been in the open sun. He had done it all with ease and simplicity . . . all because it was the unwritten law of the outback for man to rescue man and set him on his way.

He knew that, from station owner to station owner, the Smiths would pass on their way across a continent. With the goodwill of the outback they would survive; and it wouldn't cost them a penny.

Did he *have* to smile about it?

She looked at Brad and at that moment he turned his head slightly and caught her eyes. His own very nearly smiled. In that one glance he said, "I know what you've been thinking. Now add it up for yourself. What you don't know is . . .

I gave Smith ten pounds to boot, and his wife a fiver for herself."

Even without knowing about the ten pounds or the fiver, Kylie's heart went out to Brad. He was a hard man, but he was a *right* man. He did what he had to do and made no bones about it. No, he didn't have to smile!

If only he didn't make her fall in love with him again.

Last night she had battled with herself and thought she had won a certain fight. Now here he was, sitting there, that half smile in the depths of his eyes, the muscles of his sun-browned face set and unrelenting, managing unconsciously to invest himself again with the magic that had first set Kylie Brown crossing a continent, too. Unlike the Smiths, it was in an aeroplane, but the fare must have been paid by Brad.

Mrs. Coulsell was talking to Ray about the Smiths but Kylie wasn't listening. She dragged her eyes away from Brad and prayed that Tom Flynn would come home soon. Only Tom Flynn, she knew, could save her from Brad, even if Brad thought it shouldn't go any further than *fun*.

Brad, for the second time that day, jerked up his head. Once again he heard something.

This time it was a big overlanding car, smothered in dust, but oh, so safely and well equipped. This was no wanderer to be rescued. This was a visitor.

The car pulled up at the homestead gates and a tall man got out. He lifted a large parcel from the front seat, then, closing the door, came through the gate and up the path.

Brad stood up.

" Beware of the Greeks who come armed with gifts," the man said with a friendly smile. He held out the large parcel. " A fresh leg of pork from the Harveys. I understand they keep pigs and you don't."

Brad smiled.

" I'm Brad Coulsell," he said. " And you? "

" Wilson Hendry is my name. I'm from Little and Murray. My business? The Horace Bentley estate."

The two men shook hands.

*

Kylie sat fixed to her chair. Her mouth was dry and her tongue felt like brown paper.

This was the valuator who had come to Uncle Horace's

house. She had shown him the various effects in the house and handed over to him the contents of her long-dead aunt's safe, and all the keys of the house.

He would know she was Rosemary Bentley.

She bent her head downwards and sideways and rose stiffly from her chair. How long she hoped to hide from him by going away now she had no idea. Her one instinct was to flee. If only she could escape to her room now she would have time to think what she would do about it later.

Mrs. Coulsell had risen from her chair to greet the visitor and she forestalled Kylie.

"Don't go, dear," she said. "You're one of the household now and you must meet our visitor." She held out her hand to Wilson Hendry and shook hands with him. "We've been expecting you," she said. "We didn't quite know when. . . ."

"I asked the Harveys not to tell you over the air. I thought you might work up some pleasant harassment over having a valuator around. By the way, I'm afraid I've come to stay awhile."

He then noticed Ray sitting very straight-backed and looking interesting with her bandaged foot resting on a stool in front of her.

"My daughter Ray," Mrs. Coulsell said. "Ray dear, Mr. Hendry."

Wilson Hendry went across the veranda and with a pleasant show of gallantry bowed a little as he bent forward to shake hands with Ray.

"How do you do?" he said. "You look as if you are a casualty. A very attractive one, I must say. Nothing serious, I hope?"

Ray adopted her cool sister-of-the-squatter manner but nevertheless it could be seen that she was pleased with the manner of Wilson Hendry's greeting.

Brad had gone down to the car to lift out the cases and Kylie stood stiffly, her mouth growing drier, longing for the earth to open and swallow her up. Preferably before Brad came back.

"And this is Miss Brown," Mrs. Coulsell said, indicating Kylie. "Miss Kylie Brown. She's my right hand. . . ."

"Companion, Mother," Ray reminded her as Wilson Hendry turned round.

He had to turn right round to meet Kylie and he had his back to Ray, screening Kylie from Ray with his tall strong body. Mrs. Coulsell had gone to the veranda steps and was calling out something about . . . "Do leave those cases for the men when they come in," to Brad.

Wilson Hendry, holding out his hand, looked at Kylie's stricken face. His hand stayed in mid-air, as slowly Kylie's hand crept up to meet it. His face expressed puzzlement, then surprise.

"Did Mrs. Coulsell say *Miss Brown*? " he asked, as their hands at last met.

It was a hot evening at the end of an outrageously hot day yet Kylie's hand was as cold as ice. He felt its chill against the palm of his own hand.

"Kylie Brown," she said through lips she tried to moisten but failed to do so.

"But . . ."

Her eyes implored him.

He looked at her quickly, penetratingly.

"Miss Kylie Brown? " he repeated.

"Yes." It was almost a whisper.

"How do you do? " he said. He released her hand. "I thought for a moment we might have met somewhere before."

Kylie barely shook her head. He had recognised her but for the moment he would say nothing. What a godsend he stood in a way that prevented Ray seeing her face!

"I hope—I hope you have had a good trip," she said lamely.

"Excellent, except for the heat," he replied. His eyes looked into hers again and his manner said . . . "I'll see you later about this."

He turned away and seeing Brad bringing his cases went hastily across the veranda and down the steps to meet him.

"Let me carry one of those," he said.

Brad handed him a case.

"Nice place you've got here," Wilson Hendry was saying as they came, one after the other, up the steps. "Quite an oasis to come on after that barren drive across country. Tell me, will you, how the heck do you raise cattle in this country? "

"Artesian wells," said Brad. "Underground water. Then the Wet, of course, brings up the grass."

They were talking together as they passed Kylie and so into the house where Brad would show Wilson Hendry to the spare room.

Kylie drew in her breath. She had respite. He wasn't going to tell on her *yet*. Even down the passage and into his room he was still talking to Brad about cattle.

Brad's voice sounded suddenly endearing to her ears. It made her feel nostalgic, as if it was something she loved and was about to lose for ever.

" Why, Kylie! " Mrs. Coulsell said, turning and noticing her. " You're as white as death. Sit down, dear. You're not going to faint, are you? "

" Kylie's not the fainting kind," Ray said in a manner that meant . . . " No more stunts. Don't be ' interesting ' for this man too. Quite a girl for the men, aren't you, Miss Kylie Brown? "

Kylie dropped her eyelids then opened them wide. She breathed in deeply.

" It's only the heat," she said with a smile. " Don't worry, Mrs. Coulsell. I've never fainted in my life."

That ought to put Ray's mind at rest.

She turned to the other girl.

" Would you like to go in now, Ray? I'll help you, if you would like it. If I *do* something, I won't think about the heat."

Ray had been going to say . . . " You were really thinking about that man," in the tone of voice that would have implied that thinking about men was Kylie's only occupation, but for once even she was struck by Kylie's pallor.

" Don't bother," she said. " I'll probably stay here awhile. It's still too hot inside. Go and get yourself an iced drink or something. You look washed up."

" I think I will," said Kylie.

She turned to go inside, when she saw the lone figure of a man walking towards the house.

It was Tom Flynn.

Tom at last! Now, when she went inside she would really cry. Not faint . . . just *cry* because Tom Flynn had come home.

That wasn't going any further than *fun*, was it?

CHAPTER NINE

As THE SUNDOWN HOUR approached, Kylie, bathed and in a newly ironed dress, offered to help with the dinner. Sunday night was not usually a " dinner " night but suddenly here was a guest who had travelled far and would certainly be in need of something substantial.

Mrs. Coulsell looked at Kylie anxiously and seeing that her colour had returned and that she looked refreshed, accepted her suggestion eagerly. She was in quite a flutter herself over the arrival of the new guest. For one thing, she *liked* guests; for another, she felt she was coming to life again herself with the bustling and surging of life all around her.

A month ago, before Ray had come home, or Kylie arrived, she had felt overwhelmed by the loneliness and silence of the homestead during the daylight hours. With the growing up of her children she had been afraid that she herself might now be useless.

Now all was changed. The homestead was full of people and she had much to do.

Just now she must bustle off and see that shining glasses were on the tray beside the whisky bottle and the soda siphon in the office. The men would want to talk a little . . . by themselves. Mrs. Coulsell was a great believer in leaving men a little privacy. Later they could come into the living-room and have a drink with Ray and herself. And yes, Kylie, of course. How sweet Kylie looked! A little pale but really quite perked up, all things being considered. Ray, thank goodness, was looking after herself.

Mrs. Coulsell didn't really register it, but she herself was in her own seventh heaven.

" There's no need to cook anything, dear," she said to Kylie. " Two of the girls came up when they saw the car arrive. They got back to camp early for once. They've managed a small quick roast of beef. What a pity those Smiths couldn't have waited. Yes, I know they weren't really the nicest of people. But it was an awful ordeal for them, wasn't it ? "

" If I hover in the area of the pantry I can make sure the roast comes to the table piping hot and the dessert is not taken out of the refrigerator one minute too soon," Kylie said.

" That's a splendid idea. Of course we don't really have
to be quite so formal about Mr. Hendry. I think he'd rather
be called ' Wilson Hendry.' We do that sort of thing in the
outback, you know. But it does give me an opportunity to
look after the men in the office."

Kylie dreaded once again catching that man Wilson
Hendry's eyes. While bathing and dressing she had faced
up to the fact that sooner or later she might be " found out."
She wanted badly to put that hour off. In spite of small
worries and perplexities she loved the life on Rock Hill.
She loved one man and was in love with another. There
were heartaches and wakeful hours in this situation but she
couldn't bring herself to face the fact she might leave it all
. . . with these complexities unresolved.

On the other hand there was the hope . . . the faint, faint
hope . . . that Wilson Hendry would be on her side, and keep
quiet.

She went eagerly to the pantry to find the cruets, polish
them up, get out the right cups and saucers for the after
dinner coffee and generally do the little things that would
make the serving of dinner go forward easily.

The moment came when she could no longer avoid going
into the living-room where the men had now joined Mrs.
Coulsell and Ray and the clink of ice-cubes in glasses told its
own story.

Kylie was very careful about making an unobtrusive
entrance. Slim, and more attractive in the simple polished
cotton dress than she realised, she slipped in while everyone
was gathered in the far corner of the room, talking.

She was not as unnoticed as she thought. Wilson Hendry
had been watching for a glimpse of the girl whom he was
certain he had met in Horace Bentley's house as his niece.

He was a tall man with hair touched with grey at the
temples: older than Brad, not as distinguished looking, but
still very nice looking. He had the shrewd eyes of any man
engaged in his profession, but the lines round his mouth
showed the more human, even humorous, of his qualities.
His movements were agile enough for a younger man.

He tried to remember the facts about the girl. There was
some story of her being dispossessed, he thought.

But how did she come by the name of Brown?

His memory went back to the day when she had stood by

the old photograph in her aunt's former room in that old mausoleum of a house in Mosman. She had twisted the dials of a wall safe and then placed in his hands a handsomely tooled leather jewel-case.

" I'm sure Uncle Horace has never touched these since Auntie died," she had said. " I sometimes think he never knew they were here, though I can't imagine his not knowing Auntie had jewellery of some sort." She had looked at him, slightly puzzled, vaguely sad. " I never saw her wear any of it," she had added. " But then I was young when she died."

He had said, professionally, the next thing he *had* to say.

" Is this all of it? "

" Yes, all," the girl had replied. " If you look you will see the safe is empty."

" No more anywhere else? In drawers, cupboards? Your own room, perhaps? Do you wear any of your aunt's jewellery? "

" No, it has never been touched. I knew it was here because my aunt told me. She let me take it out and play with it sometimes when I was little, and then put it back and turn the dials."

Kylie had never mentioned to him, or to her uncle's lawyer, that she remembered her aunt saying on more than one occasion, " It is all yours, dear, when I am gone. You won't forget where to find it, will you? You won't forget how to turn the dials? "

That all belonged to a childhood age, and of course her aunt had not mentioned the jewellery in her last illness. To Kylie, at the time of Horace Bentley's death, it quite naturally belonged to him.

The valuator had called his assistant and together they had sat down at a small table and counted and listed the pieces. They then asked the niece to sign a statement acknowledging the receipt of the listed pieces by the valuator. As she had put out her hand to sign the paper he had seen the gold bracelet on her arm. It corresponded to a similar bracelet, smaller, in the case. He then had had to do what he thought was his duty. He had pointed to her bracelet.

" That is your own, I suppose? Not one of your aunt's pieces? "

The girl had flushed, drawn herself up and said quite proudly:

" This bracelet is mine, and I shall keep it. My aunt gave it to me."

She had moved the circle of gold on her arm and shown him the inscription inside—*Rosemary Kylie Bentley 1948.*

That had been good enough for him. The bracelet must belong to the girl. He had not thought of it again.

As Kylie stood now at the small side table in the Rock Hill homestead and picked up the drink that had been poured for her, Wilson Hendry looked at her back speculatively.

There was some mystery here. That change of name, for instance. Unless she had married of course. But then hadn't she been introduced as *Miss* Brown?

Unless he, Wilson Hendry, was much duller than he thought he was, her eyes had distinctly pleaded with him to accept her as no one but Miss Brown.

Yes, that girl was Rosemary Bentley all right. Otherwise Miss Brown would not have had to plead, would she?

But why was she in the home of the Coulsells, disguised as some kind of superior servant, when they themselves were so tightly woven into the Bentley estate?

And a whopping big estate too, if he judged rightly.

He did his best to catch Kylie's eye when she turned round. But Kylie was not looking at anyone to-night. Her eyes looked elsewhere as she crossed the room, a tray with the second drinks in her hands so precious a charge she dared not take her eyes from it.

He watched her progress, forgetting that Brad Coulsell was showing him plans of the estate—things that it was his business to see.

Brad, seeing Wilson Hendry's attention elsewhere, looked up and watched Kylie coming towards them. He looked first at the man, then at the girl, then back at the man. Something about Kylie Brown absorbed his guest's attention to the exclusion of everything else, including the first rumble of thunder that promised the possibility of a thunderstorm.

Mrs. Coulsell, ensconced gracefully in a chintz-covered chair, was talking to Tom Flynn, who stood, hands in pockets, rocking backwards and forwards on his heels as he listened.

For once Tom's back was to the room, and Kylie didn't have to worry about what impudent messages he might care to transmit to her through those challenging eyes and those instructive brows. He was unaware of the affectionate, almost appealing glance she cast at his broad-shouldered back.

For the one minute before Kylie presented the silver salver with the drinks on it there was only herself and the two men in front of her—Brad and Wilson Hendry—and silence.

She looked up in the end, as perforce she had to. As she offered the drinks she saw they were both looking at her.

It would be a relief to look at Brad for once but she dared not take her eyes from Wilson Hendry. He was her friend or her enemy, she did not know which, but at the moment she had to wait on his whim to disclose it.

" Will you have another drink? " she said quietly.

Brad took a glass from the tray and gave it to Wilson Hendry, who put his empty glass in its place. He did not take his eyes from Kylie's face, and Brad knew it. Brad himself looked from one to the other, puzzled, withdrawn, enigmatic.

The light reflected in the crystal lampshade above shone on the silver tray and shone on something yellow and gleaming on Kylie's wrist.

" A beautiful bracelet, Miss Brown . . . I think you said *Miss Brown* ? " Wilson Hendry said.

Kylie's eyes looked into his. They did not plead. They seemed to await judgment like a blow.

" Yes. Kylie Brown," she said, then added: " I'm glad you like my bracelet."

" It is interesting," he said, inspecting the bracelet because Kylie, holding the small round tray in her hands, could not withdraw it from his gaze. " I have seen one like that before." He turned his eyes thoughtfully to the ceiling, then back quickly to Kylie's face. She no longer pleaded, she waited with a small angry bitter smile on her lips.

" There is at least one other like it that I have seen," Kylie said evenly.

" Yes, I remember now," he said, smiling at her. " It was in the estate of a man whose property I had to assess some time ago at Mosman."

" Indeed? " said Kylie, and she turned to Brad. " Will you have another drink, Brad? "

With a shock she realised she had never called him by his Christian name before.

He took a glass: his former empty one was on top of the piano. He looked up and directly into her eyes. " Thank you, Kylie," he said quietly. At the back of those grey eyes was a message, distant, cold, yet promising security. They said: " Is this man bothering you? If so, I won't permit it, of course. You are under my protection in this house."

Kylie shook her head imperceptibly, but the rue went out of her smile.

" I like my bracelet to be admired," she said generally and then turned to carry the drinks to the other corner where Tom Flynn and Mrs. Coulsell were talking.

While she served them Wilson Hendry hastily swallowed his drink and reached the side table to place his glass on it as Kylie returned with the empty tray.

" I think you and I have a little talk in front of us, *Miss Brown*," he said quietly. " Do you ever walk in the garden at night? It's a common form of exercise on these lonely homesteads, I think."

" Yes," she answered in a low voice.

He glanced at his watch.

" At half past nine," he said. " I always have a last turn and a last cigarette under the stars."

" Thank you," Kylie said formally, moving the glasses on the table with her hands, and looking down at them as she did so. " I would like to do that. It's cooler in the garden at night, isn't it? "

Her long lashes swept up and she looked at him. Wilson Hendry thought he had never seen anything so clear, and so honest, as those grey eyes that had a hint of green in them. He drew in a breath, then leaned forward and stubbed out his cigarette on the ash-tray on the table.

" Good," he said briskly. " I shall be certain to enjoy myself."

He turned and strolled back to Brad who was occupied with packing away the station plans in a very battered leather portfolio.

*

Dinner passed easily and even with a touch of gaiety. Mrs. Coulsell was very much the slightly breathless eager hostess and Kylie could see how charming she was when she overcame the slight nuances of anxiety that had seemed a characteristic when Kylie had first arrived on the station.

Ray was quite engrossed in Wilson Hendry and as he and Brad talked about station affairs Ray joined in in a way that showed she was not only knowledgeable about these affairs but had the kind of judgment that both Brad and Wilson Hendry listened to. Not for the first time Kylie thought it

vas odd that Ray had this mixture of interest in the station
and longing for the bright lights of the south. Perhaps she
oo had a loneliness of a kind . . . a longing for company,
other than station company; of people of her own age, both
nan and girl.

Tom Flynn and Kylie were left to one another.

" Did you miss me to-day? " he asked her with a grin.

Kylie nodded.

" You'd be surprised," she said. " So many things happened that you wouldn't think I had time to miss anybody.
But I did think of you once or twice."

" Nice or nasty? "

" Nice. Every time I got worried about whether I was
doing the right thing or not . . . about the Smiths, you know
. . I wished you were here to tell me."

" You went out with Brad. Why didn't you ask him? "

Kylie looked at Tom Flynn gravely. She did not answer
that question.

" What did you do—whacking it up—out there at the
boundary? What does ' whacking it up ' mean, Tom? "

" Not just opening the barrel, young lady, if that is what
you're thinking. We try out the horses. The men go in for
stunt riding, far from the station owner's eye. Tell yarns.
Have a pot or two at a cockatoo if we can't find a bush
turkey or a 'roo. Generally forget our sorrows."

" Have you got sorrows, Tom? " Kylie asked seriously.

He grinned.

" And then some! " Though his eyes laughed he somehow
sounded as if he meant it.

She did not tell him how overwhelming had been her sense
of relief when she had seen him coming home.

*

At half past nine exactly Kylie slipped out of the screen
door of her room on to the side veranda.

The night was heavy with the sudden threat of storm and
the heat was damp, not cool, as she had hoped.

" Anyone would walk outside on a night like this, anyway,"
she thought. " But I feel like a foolish heroine hastening to
a fateful assignation."

This phrase made her smile because she thought of Tom
Flynn's reaction to it, if he ever heard it.

*

Tom Flynn was, at that moment, bracing his shoulders

against the outside door-frame of Brad Coulsell's office. The door led on to the veranda and Brad and Tom were having their last-minute discussion on the next day's activities. Their visitor was walking in the garden.

Tom, shaking the ash from his cigarette, was looking out idly into the pitch darkness of the garden and the paddocks beyond.

" It's going to storm good and plenty, Brad. If it cuts a swathe through the muster camp that youngster will catch it plenty."

" Youngster? You mean Nonie? " Brad lifted his head sharply.

" The women left her out at the muster camp, after their picnic. You know what the kid is, Brad. Nothing would make her come up if she knew there'd be a horse round-up to-morrow."

There was a short silence.

" Nonie is at the muster camp," Brad said thoughtfully, his tone carefully even.

Tom threw his cigarette butt on the veranda floor and put his foot on it.

" I don't like it, myself," he said briefly.

" I don't like it either," said Brad, equally briefly.

" What are you going to do, then? " Tom asked.

" I'm going down after Nonie."

" You can't do that, Brad," Tom said. " All hell will let loose when that storm hits. You know how it can be. Anyway, you wouldn't ever get back through the creek gully when the cloud-burst hits it."

" You would, I suppose? "

" Too right I would. I'm a horseman." Tom paused. " You wouldn't be thinking of taking the jeep, Brad? It would never get through if the creek comes up."

" I'm thinking of going on horseback."

Tom straightened up.

" Good. That's two of us," he said amicably. " I'll go get the nags."

" Just a moment, Tom. I'm sorry, old chap. I know you like Nonie but you've got another charge to-night."

" Me? Who wants looking after by me? "

Brad nodded his head in the direction of the garden. In the darkness Tom barely saw the movement.

" I do not doubt my guest," Brad said with a smile. " Nor

would I put a curb on the freedom of the staff. But I do not intend to leave Kylie walking about in that darkness."

Tom Flynn shot bolt upright and took two steps to the edge of the veranda and peered into the shrubbery.

" For heaven's sake, Brad——" he said.

" Just a moment, Tom," Brad said coldly. " There is no earthly reason why they should not have a quiet stroll in the garden. Nevertheless, I've never left the homestead without a man in charge in my working life."

Tom turned round.

" If you think they can safely walk in the garden with a storm like that coming up, then so do I," he said belligerently. " Only I just can't understand . . ."

" Understand what? "

" She's a nice girl," Tom said sadly. " She must make friends awfully quickly. 'Course, she's darn' pretty. . . ."

" You have an observant eye," Brad said dryly.

" She didn't get my permission to go walking out there with any other chap bar me. You know what, Brad? I feel kinda hurt. I reckon I'll go break it up. I'll give 'em another ten minutes."

Brad's voice was slightly sardonic.

" Are you going to give her the choice of walking with you or with him? "

" I'm going to sock him one," said Tom. " Hell, he's only been in the homestead half a day. . . ."

" You'll just have to leave them to their own devices, I'm afraid," Brad said, " since they're grown up and civilised. Besides——"

" Besides what? "

" I have a feeling they have met before."

" Then why didn't they say so? "

" That is their business, Tom. In any event, you stay here and I'll go for Nonie."

There was a long minute of silence, then Tom spoke again in irritation.

" Why don't you go and get that nag of yours, Brad? The storm's going to break any minute. You make me nervous standing there breathing down my neck and saying nothing."

Brad made a sharp movement and closed the door of the darkened office behind him.

As he walked away, already heavily booted, Tom called after him:

"Take care of yourself, Brad."

"I will," Brad said over his shoulder. A minute later he had stepped down over the veranda edge and could be heard walking rapidly in the direction of the stables.

"Guess he can see in the dark," Tom muttered to himself. "All the same when that young Kylie Brown comes indoors I'll give her a Dutch uncle talk, twentieth century or no."

Then with an air of astonishment he posed himself a question.

"I wouldn't be jealous, for crying out loud?"

CHAPTER TEN

A HUNDRED yards away, in the garden, Kylie walked along the footpath with Wilson Hendry.

"Yes, you are quite right. Or nearly right," she was saying. "I am—or at least I thought I was—Rosemary Bentley."

In a few words she told him of the fact that Horace Bentley and her aunt had never changed her name to theirs; or formally adopted her as she had always assumed. All along she had been really Kylie Brown. Her aunt had added the "Rosemary" as a name in front of the Kylie for some sentimental reason. Brown had been her parents' name.

She told him how she had been left penniless except for a few bonds given to her by her aunt long ago . . . and the gold bracelet. She had simply taken the job on Rock Hill as a means of earning a living. When she had discovered how closely associated the Coulsell family was with her uncle's estate she had decided to remain silent about her identity to save everyone embarrassment.

"The situation is a foolish one," Wilson Hendry said. "You know, of course, of Mrs. Coulsell's relationship to Horace Bentley? She is his sister and a beneficiary under the laws of next-of-kin."

Kylie stood stock still.

"I didn't know," she said. "*Of course!* How stupid of me never to have seen it. Yet . . . the day I came I thought I had seen Mrs. Coulsell before, somewhere. Then I thought I was mistaken. I *was* mistaken. It's the likeness. . . ."

"The situation is still a foolish one, whether you know the relationship or not," Wilson Hendry said kindly but bluntly.

"You can't possibly let it go on, you know. To begin with, the family lawyers are hunting high and low for Rosemary Bentley, and here you are roosting under the family's own roof."

"Why are they looking for her?" Kylie asked. "Why can't they leave her dead and buried? She was a poor lonely frustrated nobody. There's only me now."

"I haven't the faintest idea why they're looking for her. That part of their business is none of mine. I'm merely employed to assess the value of their various estates for probate and for the distribution amongst the next-of-kin. But I don't think it's advisable to remain in obscurity when you know there are advertisements out for you."

"Advertisements?" said Kylie incredulously. "You don't mean I'm on the Missing Persons list or something?"

"Not quite. Merely in the personal columns. I happened to see it in the papers. And incidentally I brought all the recent papers with me from the Harveys' station. They told me you didn't get an air drop here and asked me to bring the mail and papers on. The Coulsells will see the advertisement —if they don't know about it already."

"Please," Kylie pleaded, "would you give me that paper? If you have brought a whole bundle, they won't miss one paper, will they?"

"Listen, Miss Brown! Or Bentley, or whatever you must be called. You are being strictly dishonest stealing as much as one newspaper. Maybe they want you for some information only you can give. There may be other missing pieces of wealth, like the jewellery, hidden round that house in Mosman. And only you can help them. Maybe they even want that bracelet back. It's a pair with the other one and I, being a valuator, know just what the pair, as a pair, is worth. Those bracelets were made by the London goldsmiths in the seventeenth century. They're museum pieces and as a pair are worth a lot more than their face value."

"I know that house from top to bottom and backwards and forwards," said Kylie slowly. "There was nothing in it hidden at all except the papers and stock script in Uncle's safe and the jewellery in Auntie's safe. As for my bracelet—I left behind everything else I had, even though it wasn't very much. My bracelet I will never give up. Auntie was the only person who had ever loved me——" Kylie's voice suddenly broke.

Wilson Hendry was silent a minute.

"There, there," he said at length. "I'm sorry I upset you. Forget it. I promise I'll forget all I know. I apologise. I say those sort of things because it's my profession to inquire about other people's property and squeeze every ounce of value out of it I can. Sometimes I don't even like my job."

"It's all right," said Kylie more calmly. "In some ways I'm being foolish about this business, but in others I am not. It's just that I felt so dreadful—so alone and deserted when I learned that I had nothing, not even the Bentley name. I don't want to have to tell the Coulsells because I like being here. I even like——" She broke off. She couldn't possibly tell him about the day she had seen Brad and taken a job here on Rock Hill, because he was there.

"Yes? You even like what?"

"Oh, I don't know, Mr. Hendry," she said haltingly. "I suppose I sound dreadfully foolish, but I want to stay with them, and be with them. And have a *home*. They'd never permit it if they knew I was Rosemary Bentley."

"As a matter of fact," he said flatly, "I think that old miser of a Bentley deserves a heel on his grave for leaving you stranded. You keep that bracelet, my girl. It's yours and any squabble over it would spoil your love for it."

"I'm glad he didn't change my name," Kylie said simply. She was more composed now. "I like being me. I like being Kylie Brown. And he wouldn't have changed my name for the same reason he didn't make a will. He was a great autocrat, and quite often a law unto himself."

"The god complex, eh? All right, I'll keep your secret for you, young lady. And good luck to you." He paused and looked round in the darkness. He steered Kylie to turn about in the path. "That thunder has been groaning and rumbling to some effect," he said. "And that padding on the earth is an occasional large raindrop. I think I'd better take you indoors."

As they felt their way in the tense darkness towards the veranda steps he held Kylie's arm firmly.

They came quite suddenly on Tom Flynn sitting on the top step waiting for the finish of their evening walk.

"Man alive, you gave me a fright!" Wilson Hendry said. "What are you doing? Guarding the house, or keeping a watchful eye on Miss Brown?"

There was an unexpected chuckle in his voice and Kylie warmed to him.

"Both," said Tom ungraciously. "Since Brad's gone out in that raking storm, we've got to have some capable man-power around. As for walking out with Miss Brown—I'll have you know that's my girl you've got on your arm."

"Oh, Tom!" Kylie protested. Her mind was only half on what Tom had just said. Why, she wondered, had Brad gone out in the storm?

The rain had not yet begun but far away on the western skyline vivid flashes of red and yellow were intermittently lighting up the whole world. Between each flash the thunder rolled and darkness hooded everything again like a thick black cowl. The heat was oppressive. The whole atmosphere seemed to be one great violent threat of wildness soon to come.

"Where is Brad?" she asked as Tom stood up and stretched to his full height.

"Gone for Nonie," he said laconically. "You don't suppose he would let Sara Allen's child stay all night in that rain, do you? Believe me, it's raining plenty down at that muster camp right now."

Wilson Hendry felt Kylie stiffen under the touch of his hand on her arm.

"He'll get drenched himself," she said. "How could he find his way?"

"Of course he will," said Tom as if not interested. "Mister Hendry, do you think you could relieve that young lady of your right hand long enough to accept a cigarette from the temporary manager of Rock Hill?"

"Thanks, Flynn. If Miss Brown will forgive me, I will."

In the darkness the packet was passed and presently a match flared and a cigarette was lit.

"And don't take her arm again while I'm the boss," said Tom truculently.

Until that moment Kylie had thought he was joking. One never knew with Tom.

"Oh, Tom," she said chidingly, "you sound like an irate brother. And just how long are you going to be the boss?"

"A long time if Brad doesn't come back alive. And he just mightn't. It's going to be pretty wild before the night's out."

" Please let me come up the steps," Kylie pleaded. " You are trying to frighten me."

" Why shouldn't I? I'm frightened myself."

*

Long after Kylie was in bed she lay listening to the storm. Somewhere out there Brad was riding to fetch a little girl who was the daughter of a woman who she thought had once loved him and whom, perhaps, he had once loved.

" But he loves Nonie too," she thought. " He would have gone for her even if she hadn't been Sara and Bill Allen's child."

Kylie, like Tom, was afraid for Brad in that storm but somehow she was glad he had gone for the child. She was glad he was that kind of person. Intuitively, she had known he was like that.

It was funny, but this going of Brad out into the storm to bring Nonie home had chased all the other events of the day from her mind. She did not give a thought to the morning, the strange adventure with the Smiths, the dinner, or her evening walk with Wilson Hendry; and its conversation. She did not even give a thought to Tom and his half-playful, half-belligerent challenging of the other man for having his hand on her arm. It had all gone out of her mind, washed by that same rain that was pelting down now as if the heavens had opened and were delivering themselves of every drop of moisture that had ever been gathered there.

In the torrid heat of the night Kylie lay on her sheet, un-covered except for her thin cotton pyjamas. She looked out at the wire screen wall that gave on to the outside paddocks and every time the world was lit by a jag of lightning she half raised herself, hoping to see a horseman coming over the rise.

All the time, between loud rolls and crashes of thunder, her ears strained to hear, through the heavy plodding of rain on the ground, that heavier sound of a hoofbeat on the stable run.

Twice she got up and bathed her face because the wetness of cool water was preferable to the dampness of blanketing heat. Each time she lay down again she listened until her head ached with the effort of listening. Already she knew by heart the silhouettes of the fence and shrub trees that grew along it and the awful faceless desert of the rain-drenched plain.

" Next week there will be green grass, and even wild

flowers," she thought, but in another minute even that thought had disappeared in the tedium of her waiting.

She would never sleep until she knew that man and child had come home again.

Everything else—the trivialities of being or not being Rosemary Bentley—had evaporated into nothing compared to the realness of her anxiety and the long waiting.

*

It was getting past the small hours of the morning when she heard Brad come home. The sound of the veranda door banging was the first warning. For all her listening, and the watchfulness of the night, she had been unable to detect in the storm racket the sound of horsehoofs on the track, or of heavy booted steps on the garden path.

Kylie sprang off her bed, remembering to grasp her light dressing-gown as she ran through the door of her room and down the passage. She was in the kitchen doorway before Brad, water pouring from the brim of an old hat and from every inch of a waterproof cape as ancient as the hat, had time to set Nonie down.

They stood and looked at one another across the distance of the big room.

" Oh, *Brad*! " Kylie said, and there were tears like raindrops in her eyes. Quickly she recovered herself and wiped the tears away with the back of her hand. " I was afraid something might have happened to Nonie."

She could have stood an hour and looked at him. He was drenched and water streamed from him and his burden, on to the floor, making a widening puddle round his feet.

He grinned.

" Do you think you could find something warm and dry for Nonie? " he said. " I'll take my share of the storm outside, then we'll have a cup of cocoa."

" Of course," said Kylie, moving quickly towards him, ready to take the tired but wide-eyed child.

" Don't touch," warned Brad. " We're both water-logged. I'll carry her into your room and you can strip her off there. We might have to bed her down for the night."

" In my room," agreed Kylie eagerly. " There's room for two in my bed. If not, I can sleep on the sofa."

Brad carried Nonie down the passage and through Kylie's open door. He stood Nonie on the floor near the far door leading to the veranda.

" Right, Nonie? " he asked, looking down at her.

She nodded, smiled weakly, more from fatigue than anything else, and said:

" Isn't Kylie's room nice? Better than the wind and the rain, Brad."

He looked around as if Nonie had pointedly drawn his attention to bright and sheltered security after their adventures in the wild night.

" It's always a fine thing to come home," he said quietly.

Kylie was glad she had hung away her day clothes and that though the bed looked a little tousled, the fact she had folded back the top clothes before she had lain down on it gave it a reasonably tidy aspect.

The bougainvillaea flowers she had put in a vase on the small table that morning liked the damp heat and they shone, a brave gay splash of colour, against the white embroidered cloth.

Everything else was tidy except Kylie's shoes which stood at an angle to one another, the toes touching and the heels not playing neighbours, like two naughty children caught unawares playing truant from the cupboard.

Brad glanced at Kylie then looked down again at Nonie.

" It's a nice home to come to," he said to the small girl.

Nonie sank backwards on to the padded seat below the ledge of the screen wall.

" You're putting water on Kylie's carpet," she told Brad reproachfully.

" So are you," he said reprovingly. He moved over to the door leading to the veranda and taking off his hat shook it outside. He turned back.

Kylie had never seen Brad looking so human, even friendly, before.

" I think you'd better dry her and put her to bed, Kylie," he said. " Then we'll brew in the kitchen. You'll have some cocoa too? "

Kylie was thrilled. She had an invitation to an early morning cocoa-party with Brad in the kitchen, and she didn't care if she had no sleep that night at all. She would be there. She nodded " Yes " as he went out on to the veranda.

All through the long wait she had thought of it being the day of a hundred disasters, and suddenly it had ended in heaven. Everything that had happened . . . Brad's warning not to let her friendship with Tom become anything more than " fun "; the plight of the Smiths; the arrival of Wilson Hendry; Brad and Nonie in the storm . . . had been wiped away as mere incidents.

From Mosman, in the far south, she had followed her star and now she was to have cocoa in the kitchen with Brad.

All the same, at the back of her mind she had a feeling there weren't green lights everywhere, not even in the Milky Way. Somewhere a red light of warning was flashing.

CHAPTER ELEVEN

It DIDN'T take her five minutes to strip the clothes from Nonie and rub her down. A minute later she had wrapped a light cotton blanket round the child and put her in the middle of the bed. Even as Kylie pulled up one sheet and one blanket to cover her, Nonie's eyelids had drooped over her eyes and she was so near sleep she could not answer the invitation to have a cup of cocoa too.

Kylie, tying the sash more firmly round her dressing-gown, turned out the light and slipped down the passage to the kitchen. She was barefooted but past wondering where her slippers were and if she should put them on. She wanted to get to the kitchen first, and make that cocoa.

She had the electric jug bubbling, the cups and saucers on the table and the milk in a saucepan on the Primus stove when Brad appeared.

He was in his pyjamas, barefooted, and tying the cord round his dressing-gown when he came in. She turned and looked at him, barely able to keep the expression in her eyes subdued to something impersonal. Suddenly, because of this adventure of the night, she had got close to Brad. They were two people about to drink cocoa in the middle of the night as if it was a mischievous escapade.

" I'll make toast," Kylie said, turning quickly to light the second burner on the Primus; anything not to let Brad see how thrilled she was to see him home safe and know that Nonie was lying comforted and in good health in her own bed.

" Give me the bread. I'll hack," said Brad. " You make the cocoa."

Kylie felt like a schoolgirl again. She couldn't have cared less about her own undress or Brad's rather shabby but entirely comfortable dressing-gown. And there was something satisfactorily conspiratorial about their two pairs of bare feet side by side on the kitchen floor as together they hastily got supper.

There was a soft plodding on the veranda floor and Brad, smiling sideways at Kylie, said:

" If you can hear what I can hear—it's the late acting-manager of Rock Hill coming to find what goes on in the kitchen."

There were no more subtle inquiries from Brad about her " friendship " with Tom, thank goodness!

The screen door opened and Tom Flynn stood, dressing-gown draped over his shoulders, yawning in the doorway. His hair was so tousled it stood on end.

" Ha! " he said. " So you made it safely? " He rubbed one hand over his chin then scratched the back of his head. " What goes on? Can I smell toast? "

" You butter that lot," answered Brad. " I'll make some more."

There was the sound of another slippered approach from the other end of the veranda and Wilson Hendry came in. He had the buttoned-up kind of dressing-gown and as his hair did not stand on end he looked a shade more respectable.

" And more toast, and more toast," said Brad dryly without looking up.

Kylie had already put a small cloth on the kitchen table and was now placing cups and saucers around it.

" Where do I sit? " asked Wilson Hendry.

" Did you get an invitation card? " Tom Flynn asked him after one more yawn. He sat down and reached for the butter dish.

" Did you? " asked Wilson Hendry as he cheerfully passed Tom Flynn a knife and a plate and pushed the mounting pile of toast towards him.

Kylie felt a surge of extra love for outback life that made of a stranger like Wilson Hendry an instant friend and intimate of the house. It had been this way with herself on Harveys' station.

" Listen," Tom was saying slowly. " I've been awake all night—on account of having my period as acting-manager cut long or short according to whether Brad got home alive from that storm, *or not*."

" With or without child? " inquired Wilson mildly.

" With child, of course," said Tom furiously.

" For your information," said Wilson Hendry, still mildly, " I've been awake all night too. For the same reason." He buttered toast very precisely.

" So have I," said Kylie, bringing the jugs of hot milk and cocoa to the table. " On account of Nonie," she added hastily.

Tom Flynn looked up and his eyes asked if that was the case why wasn't she having cocoa with Nonie instead of Brad.

" I'm so glad you've come to the party," she told him tartly, to punish him.

Tom Flynn grinned.

" Sit down, Miss Brown," he said. " Standing your full height you menace me with charm. And I'm not the only susceptible man present." With that he glowered darkly at Wilson Hendry.

This time Kylie laughed. Brad, bringing the last of the toast to the table, sat down at the end of it.

" Anyone mind if I smoke while we eat? " he said. " Funny thing but you can't light a match with a wet child on your knee and a sixty-mile-an-hour gale blowing."

It reminded Kylie of the fact Brad hadn't smoked a cigarette on the night he had brought her home across his knee on Joachim.

" Good idea," said Wilson Hendry and all three men reached for cigarettes in their pockets.

*

Kylie had the gayest half-hour of her life. The three men chipped one another wittily and treated her with a slightly affected gallantry that she didn't misunderstand but which brought her spirits to bubbling point of happiness. How wonderful everything turned out to be! Never in her life in Horace Bentley's house had she dreamed of fun like this. For others perhaps: but never herself.

Tom Flynn, in his lugubrious manner, was saying someting funny. Wilson Hendry had thrown back his head and was laughing. Brad's grin was so human and amused that Kylie was sure her own eyes were shining—and then she saw, across the room, the kitchen door open.

Ray, shimmering in a short floral dressing-gown, was standing there, leaning on a stick; she had only one slipper on because the other foot was bandaged.

Tom Flynn and Wilson Hendry looked up too. Laughter

died on the air. The stars in Kylie's eyes faded as she saw the expression on Ray's face. Brad, who was tilting back his chair, lowered the front legs on to the floor and slowly turned round.

" Come and have some supper, Ray," he said quietly.

She advanced to the table, buttoning up the neck of her dressing-gown. Her face was quite white.

Tom Flynn went round the table and ceremoniously placed a chair for her.

" Sit down, dear girl," he said soothingly. " It's a bad night for sprained ankles, and cocoa is the only remedy."

Wilson Hendry stood up and dug his hands deep in his pockets.

" I hope I haven't transgressed your hospitality, Miss Coulsell? " he asked.

Ray withered him with a look.

Brad was standing too.

The whole atmosphere of the kitchen was changed, even charged. Kylie, also on her feet, now began hastily to gather the empty cups and saucers.

" I'll heat some more milk," she said lamely.

" Don't trouble with those cups and saucers," Ray said with ice in her voice. " The other servants will do them in the morning."

In the kitchen a pin could have been heard to drop.

Over the untidy waste of the table Kylie's eyes met those of Wilson Hendry.

Brad drew in his lips sharply, then looked from Kylie to Wilson Hendry. He knew that Ray's words had some double significance for them. Then he looked at Tom Flynn.

" I guess that's about all, chaps," he said after a pause. " It's time we got to bed."

As he went out of the door he said " Good night " generally but did not look in Kylie's direction. He was back again, in spite of the pyjamas and slightly shabby dressing-gown, in the role of the station owner: an angry one.

Kylie, whipped back to her own place in the homestead by the stinging lash of Ray's words, knew that the Brad who had come home wet from the storm and stood in her room and called it " home " and who had sat in the kitchen making fun with them all was about as unattainable as the real stars.

Ray would see to that.

The sad anti-climax of the cocoa-party in the kitchen made

Kylie think again of that old warning of Tom Flynn's—not to fall for the boss because other girls had done that, and they had been moved on.

The whiteness of Ray's face and the ice of barely controlled rage in her voice told Kylie that she herself would have to be doubly guarded, to build double defences for herself, or she too would go the way of the former girls who had dared to look at the head of Rock Hill Station.

Was Ray reserving Brad for Charmian Dane, the girl whom she appeared anxious to welcome to Rock Hill? Or was she afraid Kylie was another Sara Allen?

*

What was Sara Allen like, she wondered for the umpteenth time as she helped Nonie build a china garden below the veranda ledge outside her own room.

The one person she couldn't ask was Nonie.

She had got over the shock of discovering that Mrs. Coulsell was Horace Bentley's sister, though she often wondered how two people could be brother and sister and so different in personality. Mrs. Coulsell was kind and generous, and liked to have lots of people around her. Her brother had had to do with people only if they were connected with his business.

As the days had passed, Kylie had become quite attached to Wilson Hendry and often went for a walk with him in the garden after dinner. In Wilson Hendry she found a release from her past because she could talk to him about it. He honoured his word and did not tell anybody on Rock Hill that Kylie Brown was the missing Rosemary Bentley.

Mostly, because of Wilson Hendry's visit, the men were out on the run all day. They had to show their visitor the whole estate, and all the capital equipment on it. Also the cattle had to be mustered for a tally.

Nonie took Kylie for a ride in the early mornings, after that five o'clock tea, and in return Kylie was building a garden for Nonie of little pieces of broken china she found everywhere on old heaps, at the back of drawers, even under the foundations of the homestead. Nonie too brought her own gleanings from round the cottages of those stockmen who were married.

*

It was Wilson Hendry in the end, not Tom Flynn, who took Kylie to the Wirradonga Dam. Once again the quiet spell was followed by a day of shocks.

Tom too seemed to have sensed the danger in Ray's anger for he did not see very much of Kylie. She missed him badly but at the same time knew that as record-keeper as well as book-keeper he had to be out the long, long day with Brad and Wilson Hendry.

She herself was longing to see the life beyond the horizon. It was out there, miles from the homestead, that the cattle made of the place a real station.

" What is Wirradonga Dam like? " she asked Wilson Hendry one evening as they walked down to the homestead fence, and leaning there looked up at the sky and the stars.

" I'll take you out," he said. " Brad and Tom go out a couple of hours ahead of me in the mornings. I have to keep my own books up to date. How about coming with me? "

" If Mrs. Coulsell doesn't mind," Kylie said doubtfully. Actually she hadn't had a day off for a fortnight and nobody seemed to have noticed it.

" I'll fix it. Leave it to me," said Wilson Hendry. " Ray's walking round now, hot-footed and able. I guess she'll give her mother a hand round the homestead."

" Would I be in the way if I came? " Kylie asked. " I don't think Brad likes women interfering. . . ."

" We won't tell him till too late," Wilson said. He tucked Kylie's arm under his own comfortingly as they turned to walk back to the house. " You rather mind what Brad says and does, don't you? " he asked kindly.

" Wouldn't you? " said Kylie. " He is the boss, you know."

" Fair enough," said Wilson. " All the same, I don't think he's the ogre you imagine."

Ogre? thought Kylie. *No, I've thought a lot of things, but not that.*

" I'm going out to price a mob of cattle they've got there," Wilson said. " I'll do a little subversive plotting and see if I can get the jeep. How are you at smuggling rations from pantry? "

Kylie laughed.

" I can smuggle rations all right, but how am I going to avoid smuggling Nonie too? She doesn't let me out of her sight."

" That's a left-handed way of inviting Nonie. All right, we take that freckle-faced youngster along. Now all we've got to do is fix to-morrow or the next day as D-day, and elope."

Kylie touched his arm.

"Thank you ever so much," she said. "I'm dying to know what it's like out at the muster camp. And Black-fellow's Creek sounds most intriguing. I think it's the water that flows in to make the dam, isn't it?"

"I know it is—crocodiles and all. Don't worry. Contrary to legend crocodiles are timorous creatures and you've got to be really nasty to stir them into action."

*

Wilson Hendry was as good as his word. How he worked the oracle or in what way he went about it Kylie did not know. The following evening just before dinner Mrs. Coulsell told Kylie it was really time she had a rest from homestead chores and as Mr. Hendry was going out to the muster camp near Wirradonga Dam perhaps she might like to go.

"He's not riding to-morrow," Mrs. Coulsell added, "as he can get through his work quicker with the jeep. Take a shady hat, Kylie, and don't forget to pack a nice lunch. The men out there have only the coarsest food. Of course, they like it that way."

Kylie did not mention the outing to Ray, for fear of spoiling everything for Nonie. If Mrs. Coulsell mentioned it and Ray did come, then Kylie would accept it philosophically but she knew Nonie would not.

The next morning it was clear that Ray was already aware of the arrangements and showed no interest in going. Long transceiver-set conversations with friends—particularly the much desired Charmian Dane—all scattered hundreds of miles apart, had disclosed that everyone was thrilled with the idea of a house-party on Rock Hill. A date had been set the night before and now Mrs. Coulsell and Ray were quite glad to have a day alone in the homestead so they could make their plans together.

It was nine o'clock when Wilson Hendry came up to the homestead in the jeep and Kylie, straw hat on head, gathering Nonie in one hand and her picnic basket in the other, ran down to the gate to join him.

He really is a pet, she thought of Wilson Hendry. He'd borrowed some cushions and an old bush rug from the men's quarters and had had a word with Mrs. Craddock, Nonie's guardian, for in the back of the jeep was the Craddocks' large vacuum cooler. In it was cold lemonade, iced fruit salad and a bottle of beer for himself. He was as merry as a sandboy and bent on having fun in his own way as well as getting through a good day's work.

" What some wife missed! " Kylie thought as she packed Nonie in the front seat between them and then climbed in herself. " I wonder why he never married? " She stole a glance at him over Nonie's head. " It's not too late now," she thought.

Wilson Hendry revved up the engine and jolted the jeep round in a quick circle to get it on to the track, then he smiled at her from under the brim of his battered working hat and said . . . " Quite a family man, aren't I? Bet those blackfellows down at the creek will think I'm arriving with wife and child."

" You might be old enough to have Nonie for a child, but I am not," Kylie reminded him with pretended asperity.

" Let's adopt her," said Wilson, slipping into a higher gear.

" Sounds like a proposal," said Kylie with a laugh.

" That sounds like a hint," said Wilson. " With Brad Coulsell and Tom Flynn around, you don't want a ledger-keeping business man as old as I am."

" *Old*," said Kylie. " *Poof!* You haven't got truly grey hair. Only the distinguished kind. We'd like him, wouldn't we, Nonie? "

" I've *got* a father," said Nonie firmly.

Kylie and Wilson looked at one another over the child's head.

" You see? " Wilson said. " I can't borrow a family as easy as that." He looked down at Nonie. " Don't worry, Tuppence. We'll let your dad keep you and we'll look around and find someone rich and handsome for Kylie."

" What's wrong with you? " asked Nonie, entranced but not quite understanding this conversation.

" I might aspire to the hand of Miss Brown," Wilson said deliberately, talking down to Nonie, " but not to that of Miss Rosemary Bentley. That would be aiming high."

" Who is Rosemary Bentley? " Nonie asked.

" Someone I fell in love with long ago," he said, lifting a quizzical eyebrow at Kylie. " Now and again I see her ghost flitting about and it stops me ever thinking of anyone else."

"Did she die?"

"Yes," said Kylie hastily. "She died. And we won't talk about her any more because it makes Mr. Hendry sad—and me sad too."

"It's a picnic day," said Wilson with determination. "Let's talk about us and how much fun we're going to have."

The jeep was rollicking down the long grade that passed over the undulating ground of the blue-grass plain and the bumping about made them all laugh.

"Can we swim at the dam, Nonie?" Kylie asked.

"Yes," said Nonie in between a shuttle hurl from Kylie's side to Wilson Hendry's shoulder. "An' ride horses too. The stockmen lend us their change horses, only we can't ride them far 'cos they might need them."

"Good!" said Wilson. "The sooner we get there the sooner the fun will begin."

CHAPTER TWELVE

IT WAS an hour later, and after a stop for lemonade and biscuits and one stop for Wilson Hendry to light a cigarette and let Kylie have a turn at learning to drive the jeep for a few miles, they arrived at the mustering yards below Wirradonga Dam. For the last mile they had seen the dust cloud that meant cattle were on the move.

Here at the dam the whole world was changed. Way over to the right of them the creek bed could be seen along the bottom of a narrow gully. Its course was marked by the green trees on either side and here and there the glinting red wall of low rock cliff on the farther bank. Birds flew overhead and the flat plain had given way, in places, to rocky surfaces out of which sprouted the tussock grass. Down the sharp stony track that led to the second land-level below the dam lay a new world. The creek water spread out in a still, wide lagoon covered in places with lilies. The water of the lagoon narrowed into a head and finally into the lower creek, then went bravely on across another brown treeless plain.

To the left, some two hundred yards away from the dam's waterfall and its consequent lagoon, were the muster yards.

Big trees stood here in clumps and under them were the men's camps, more a huddle of gear and an occasional piece of flapping canvas than civilised habitations.

No wonder Brad had ridden out to bring Nonie home!

As the jeep swung around the stockyards and into the shady area of the men's camp the stockmen could be seen emptying the dregs from the billies as they were breaking up from their morning smoke-o. Farther away other stockmen were driving in a mob of cattle to be counted and valued for Wilson Hendry's benefit.

*

A man came across from the drovers' camp, his dusty shabby hat pulled well down on his brow, and it was only his walk, his tall lean well-built body that made Kylie realise it was Brad.

" Oh, Wilson! " she said. " You told me you wouldn't tell him."

Wilson's left hand was pulling on the handbrake as they came to a stop.

" Dear girl," he said with raised eyebrows, " I can't stop a man working on his own property where he likes. The chances were a hundred to one he'd be here. After all, it's his business I'm inquiring into." He looked at Kylie quizzically. " Do you mind so very much? " he asked curiously.

Kylie could have wrung her hands. What would Ray say when she heard? Ray would think it had all been planned and that Kylie had come out to find Brad, using the subterfuge of going for a picnic with Wilson and Nonie.

Oh, why couldn't one do things openly? Why had she always to be on guard?

Wilson Hendry was looking at her and noticing her undisguised distress and that she hadn't answered him.

" He's not such a bogy, Kylie," he said quietly. " Look at Nonie. She's thrilled."

" She belongs," said Kylie. " I don't. Can't I ever have a day free of the bosses? Wilson, don't you understand? Sometimes I want to run away from them . . . just for a day."

" I think it's more likely you want to run away from yourself," he said dryly as he got out of the drive door and closed it somewhat sharply after him. " Here he comes, so cheer up. I'm ready to bet you a pound to a penny he won't eat you. He probably won't even mind you've come."

That jolted Kylie. So Wilson thought Brad probably *wouldn't even mind*!

Brad's sun-tanned face was well coated with dust, along with his boots, hat and clothes. This was a stockman who rode with his stockmen, not the well-dressed station owner of the homestead. If anything, in this working dress, in the slightly rolling slouch of the horseman wearing cattleman's boots, one spur on his right heel, he was more striking than ever. Kylie could not unfreeze enough to return his smile, or raise her hand in an answering salute.

" So you've brought a party? " Brad said to Wilson as he came up. He raised a foot and rested a dusty boot on the jeep's bumper-bar. His voice drawled more because when he was with the stockmen he spoke as they spoke . . . softly, between half-closed lips, the voice coming with the curious sing-song of the diphthong that only outback men used attractively. He was smiling a little, so he didn't mind. At least no one would suspect he did. His manner was easy, pleasant, and his fingers were busy taking out the makings of a cigarette from his pocket and beginning to roll tobacco into a thin spiral along the narrow strip of rice paper.

" Hallo, Nonie! " he said. His smile was a special one for the child and it had great charm. For once Kylie was seeing Brad Coulsell completely natural. Gone were all the inhibitions of the homestead—the careful grooming of a manner for a household of women.

Nonie bounced up and down excitedly on the cushion seat.

" Hallo, Brad! Hallo, Brad! Hallo, Brad! " she chanted joyously. " We've got sandwiches, and cakes, and lemonade. And we've got our swim-suits. Can Kylie have a ride on one of the stockmen's horses? "

" Kylie can," Brad said, licking down the edge of the cigarette paper meticulously. " On Goldie. She's with us to-day." He looked up and his eyes held a hint of a welcoming smile in them. " Good morning, Miss Brown," he said. He'd been gone out on the run long before early morning tea to-day.

" Good morning," Kylie said a little awkwardly. The " Miss Brown " was meant as a joke. He didn't mind her coming, but that didn't get over the feeling of illicit *rendezvous*; of being about to partake of stolen fruit, as Ray would see the escapade. But, oh blessed fun! Goldie was here.

Enjoy it, Kylie Brown. Enjoy the day. *Enjoy* Brad, she told herself. It's just for one day, and let to-morrow, when Ray finds out, look after itself.

Brad handed Wilson Hendry his packet of cigarette makings.

" Do we get out here? " Kylie asked.

" In just one minute," Brad said. " I've got a surprise for Nonie. It's coming in with that mob of cattle easing over towards the number two yard."

He lit his cigarette and through amused, half-closed eyes, smiled at the child. Nonie raised herself on her cushion and looked through the glass windscreen. She watched the stockmen winging in the bullocks to a narrow stream. There was a curious excitement dawning in her face.

" It is! It is! " she cried, jumping up and down. " It's *Daddy*! "

Brad, one foot still up on the bumper, turned and looked across the yards. Then he turned back again to Nonie. All the time Kylie felt like an unimportant onlooker. Wilson Hendry was as interested, if not as excited, as Nonie. He too looked at the stockman who had just handed over his job to another man.

" That all? " asked Brad casually.

" All? What . . . ? Why . . . ? " cried Nonie, so excited she was scrambling over the drive seat and trying to turn the stiff handle of the drive door.

" You're looking the wrong way, Nonie," Brad said in his soft drawl. " Look who's coming round the other side of the wing."

Nonie left the door handle alone and turned to look back through the windscreen.

For one minute Kylie thought the other stockman, now riding round the near side of the yards towards the jeep, was a slim youth. Then suddenly she too saw why there was a difference. Nonie had seen and there was a squeal of delight from her. The other figure was that of a woman. Under the sombrero-like hat was a face that no dust could disguise from being anything but that of a very pretty though sun-tanned woman. The yellow hair was tucked up under the crown of the hat.

So at last Kylie knew what Sara Allen looked like!

Sara rode right up and swung off her horse, as easily and as professionally as a stockman. Kylie could see sun-weathering had put fine lines at the edge of her eyes and round the corners of her mouth. Her hands, though slim and feminine, were as firm, brown and hard as any of the men's.

She let the reins slip over her arm, as she leaned forward and stared into the jeep.

" *Nonie!* " she said.

" Mummy! Let me out, let me out! " squealed Nonie, so excited she couldn't manage the door handle at all.

" I think I'd better get out and let Nonie out too," Kylie said quietly.

Sara was more than pretty. She batted in Brad's league. She was a station woman and a horsewoman. She, like Brad, lived a world away from anyone as town-simple as Kylie.

Brad moved forward and opened the door for Nonie. He remained, an amused and silent onlooker. Kylie got out and stepped aside so that Nonie, almost falling out, managed to be caught in her mother's arms.

Wilson Hendry was watching the scene and Kylie's eyes went from his face to Brad's, to the woman who was Sara, back to Brad. There was something almost tender in the expression in Brad's eyes as he watched mother and daughter.

Sara straightened up, one arm round Nonie, and looked at Brad with a smile. There was something tender in her face too.

" Brad, you are a darling," she said. " Thank you."

Kylie moved round the back of the jeep and came up beside Wilson Hendry.

" So it was all arranged beforehand! " she said quietly.

" I'm afraid Brad turned the tables," Wilson said. " He put one over *me*. He asked me to bring Nonie." He looked back at Brad. " He's a downy bird, isn't he? I think I'll go count those cleanskins in case he puts one over the estate trustees too. You can't beat these outback cattlemen for playing simple and having the mendacity of rogues in their make-up."

He was joking as he spoke but all the same Kylie knew he was surprised that Brad had so easily got Nonie down to the muster yards to meet her mother—without Ray's overseeing and suspicious eyes on them; and, of course, letting Wilson Hendry think he was organising a picnic for Miss Brown!

As Wilson moved away Kylie too went across to the nearest stockyard and leaning on the rails looked with unseeing eyes at the wide-horned cattle inside the yard.

The stockman who was Nonie's father had joined the little

group by the jeep now, and Kylie, leaning on the stockrail, kept her back to them. It was a family meeting and she must not intrude.

Why did she feel her heart had dropped somewhere in the region of her boots?

Wasn't she glad that Nonie's mother and father had come to see her? Wasn't she glad for Nonie's sake? Of course she was. Dear little Nonie! How thrilled *she* was!

Was it something to do with an awful doubt of Brad? How long had Nonie's parents been out there at the Rock Hill muster camp without anyone in the homestead knowing? And why shouldn't they be here? Or was it that she recognised that no one could compete with Sara Allen, the cattlewoman?

Kylie did not turn round as she heard the sound of boots coming towards her. A minute later someone was beside her at the stockrail, a cattleman's boot went up on the foot fence and a pair of strong brown arms, shirt sleeves rolled up, leaned on the toprail.

" I'm glad you came. I hope you will find it interesting. It will be hot and dusty, I'm afraid." It was Brad's voice.

Kylie looked at him with guarded eyes. She didn't know it, but it was very hard to guard eyes as clear as hers.

" Thank you very much," she said. " I find it very interesting already."

He could make what he liked of that.

" So I've come to Wirradonga Dam after all," she said, determined to be cheerful. " It's the upper stream, isn't it? "

" We call the upper stream Blackfellow's Creek," Brad said. " We'll have lunch there. Sara will come too. I don't think Nonie would go without her."

He smiled cheerfully and Kylie knew it was her job to stay that way too . . . until sundown, anyway.

*

All that day Kylie felt as if she were divided in two parts. One part was madly enjoying herself and having the most extraordinary adventures. The other had something inside it that wept a little.

Funny how you could laugh and talk, watch the stockmen driving in bunches of cattle and breaking them out for different muster yards with an almost feverish interest, yet feel all the time that this must come to an end . . . when the sun went down. Then she was going to be once again that very lonely girl who had left Horace Bentley's house in the vain hope of following a star.

Sara Allen was amazing on horseback, as were, of course, all the stockmen.

Nonie amidst all her thrills and excitement did not forget Kylie. They had no sooner finished emptying the dregs of a fresh brew of tea on the ground—one made by the camp cook specially for the new arrivals—than Nonie, a pebble in the saddle of a big horse, rode up with Goldie on a lead.

" Come on, Kylie. Come on! Quick! Quick! Quick! We're going mustering with Mummy. She's only got a quiet mob this time."

" Oh, Nonie, you darling! " Kylie cried, jumping up from where she was sitting on a burnt-out old log that must have been the sitting place for hundreds of stockmen in its day. " Where can I change into my slacks? "

" In the jeep," said Nonie. " Get in the jeep. No one will look."

Kylie, as she did as her mentor commanded, wondered where Sara Allen camped. Then she remembered that Bill Allen was here too. They would be camping together somewhere along the bank above the lagoon. There were canvas camps dotted along like mushrooms.

In no time Kylie was out of the jeep, her slacks tied on tight round the waist with a businesslike snake belt that Tom Flynn had given her when he heard about her early morning rides with Nonie. She punched out the crown of her straw hat and pulled the brim down all round. Now it looked as near to a stockman's hat as she could get it. The next thing was to ram it well down on her head and push her hair up into the crown, out of sight. Like Sara!

Now she felt braver. She mightn't be going to be much of a stockman but at least she didn't look too dreadfully like a " townie."

Nonie didn't even notice; or she took it for granted that Kylie was looking as she ought to look when out at a muster camp.

" Now," thought Kylie, " if only I could swagger or roll across the ground the way those men do. . . ."

But she didn't try going that far. That way she would really raise a laugh.

Sara Allen was back on her horse and away round the

wings of a mob well out on the plain. Brad and Wilson Hendry had disappeared into a pall of dust hanging over a welter of men, horses and bullocks in one of the yards.

Kylie could hear the shotgun cracks of stockwhips and the quiet yet penetrating " Yip-yip-yip " of men calling to cattle.

" Come on, Kylie, do get up! " Nonie cried impatiently.

" Anyone watching, Nonie? You know I can't jump up in the air *yet*. . . ."

" You can. If you don't try hard, Kylie, you won't ever. Put your left foot in . . . hold her mane . . . *Up!* Gee, Kylie, you looked good! You went right up and over her like anybody does."

Anybody to Nonie meant anybody who had been riding since childhood, and Kylie was flattered. Also she was pleased with herself. She had *felt* she mounted well then.

" Come on," said Nonie, dashing away, a diminutive lump on a big horse's back.

Kylie lifted her reins and Goldie followed Nonie.

They rode at a fast canter round past the stream of cattle passing into the yard out towards another mob just coming through the middle distance. Ahead of them Sara Allen was galloping. She sat up from her saddle and leaned forward, her feet long in the stirrups.

" Ah, if only I could do that! " thought Kylie.

To her surprise in another minute she felt Goldie break into a gallop, following Nonie who was heading towards her mother.

As Sara Allen rode out wide of the bunch of cattle, so Nonie followed her and Kylie followed Nonie. When well out Sara reined in and the others caught up to her. She looked across the short distance to Kylie from under the brim of her hat.

" You'd better stay here," she said rather shortly. " I don't suppose you know anything about cutting-out so you'd better keep away from the business-end of rounding up." Her eyes were a forget-me-not blue in her tanned face but they were not as kind as flowers. She relented a little. " If a stray breaks out you can stop him. That's easy. All you've got to do is head him off, then back to the mob. Otherwise the whole mob will stream after him." She looked at her daughter. " Come on, Nonie," she said and galloped away in a wide arc to reach the cattle from behind them.

Nonie, for once, forgot Kylie and dashed madly after her mother.

Kylie sat in her saddle, Goldie obedient and standing still under her. She seemed all alone on the plain except for the various small mobs in the distance that were enveloped in their own dust clouds. She could see horsemen riding round them now and again, and occasionally hear the crack of a stockwhip. Mostly the cattle were coming in quietly until they got near the muster yards. Then they seemed to become nervous.

Sara Allen's words must have been foreseeing for as the mob which she and Nonie had joined came abreast of Kylie, still quite a distance away, a bullock broke away and headed past Kylie.

She stiffened. Unconsciously she lifted the reins and pulled on them.

" What do I do? What do I do? " she thought wildly. " Head him off, Sara said. How do I head him off? "

Goldie might have been a quiet riding hack but she was also stock-trained. She rose up on her hind legs, wheeled, and was off across the plain after the bullock. She dragged her head on one rein for she knew she had to go round the beast and not behind him.

Suddenly Kylie was unafraid. She found herself doing what she had seen the men do while she was having tea. She leaned forward in her saddle and let Goldie have her head.

The little horse raced on the wind and overtook the bullock. When past it, Kylie thought it was the moment to turn and head him back. She pulled one rein.

Goldie was on the gallop, and that pull on the one rein was the signal to wheel. A stock-trained horse wheels only one way, up on his hind legs, body almost vertical, and turns on a sixpence. Goldie did just this and Kylie came straight down and off her back and was on the ground before she knew what had happened.

Even lying on the ground she did not quite know what had happened or where she was.

All of a sudden there were pounding hoofs all round her. There seemed to be a whole world of stockmen, sliding off horses, leaving their reins dangling to the ground and standing around her in their fine-leathered high-heeled boots.

Oddly enough Kylie thought only about their boots. She

couldn't seem to think of anything else . . . not even where she was.

Somebody lifted her head. Somebody straightened her legs out. Somebody began feeling her body, beginning with her neck. It was like a doctor feeling if she had glands or mumps or something. He caught her head and waggled it from side to side. Then his hands slid down over her arms, under her back, dug into her stomach, worked firmly down her thighs and legs. They were strong, yet sensitive, fingers that searched her so thoroughly.

She wasn't very much troubled about *who* it was, or why. She was only troubled as to why stockmen wore high heels. She must remember to ask Brad, sometime.

She must have said it aloud.

" Ask Brad what? " It was a man's voice . . . a familiar voice that somehow made her want to cry.

She blinked her eyes and shook her head and looked up. The cobwebs were beginning to fade from her brain. She was looking at Brad.

He had been on one knee beside her and now he stood up.

" All right, you chaps," he said. " Get back to the mobs. You'll have to break them out again. Sandy, take Jim and cut out the steers. Bill, give Sara a hand with the cleanskins, will you? Scram off back to the camp, Nonie, and get Tom to haul out the first-aid kit. She's got a few abrasions, that's all. I'll bring her in." He turned to two other men who were standing behind him. " 'Fraid you'll have to go after those raking break-outs," he said. " Don't lose any if you can help it."

Kylie was lying on her back, looking up at Brad, but she heard the sound of boots moving away and then of horse-hoofs beating the ground in a tattoo of gallops.

He turned round again and looked down at her.

" Feeling okay? " he asked, quite kindly.

" Did I do much harm? " she asked, still looking up a very long way to a very tall man standing much nearer the sky than she would ever reach. Star-high, in fact.

Brad had a slightly sardonic smile as he answered.

" All the big heroes round here came to your rescue. I don't advise you to look around and see what happened to the cattle. They just scrammed."

" Oh, I'm so sorry."

He knelt down and lifted her head.

" That okay? " he asked.

" Yes. I think I'll sit up now. I was a bit groggy in the head," Kylie said.

When she sat up she was dizzy and had to hold her head in her hands. Brad, standing up now, waited patiently.

" Give it time," he said quietly.

In a few minutes Kylie's head cleared. He held out his hand and helped pull her to her feet.

" Guess I'll have to ride you back to camp," he said as she swayed a little. He held her firmly by the arms. Beyond him she could see Joachim standing quite still a few yards away, his reins dangling on the ground.

No, Kylie thought. Not again. Not in front of all these people. One ride home after a " stunt " had been enough. Two rides home on Joachim would turn that method of transport into a farce.

" I'll ride home on Goldie," she said with considerable dignity.

Brad was still holding her. He looked searchingly into her face. Then he dropped his hands.

" That's just what I'm going to let you do," he said unexpectedly.

He flicked his fingers and Goldie, who had been standing mute and waiting behind Kylie, came quietly up. Brad threw her reins back over her head and held the stirrup for Kylie.

" Now I've got to fly up in the air again," Kylie thought desperately. " In front of Brad. And my head's still wuzzy. . . ."

As she put her foot in the stirrup she seemed to hear Nonie's half-impatient voice . . . *If you don't try hard, Kylie, you won't ever.*

Kylie had tried hard and she had mounted to suit Nonie . . . was that an hour, or a week, ago?

She pressed her foot in the stirrup Brad was holding, and jumped off her right foot. She went up in the air and her right leg swung over Goldie and she was in the saddle. A little dazed by her success, Kylie shook her head and then looked down at Brad as he handed her the reins. He was looking at her face, closely, she thought. She couldn't believe he had something of a *smile* in his eyes!

Was her face dirty from that fall? She supposed it was. Oh, well! Not to worry. She had made such a mess of everything now, including at least three cattle mobs, nothing much could matter any more.

Brad dropped his hand from Goldie's chinstrap and walked away to Joachim. He, Kylie thought, still in a slightly unworldly haze, didn't mount a horse. He flew into the saddle.

"Now give her her head," said Brad. "We'll gallop."

That was exactly what they did, Kylie feeling she had galloped all her life and there was nothing to it.

In ten minutes they were back at the muster yards. Goldie reined in automatically beside Joachim and Brad slid off his horse and came round Goldie's side.

"Good girl, Kylie," he said quietly. "That's the only way to come home after a fall. I'm glad you made it."

It occurred to Kylie that she must have done something to earn Brad's praise. She knew by the way he looked at her that he was praising her.

Her head was clear now, and she was a little ashamed. She couldn't tell him, of course, she had ridden Goldie home because she couldn't make a farce of riding home on Joachim *twice*. Not now, anyway. Perhaps when she was an old, old woman she might tell him.

Sara Allen came thundering in and pulled up beside them. It occurred to Kylie, looking at Sara's set mouth and forget-me-not blue eyes that were not as kind as the flowers, that she, Kylie, would have to *write* it to Brad. She wouldn't be near enough to him to *tell* him.

If Ray didn't "move her on" from Rock Hill Station, Sara Allen probably would.

CHAPTER THIRTEEN

KYLIE HAD no sooner dismounted than Nonie and Tom Flynn took charge of her. Kylie was so pleased to see Tom Flynn that in some peculiar way she felt a little tearful about it. To begin with she hadn't seen him when they had arrived at the muster yards and she had supposed he was working somewhere else on the station.

She did not see Brad and Sara, leading their horses, walk away once she herself was out of the saddle, but she just knew they did so. She felt their going. It made her all the gladder to see Tom. She rubbed the back of her hand across her eyes.

" I'm not crying, Tom," she said emphatically. " It's just that my eyes are watering."

He took hold of her chin with one hand and tilted it up.

" Smoke in your eyes, huh? Like in the song? "

" I don't quite know what it is . . ." Kylie was saying, one word at a time, trying to appear as if considering.

Tom's hand slid away from her chin, gently down the rounded curve of her neck, then round her shoulders.

" You want something to cry on, Kylie? " he said. " You've had a fall, and you're hurt. And you're not very grown-up, after all. Here's Tom Flynn's shoulder begging to be cried on."

For one minute Kylie did rest against him. She would have stayed there for a long time only somehow she had to keep up this brave front with which Brad had invested her. Maybe she would tell Tom Flynn about not riding Joachim *twice*. That would prevent her feeling such a fraud.

For a moment the tears blinded her but just then she heard Nonie's best school-mistressy voice.

" Everyone cries after their first fall, Kylie," she said. " It's not because it *hurts*. It's because you get a shock. My Daddy says so. And he says if you don't cry it's bad for you, because five years afterwards you still dream about falling off horses."

Kylie's tears dried instantly and she lifted her head from Tom Flynn's shoulder. She stared at Nonie.

" Don't be precocious, Nonie! " she said in a slightly astonished voice.

Tom Flynn gave a shout of laughter.

" As a matter of fact the kid's making a plain statement of fact," he said. " Cry now and there's no delayed reaction."

" My Daddy also says you have to put acriflavin on your scratches at *once*. Else you'll get weed-poisoning. The same as the Whip Man had in his water-bottle."

" For goodness' sake, where is it, Nonie? " asked Kylie hastily. " I don't want to lean against a rock and frizzle in the sun again as long as I live. That's what happens to Whip Men when they get weed-poisoning anyway. . . ."

" He didn't die," said Tom laconically as he helped Nonie wipe a swab saturated in the antiseptic over Kylie's bruises and cuts. " He's over there in the cook's camp, making whips for the stockmen who've come in from Eagle Eye. They help with the muster."

"Is that why the Allens are here?" asked Kylie, lifting her head. She had been watching Nonie's operations on her grazed hands.

"Sure," said Tom, applying a swab to the back of her neck which was now beginning to feel a surface soreness. "They always do. Same as our men ride over to Eagle Eye when they have a big muster on."

"Now I'll make you a cup of tea," said Nonie. Having gone through the transition from schoolmistress to nurse, she was now the mother. "Come and sit over here in the shade, Kylie."

Kylie allowed herself to be led obediently to the group of trees standing a little back from the yards.

"Sit down there and lean against the tree. That's right," said Nonie. "I won't be long."

Tom Flynn stood above Kylie, balancing himself on feet a little apart, his hands dug in his belt.

"Tom, why do stockmen wear high-heeled boots?" Kylie asked. From her lowly position on the ground, back to the tree, Tom seemed all boots. "I've been wanting to ask ever since I came to Rock Hill," she finished.

He grinned down at her.

"So that when they throw a bullock . . . they swing off the horse and catch him by the tail, you know . . . they use the heels of their boots as a brake. Otherwise the bullock would run away with 'em. Got it?"

Looking up at him, Kylie nodded seriously.

"Excuse me asking silly questions, Tom. I'm still a little bit wuzzy in the head."

"I know," he said, shaking his own head wisely. "So does Nonie know. That's why you're getting some pushing around just now."

"Brad didn't know, because he went off and left me . . . just like *that*." Kylie made a little flick in the air with her hand.

"He didn't go off; he got taken off," said Tom. "Besides, he could see I was here to look after you."

"Nice for you," said Kylie a little abruptly.

"Very nice," said Tom. He was still standing, feet a little apart, hands dug in his belt. "Very nice indeed. You see, I'm just a little in love with you, Kylie, and with

that pretty little smudge on your pretty little nose ...
together with the fact your hat is all awry and the shoulder
of your shirt has got half the red dust of the plain on it ...
you are more endearing than ever. I feel like proposing
to you."

" And me with a wuzzy head? "

He nodded.

" That's exactly it. You might be silly enough to accept me."

" Oh, Tom! "

Did he mean it? Was he joking? What if she did say yes?
She would like to be engaged, have a ring, make a " box,"
get married. She'd rather die than never get married.

" Please, Tom . . ." she pleaded.

" Here's Nonie with the billy," he said. " You're saved
from answering. Never mind. Don't forget I did ask you."

He grinned back in his old wicked style, as he turned to
take the billy of boiling tea from Nonie.

*

Half an hour in the shade was enough to clear Kylie's
head. She was a little anxious about how she had been talking
in that " wuzzy " state. It seemed to her that it might have
sounded to others a little " drunk." Kylie had never had
more than half a dozen drinks spread over a few weeks on
Rock Hill, but she imagined that this was how to describe
the feeling she had had.

At all events she was sure Tom Flynn had proposed to
her. She had a sudden jump in her spirits. She had actually
received a proposal of marriage. It was only weeks ago that
she had thought she might never even meet a man as a friend.
Now she had them all round her. Maybe he was only joking,
but he had proposed. That was the great thing.

She got up, a little stiffly, and began dusting the knees of
her slacks. She looked up under the brim of her self-arranged
" stockman's " hat and saw Wilson Hendry approaching.
Everyone seemed to appear out of a dusty middle-distance at
a muster, Kylie noticed. First there was only red dust,
then someone emerged out of it, rather wraith-like at first,
then very dusty and heavy-booted in reality.

" I heard you had a spill," Wilson Hendry said.

" Pooh! " said Kylie airily. " That was nothing. Just
came off, you know." She looked up at him quickly to see
how he was taking it. His face, like everyone else's when
they got away from the homestead, was dead-pan. " I rode

Goldie home at a smart gallop, of course," she said even more airily. " I've been sitting here just waiting for everyone. Seems like it takes some people all day to muster a few cattle. . . ."

Wilson Hendry could no longer control his face. He burst out laughing.

" Good for you, Kylie Brown," he said, taking her arm. " I'm beginning to think I like Kylie Brown even more than I liked Rosemary Bentley."

Nonie too had emerged out of that red dust screen and came up just as Wilson Hendry was speaking.

" Rosemary Bentley," she said, looking up at him with a wrinkled brow. " You said that was the one you fell in love with . . . and she died."

Wilson Hendry and Kylie stood looking at one another. Suddenly Kylie wasn't trying to be airy any more.

" Quite dead," she said softly so that Nonie would not hear.

Then Wilson Hendry did an unexpected thing. He picked up Kylie's hand and lightly kissed it.

" The Queen is dead. Long live the Queen," he said. He dropped her hand and turned to Nonie. " How's the picnic going, young 'un? When do we get that swim in the billabong? "

" Right now, if you hurry," said Nonie. " Mummy's riding up with Brad, but you've got to go in the jeep because somebody's got to take the things and Tom Flynn's pretending he can't drive jeeps any more—that's 'cos he wants to ride too—and Kylie can't drive a jeep, only the little bit you showed her coming out here. . . ."

" Listen, Gossip! " said Wilson Hendry, pretending to dust Nonie away with his hat. " Anybody would think I didn't want to drive the jeep. Have you considered who I am likely to have as my passenger? Miss Kylie Brown."

" And Daddy's staying with the musterers because . . ." Nonie was not going to be stopped until she had finished a description of all the arrangements.

" Tell me as we go along," said Wilson. He took Nonie's hand and they turned away and went towards the cook's camp.

Kylie stood and looked after them.

That was the second time in half an hour that a man had said or done something extraordinarily nice to her.

"But I'm not like that," she thought, a little bewildered. "I'm not sort-of experienced and poised ... and things girls are who get proposed to—even as a joke—and get their hand kissed. ..."

Maybe she was still wuzzy in the head, after all! By and by she would wake up and find nothing had happened to her at all. Probably she hadn't even come out to a muster and was still asleep in her bed at the homestead, dreaming.

*

The picnic lunch at the billabong was a great success, except that Sara was there, beautiful in a red swim-suit and as proficient at diving and swimming in the pool by the bend as she was at horse-riding. This made Kylie feel *low* although it also made her feel mean. She had Wilson Hendry and Tom Flynn both being very nice to her ... barbecueing her steak for her, helping her to wash up, pretending they were jealous of one another. Why should she mind that Sara was best at everything else and that the red swim-suit should make her fair hair fairer and her tanned skin golden?

Nonie, in a brief swim-suit at least two years old, took to the water as easily as she took to horseback. Kylie wondered if the child had been born proficient in all things pertaining to an outback life.

Brad, suddenly, was quite different from anything he had seemed before. He smiled all the time—really smiled—his white teeth flashing in his brown face, his eyes full of colour as well as full of life.

Sitting there by the camp-fire his dark hair damp and his skin glistening, he seemed to Kylie more than mortal. He was like royalty, born with something extra, and it made people look at him. People like herself and Sara Allen, anyway.

"You're doing pretty well for yourself," Sara had said to Kylie.

Sara had just come out of the pool and stood hands on hips, the water streaming from her. She watched both Tom Flynn and Wilson Hendry rescue sizzling steaks for Kylie from the bush-forks in the fire.

"I always do things in numbers," said Kylie, trying to be jaunty.

"So Nonie tells me. She had three bead bangles, a china

garden under your window and you've promised to make her a dress for the Rock Hill party?" For the first time Sara's eyes had some expression in them. They were quite kind.

"Nonie's done more for me. She's kept me company and she's taught me to ride," Kylie said.

"And spill off?" Suddenly Sara was laughing. Then quite as suddenly she stopped and asked another question. "So Charmian Dane's coming to the Rock Hill party?"

"Well, yes, I think so."

"In the transceiver-set world there are no secrets," Sara said off-handedly. "Of course Ray thinks the sun, moon, and stars rise and set on Charmian Dane." She lifted one eyebrow and looked at Kylie. "Money and ancestral position, you know. By the way, I suppose you knew Ray couldn't stand me?"

"I did not," said Kylie a little hotly. This was not strictly the truth, but her first loyalty was to the Coulsell family. "She has never spoken of you to me."

Sara laughed.

"She thought I was going to run off with her precious brother. Not that he's not a pet. He is. By the way, don't look at him twice while Ray's around, will you? Just warning you." She turned away, pulled the pins out of her bun of hair and let the hair fall down over her face as she leaned forward to shake the water out of it. She looked up between strands of hair; her very blue eyes were sprightly and just a little malicious. "And if you run off with Tom Flynn, do it quietly. That way you might get away with him." She really smiled.

"I beg your pardon?" said the bewildered Kylie. She tried to rescue a bush-fork that had fallen into the fire and burnt her fingers doing so. She dropped the stick and blew on her fingers.

"I'd try this other chap . . . what's his name? . . . Wilson Hendry. He's a few years on, but still personable. More important, the Coulsells haven't staked a claim on him."

At that minute Nonie, more a water-rat than a human being, came out of the water and ran up the bank to her mother.

"Do we have to get dressed now, Mummy?"

"Yes, poppet, if you want to eat with the Coulsells. They always dress for dinner. Just look at Brad right now. . . ."

Brad was standing up talking to Tom Flynn. They both had glasses in their hands and Kylie could see why suddenly she had lost her helpers. Wilson Hendry was officiating at a small keg that had been loaded in the back of the jeep by the camp cook.

Brad had shed his mustering clothes in honour of the picnic. He was shining clean and laundered in his spotless khaki-drill clothes. He'd even removed his riding-boots in favour of brown calf shoes.

Mournfully Kylie wished she had brought a fresh shirt and had owned two pairs of slacks instead of one.

Sara turned away to find a towel and made for the " dressing-room," a bush-screen behind a tree. She looked over her shoulder at Kylie and said quite genuinely:

" Thanks for looking after Nonie. You've been sweet to her."

*

After the picnic they packed up hastily, for the men had to be back at the muster yards. Lunch was a mere interlude, and the day's work had to go on.

Kylie spent the afternoon round the yards, watching the men cut-out wanted bullocks from the middle of mobs and from the cattle bunched round the dividing gate.

She watched Brad more than anyone else because everything he did he did well; his tall figure seemed to stand out whether he was on horseback or on foot. She sat on the stockrails with Nonie, feet twined in the middle rail and hat pulled well down to keep out the glare, and watched ecstatically.

As each mob was brought in to the gates Brad, on horseback and with the help of one or two men, rounded them into a mob against the double gates.

" The cleanskins have to go in one yard," Nonie explained. " They've got to be branded, you see. An' we can't brand them till the Eagle Eye men all come in. We divide them equally between the two stations because cleanskins can be calves of loose cattle round the boundaries from either station."

" I see," said Kylie. She was learning fast and this seven-year-old child seemed to know as much as the grown men.

" Then, if there's a good bullock for prime beef they cut him out too. He has to go through the other gate first and right through the yard to the inside yard. That's what Brad's doing now. Cutting out the young primes."

Brad was on horseback on the edge of the mob milling round the double gates. His long stockwhip lashed out towards the middle of the mob and a young bullock started forward.

"Yip-yip-yip!" Brad called. It was a short staccato sound, not very loud, but the other bullocks started up too. They couldn't go forward because of the crush so they pressed sideways. Gradually, inch by inch, Brad eased the picked animal through the mob until it was pressed against the part of the gate that would presently open a crack and let him through—alone.

Kylie thought it was the cleverest thing she had ever seen. A man sat quietly on an unmoving horse and with his stock-whip picked out and moved through a bellowing, horning, startled mob one animal to the exact position where it could be drafted into the yard, leaving others outside.

"I wish Brad didn't have to whip him in," Kylie said, grieved for the young bullock.

"Don't be silly, Kylie," Nonie said, pitying Kylie's ignorance. "The whip doesn't touch him. It's the crack that makes him start forward. The end of the whip just curls an inch from his backside and goes off like a cracker. He gets a fright."

"Goodness, what judgment!" Kylie said. "How long is Brad's whip that its tip can reach the bullock from the edge of the mob?"

"That's about the longest you can get," Nonie said proudly. "The Whip Man makes them specially for Brad. He says they're the longest in the north. Twenty-eight feet." Nonie said this as if she were talking about pound notes, and in millions.

No more mobs were brought in after the tea-break but the cutting-out went on until nearly sundown.

Kylie, like everyone else, was covered with a thick pall of dust. She had heard enough bulls bellowing and enough men "Yip-yip-yipping" to last her a week. She was glad when it was home time. Her bruises from her spill in the morning were beginning to make themselves felt.

She was just getting into the jeep, after the camp had been broken, when Brad came riding up. He had three horses on the lead behind him. One of them was Goldie.

"Kylie," he said. "I think you'd better ride home. I'm going up now and I'll take you."

Kylie was so surprised she didn't know what to say.

"Me too, Brad?" clamoured Nonie, who had just said a slightly tearful farewell to her parents but now seemed quite happy to go back to Rock Hill homestead.

"Not this time, Nonie," Brad said quietly. "Kylie has to ride those bruises out of her system. It wouldn't be very kind of you to let Wilson Hendry drive up to the homestead alone, would it? After all, it was he who invited you for a picnic."

"Wilson Hendry and who else?" the last-mentioned said. "I still think you had a hand in it somewhere, Brad."

Kylie was a little staggered that, bruised, tired, the scratches on her hands and the back of her neck stinging as if salt had been rubbed in them, she now had to make that long ride up to the homestead. Why, it was miles away.

All the same she was not going to say no. An invitation from Brad always seemed to be something in the nature of a command. It wasn't only this fact. It was that he had *asked* her: and had thought of her again after that long day. There had been periods in the middle of it when he had seemed to pay attention only to Sara Allen and forget she, Kylie, was even present.

It was something of a test, she knew. That was a long way to ride, but if she made it, uncomplainingly, Brad would think better of her.

Above everything else, she was going because he had asked her.

"All right, Brad," she said cheerfully. "Do I ride Goldie?"

"I think you're safest on Goldie." He nearly smiled. "Don't try to turn her on the rein again, unless you know what's likely to happen next, will you?"

"Oh, no," Kylie said firmly. "I shall behave like a passenger in a railway train."

Brad swung himself off Joachim, handed his reins to Nonie, and those of the lead horse, and came across to help Kylie mount Goldie. He held the stirrup for her.

"Put your foot in. Right," he said. "Now stand steady." He dropped Goldie's cheek-strap and taking a step round Kylie, he put both his hands on her waist and lifted her up into the air and on to the saddle.

Kylie could have cried with gratitude. She was so stiff she had been desperately afraid she was going to muff that mounting. She knew she couldn't "fly in the air" the way Nonie had taught her, and dreaded making a clumsy climb up on to the saddle in front of everyone. Brad must have known just how stiff she was for he hadn't waited to let her make the clumsy effort. He had simply lifted her gracefully up.

He put the reins in her hands, took Joachim's reins from Nonie, and the lead from his change horse.

"Thanks, Nonie," he said. "See you later. Tell Ray to have that bath water hot. We'll need it."

Again Kylie was grateful to him. He hadn't said—"Kylie will want a boiling bath and several pounds of salt because she will have *had it!*" He had said "we" as if tumbling off horses and then making long sundown rides home to work out the bruises was a matter of course to him too.

CHAPTER FOURTEEN

It was a long sundown ride home. The lead horse slowed them up and they trotted most of the time. Trotting was more painful to Kylie and a dozen times she was near begging Brad for mercy with the plea to have a short canter, even a gallop. The rising up and down from the saddle in the trot tore at her tired muscles and stinging bruises.

They made a silent cavalcade for Brad too was evidently tired. He went ahead with the lead horse but every now and again turned his head.

"All right?" he called.

Kylie nodded. What's more, she smiled. She had to grit her teeth to do it.

All right, indeed? She had moments when she hoped never to get on a horse again. Yet at the back of her mind she knew that she would. And she knew all was worth it because Brad had asked her to ride home; and they were alone.

As the sun declined over the western slopes and hid finally behind a clump of trees behind them, so the cockatoos flew, flight upon flight, home to wherever they roosted at night. The lizards disappeared, the little creeping crawling things in the grass beneath their horses' feet, disappeared. The scrub, two hundred yards away on their left, became still with silence. The red plain had become grey and there was silence everywhere. They were indeed alone.

Presently Brad slowed down to a walk to negotiate a short rocky rise with the lead horse drawn up abreast of Joachim.

At the top of the rise he stopped. As Kylie, on Goldie, climbed up beside him he held out a hand that meant silence. He sat, graven still in his saddle, and looked away to the left towards the scrub.

For a moment Kylie could not see what Brad was looking at. Then she discerned the black shape of an animal, one of the bullocks she supposed, grazing out on the plain fifty yards from the fringe of the scrub.

" Wouldn't it! " said Brad, exasperated.

" What is it? " asked Kylie. She kept her voice as low as Brad's voice for it seemed important not to make a noise.

" The Kelly bull! " he said. " He's been loose in that scrub since the last round-up, twelve months ago. We lose endless heifers to him. He lures them in the scrub and it takes us weeks to comb out the few we can retrieve."

" Can't you get him? " asked Kylie.

Brad turned his head and looked at her. He shook his head slightly.

" Not with you, Kylie, I'm afraid. It needs three of us."

" How? "

" One rides into the scrub behind him, so he can't beat back into the scrub. We startle him well out on to the plain, if he's a wanted stray. We need a man on the north side to prevent him racing north and a man in waiting out on the plain to the south who can race alongside him as he breaks out. That man would throw him."

" I couldn't chase a bull and throw him, Brad," Kylie said ruefully. " But if I rode in the scrub behind him maybe I could frighten him farther out, and you throw him."

Brad smiled.

" Kylie, you're a novice."

" I know. But we've lost the stray anyway, haven't we? Well, why not play our luck? It wouldn't hurt to try. The worst that could happen is we lose the stray . . . same as now."

Brad looked at her thoughtfully.

" Could you ride Goldie in that scrub? "

" I think Goldie would know what to do, wouldn't she? "

" Yes. But don't wheel, on the gallop, Kylie. She'd come up like she did when you fell."

" I won't, but if she does, I won't fall," said Kylie. " I know what she might do now, and I'd just stick on."

" You're a game chicken," he said. " All right, we'll give

it a fling. Now listen carefully." He nodded his head in the direction of the grazing animal. "Those chaps come out early in the morning or after sundown to graze on the plain because they *know* there's no one about. So he won't be on guard. I'll ride into the scrub with you . . . we'll go way back about five hundred yards. I'll station you in the scrub well behind him. I'll take Silver, the lead horse, farther along the line and leave him haltered just on the edge of the scrub. When you break through the scrub the stray will get a start, instantly become aware of Silver tethered inside the scrub fringe. Given luck, Silver will kick up his heels too. The stray will head out on to the plain southwards. I'll be waiting. Got it? "

Kylie nodded.

" When I've placed you in the scrub I want you to wait ten minutes by the clock while I place Silver and ride back in an arc into the plain. Have you got a watch? "

Kylie shook her head regretfully. Without a word he unstrapped his own watch and handed it to her over the space between them.

" Good," he said. " Let's get cracking. The less noise the better."

They rode back in a wide arc into the scrub. Brad had taken a line on some trees and the grazing stray.

" All right," he said. " Sit here. Don't snap so much as a stick. When ten minutes is up come out with as much racket and row as you can manage. Ride straight for that tree over there . . . round it, when you come to it, of course. The stray is straight out in front of it. If we have any luck, and Silver plays his part, the stray will make for the open plain. I'll be waiting. Got it? "

Kylie nodded.

She hardly heard him ride away for Joachim also was trained for this kind of scrub hunt. He picked his way over fallen scrub limbs, through stick-bush and tree-creeper as delicately as a dancer.

Kylie had Brad's watch strapped on her wrist by this time. And she sat watching it. Goldie had her ears pricked but she did not make a movement. The only sound in the sundown world was an occasional leaf or nut dropping; an occasional dried stick cracking. The stray was used to these noises and they did not frighten him.

Second by second Kylie waited as the big hand on the watch

left the nine minute mark. Dead on the ten minutes she stiffened. Goldie under her knew the sign and she too stiffened.

"Go on, Goldie. Go on!" Kylie cried, shaking the reins.

The little horse plunged through the bush, thrashing and crashing through the scrub with the sound of a legion of bush-whackers.

The only noise Kylie could think to make herself was the one she had heard man-made all day.

"Yip-yip-yip!" she cried. "Yip-yip-yip!"

Goldie dodged the big tree, crashed through the scrub fringe, and a minute later they were out on the plain.

Several hundred yards north of them, Silver was thrashing the bush with his legs, his head straining on the tether. Away across the plain the stray was charging madly and then, at that moment, Brad came full gallop from behind the rock rise he and Kylie had ridden up a short time ago.

Goldie reined in obediently and Kylie sat on her horse and waited, breathless. Man on horse, and the stray, were riding madly side by side now.

"But how does he catch him? How?" cried Kylie, nearly sick with apprehension and excitement. She knew Brad had no rope on his saddle. And she didn't think Australian stockmen lassoed the stock.

Then she saw how it was done.

Joachim had measured his pace to the stray's pace. As the animal swung away, the horse swung with him and instantly Brad was off Joachim's back and on to the stray's back. After that all was so quick Kylie was never quite sure if she had seen rightly. One minute Brad was on the stray's back, then he was sliding down the backbone of the animal to the ground. He held the stray's tail and leaned back. He was a man being dragged along the ground standing, like a water-skier holding on to a balancing rope. He was braking himself by heels dug in the ground. Then Brad's hands, holding the tail, came up, flicked over sideways and the stray was on his side on the ground. Quick as lightning Brad was on the stray's back, something caught the light and glinted in Brad's hand. As quickly he jumped clear.

The stray gathered himself together and stood up. He shook his head then looked round. Slowly he moved away. There was a slight limp to his right foreleg as he walked.

Joachim was standing still, reins dangling, waiting for his master's return.

When Brad rode up to Kylie he was smiling. He had Silver on the lead again.

" I didn't think we'd do it," he said. " You're a good time-keeper, Kylie."

" What did you do to the stray? " Kylie asked. " Why did he just walk away? "

Brad looked at her under the brim of his hat.

" I could have killed him, Kylie, but I didn't. I had too much respect for him as a bushranger. I merely deprived him of the right to woo away the young heifers in the stock. I cut the tendon behind the knee of his right leg. He wouldn't feel it, and he won't have any pace again. . . ."

" Oh, *no*, Brad! "

Brad pulled in his mouth in the formidable way Kylie had seen him do before when he had to put someone right in their thinking.

" When you're in the cattle business you're in the bush-ranging business too, Kylie. That stray will get fat and jolly grazing about the scrub for the rest of his life, simply because he won't be able to keep up with the old bushranging gang of strays. Cattlemen are not without hearts. From time to time my stockmen will see him, even ride up to him, but not one of them will ever touch him. By right of one severed tendon, the pain of which he felt no more than a pricking needle, he'll be Kelly's King instead of Kelly's stray. Got it? "

This was a very long speech for Brad; quite a lecture in fact. It did Kylie good for she immediately saw the stray as happy ever after, which was exactly what he would be. It was no different from breaking in a horse to make him a homestead pet.

They reined in together to continue on the ride home.

" Why is he Kelly's stray, Brad? Who is Kelly? " Kylie asked as they turned for the homeward track.

" Ever heard of Ned Kelly—the most famous of the legendary bushrangers? Any brave robber is called Ned Kelly in the outback but this one will come to a happier end—old age in fact. The two-legged original, being a human being, was hanged."

" Oh! "

Kylie didn't seem to have anything more to say. Actually she was so thrilled to have helped Brad, and to have him talking to her like this as if she was a friend and comrade rather than his mother's companion, that she forgot her muscles had ever ached or that trotting had ever been an agony to her.

She could do anything on horseback. That is, she and Goldie! She had taken a spill, she had rounded up a stray; she was making this long sundown trek home with Brad as Tom Flynn or one or other of the stockmen must have done many a time. She was an outback girl!

She was so happy she could have cried.

If Brad would hunt a stray with her, ride home alone with her, maybe he would have just one dance with her at that party.

She would have a dress for it. She didn't quite know how yet. But have it she would.

Night had fallen when they walked their horses into the stable. Brad lifted Kylie down, as he had lifted her up out there at the muster yards. In that brief moment as he lifted her to the ground she was happier than she had ever been in her life. The light in the stables was not very bright but she could see it reflected in Brad's eyes. Beside them the rousabout was already taking the saddle from Joachim's back.

"Thank you, Brad," she said as she unstrapped his watch and gave it to him. He put it in his pocket.

"Don't thank me, Kylie," Brad said. "I was actually acting in my own interests, you know. I knew you were doing some riding with Nonie and that little venture out with the mobs this morning made me realise you were in earnest."

"Oh I was!" Kylie said eagerly.

"Exactly. I can't have mishaps on the station. We've no airdrop here and if there are accidents we can't get the Flying Doctor out here under hours. It's my duty as station manager to see that anyone who gets up on a horse knows how to ride, and ride well. That's why I made you ride home. You've got to stay the distance under exacting circumstances in the riding life in the outback. I had to see that you faced up to your own responsibilities. You, or anyone, Kylie. That's how I run Rock Hill."

*

Slowly her happiness died away and her heart dropped back to its proper place . . . a shade below the normal for a really happy girl.

It had all been for duty.

His duty, and her duty.

She turned away.

"Thank you very much," she said again as she walked away.

Oddly enough the stiffness was back, and her bruises hurt.

*

Next day, in the homestead, Ray had a few hard words to say about the Allens being down at the muster camp and nobody in the homestead having been informed.

"I'd just like to know what they're up to," she said angrily.

Kylie was furiously polishing Mrs. Coulsell's extra best silver ready for the big party, and she did not answer. When Ray had first broached the question she had had to admit she herself had no idea the Allens were there, and there had been no conspiracy to take Nonie down to see her parents surreptitiously.

"The idea of going to Wirradonga Dam was mine and Wilson Hendry's," she said. "We invited Nonie . . . because we wanted her."

"So Nonie's the draw-card, is she?" said Ray, then added as if she had suddenly had an idea, "We'll do something about that."

She had gone away, no longer limping, because her ankle was nearly well, leaving Kylie worried and perplexed.

"Please God she won't send Nonie back to her home before the party. It would break the child's heart."

Now she reversed her own feelings about Sara Allen. She hoped she *would* stay down at the muster yards, and Brad was welcome to see her all day and every day. If Sara and her husband were on Rock Hill Station, they wouldn't be home on Eagle Eye Station to look after Nonie, would they?

*

Mrs. Coulsell had given Kylie some pretty blue nylon material from the store to make Nonie's dress and Kylie felt like asking Mrs. Coulsell to be sure the child was not prevented from coming to the party. Yet she could hardly do this. She couldn't set mother against daughter or the other way round.

So troubled was she about what to do that she forgot to think any more of Tom Flynn's " proposal " or that Wilson Hendry had kissed her hand. In fact she stopped thinking about herself altogether and spent her whole time thinking about Nonie. For the next day or two she kept the child in sight as much as possible.

Every afternoon Nonie came up to the homestead, round the cement path below the veranda to Kylie's room. Kylie stitched and fitted and ruffled frills, and Nonie washed and polished her pieces of china and made more patterns, little "secret" nooks and crannies, tiny pathways and chipped houses, all of china pieces, in her china garden.

All seemed to be going well and there was no talk of Nonie going away. Kylie was beginning to decide she had attached too much importance to Ray's words. They had sounded like a threat but obviously Kylie must have been mistaken.

Nonie was nearly mad with delight over the dress. She had never had a party dress before, much less one that looked as fairy-like as the one Kylie had now nearly finished.

"When are you going to make one for yourself, Kylie?" Nonie asked.

"When I've finished this one," Kylie said, biting off a thread.

She hadn't thought about getting herself a party frock until she heard Ray discussing dresses over the transceiver set with her various friends. Kylie had thought her own role was going to be rather Cinderella-ish until Tom Flynn and Wilson Hendry had started telling her, at different times of course, how many dances she was to promise them.

Sitting stitching Nonie's dress, Kylie had a lot of thoughts. She had come all those hundreds of miles to Rock Hill to follow a star, not to be Cinderella. The more she thought of this the more she rebelled against the prospect. If only she had had one party dress in the days when she had lived in Horace Bentley's house! She could have brought it.

Then she rebelled against that imaginary dress. It would have been last year's dress anyway. She wanted this year's dress.

Suddenly she made up her mind, like the day when she had seen Brad Coulsell standing looking up at Uncle Horace's house from the path outside. She had looked at him, felt sorry for herself, then immediately rung up the agency to say she would take the job on Rock Hill. Just like that.

Putting Nonie's dress down on the bed she went to her door.

"Where are you going, Kylie?" Nonie asked. She had finished washing all to-day's china and was looking round for something more to do.

"To find Tom Flynn," said Kylie. "He didn't go out on the run to-day. He's doing the books in the office."

"May I come too?"

"No, dear. Look, here's something you can do for me . . . ready for the party. Polish the silver backs of my brush and comb set. Oh, and here, darling, you can give my bracelet a polish too. That ought to make you happy."

As Kylie went through the door she heard Nonie saying:

"I want a bracelet like this one day."

She found Tom hot, and immersed in ledgers.

"Why aren't you asleep? It's the siesta hour," he growled.

"My ideas are too bright to be sleeping on them," said Kylie. "Please, Tom dear, may I buy some material from the store and have it charged to my account. Brad said I could do that. . . ."

"Of course you can." He stood up and reached for the key bunch on a shelf. "Lead on, Lady Macduff. I like any excuse myself to escape from these infernal books."

"Oh, thank you," said Kylie. Then as they went through the door together, she went on: "Tom, I'm going to make myself a dress for the party. It's going to be lovely. It's going to have yards and yards of material in it. It's going to have petticoats and petticoats under it. . . ."

They were walking across the gravel square towards the store. He turned his head and smiled.

"You sound as if you've never had a party dress before," he said jokingly.

For a moment Kylie lost step with him, then she went on happily.

No, she wouldn't tell Tom Flynn, or anybody, she had not had a party dress before, that she had not been to a party before. She was not going to be Cinderella for anybody. She would have ever so many dances with Tom Flynn and Wilson Hendry anyway, even if Brad . . .

They had reached the storeroom door and Tom Flynn unlocked it.

Even if Brad . . . she had said to herself. No, there'd be no *even if*. She would make that dress, and make herself so beautiful that Brad would have one dance with her. Just one was all she asked. Then, when she was an old old woman she would be able to die happy.

Tom held the screen door open for her and let her go in.

He did not come in himself but stood holding the door, his head poked forward, as Kylie examined the bolts of cloth stored on the shelves.

" It might be a good idea if we announce our engagement that night," he said. There was still a joke in his voice. Kylie, her brows knit, was looking at the materials and she did not turn round.

" No, darling Tom, I'm not going to marry you . . . this time. Next world, maybe." She too had a joke in her voice.

" You mean that? "

Kylie had pulled out a bolt of palest leaf-green material, so like a chiffon it could be a chiffon, and brought it to the door to look at the colour in a better light.

" Oh, isn't it lovely, Tom! " she said, enraptured. " I wonder what Mrs. Coulsell bought it for? Could she be going to use it for something special? "

" She could not. She or Ray earmark everything they've bought for special purposes. Like you, she probably fell in love with it and so bought it. I keep the books so I know just how much stuff goes on those shelves because either Mrs. or Miss Coulsell couldn't say *no* when they were down in the city, ordering. Then they hope the stockmen's wives will buy it. When they don't . . . after a year or two . . . they just give it away."

" Can I buy it then, Tom? "

" You can—and with pleasure. One more bolt of cloth off my shelves."

" But I'll need an underskirt for chiffon," Kylie nearly wailed, suddenly struck with the thought there would be no hope of matching the colour of this lovely piece of silk or nylon or rayon or whatever it was. Kylie didn't know what it was and she didn't care. It was lovely and soft and it draped beautifully. She thought she'd call it French chiffon and be done with it.

" Easy," said Tom. He took a step inside and let the screen door bang behind him. " Haven't been a book-keeper without knowing what goes on in station stores," he said. He pulled a bolt of white net from another shelf. " This is what the ladies do," he said.

He then rooted about in a box under the counter, and brought out a smaller cardboard box of packet dyes.

" There you are," he said. " You take a bit of that white

lining-satin over there and dye it. Then you put some starch in this net . . ." He looked at Kylie and lifted his hands in a comical shrugging gesture.

" Of course," cried Kylie. " Of course, of course. Oh, Tom, you are a darling."

She had the chiffon on the counter while she happily tugged at the lining-satin. Tom came to give her a hand. They stood side by side. When they had eased it out from under a whole pile of other material Kylie realised Tom was no longer tugging and that his hands were still, and he was looking at her.

" Why aren't you going to marry me? " he said.

" Because you didn't mean it. You were joking."

Both had their hands on the material but they were looking at one another steadily.

" I wasn't joking, Kylie, and I love you. But I'll be honest with you. I love you second best."

They stared at one another in silence a minute.

" What about you, Kylie? " Tom said.

" I love you, Tom. But I love you second best."

For a moment all laughter and fun-making had left them. They looked into one another's eyes with quiet sincerity. Both had told the one truth that is the hardest truth of all to tell.

" Hopeless? " Tom asked, his eyebrows raised in question. Kylie nodded.

" And you, Tom? "

He nodded too.

He turned round, pulled out two stools and motioned Kylie to sit on one. He sat on the other and took out his cigarettes. He lit two cigarettes and handed one to Kylie. It was a sweetly intimate gesture and Kylie felt very close to him.

Outside came the sound of horses riding up to the homestead paddock. She thought of riding home with Brad that night from Wirradonga Dam. With him it had been a *duty*.

" We'd better not ask one another who, what and why," Tom was saying. " Let's treat it as a joke, shall we? "

" Yes please, Tom, do. I couldn't tell you about it. I couldn't bear you to know what a fool I've been."

" A fool? "

The barred ventilating window of the store faced west. Out there, saddled and hitched to the stockrail were the change horses she knew were to be taken that afternoon down to the muster yards. The sound of horses she had heard a few minutes ago had been the jaded ones being brought home for a spell.

She saw a group of stockmen, walking in their strange slow rolling gait to the stockrail. They slipped the reins and mounted the horses.

One figure was unmistakable. It was Brad. He was not riding Joachim, but a tall bay horse with a silver mane. He swung round in his saddle to say something to the slim rider behind him.

Kylie, sitting on the stool in the storeroom, saw that it was Sara.

CHAPTER FIFTEEN

KYLIE LISTENED to the sound of horses riding away into the distance. It seemed as if *love* had ridden away too, out there towards the west where presently the sun would go down.

She turned to Tom Flynn and smiled gently.

" Yes, I've been foolish," she said. " And yet . . ."

" Yes? "

" And yet I'm not sorry. Funny, isn't it? "

" That's what I said—we've got to make a joke of it. It's very, very funny, Kylie. And we've got to live with our jokes."

Tom was smoking with his left hand and with his right hand he picked up Kylie's left hand.

" One day we might figure out that second best is worth a fling," he said. " Shall we bear it in mind? "

Kylie looked at him and smiled. She nodded.

" I couldn't bear not ever to get married," she said. " And Tom . . . I do love you."

" Same here. You heard me the first time," he said lugubriously. His blue eyes looked up and caught Kylie's clear grey-green eyes. He put his head on one side and looked at her eyes intently. " Now I know why you picked that chiffon. To match your eyes."

" They're not green, they're grey."

" That's what you think they are." He leaned forward and kissed the tip of her nose.

Nonie's shadow darkened the screen door. She was outside,

pressing her nose against the wire screen, staring hard into the inner shadow.

" Kylie," she said. " When are you coming? I've finished the polishing, and you haven't fitted my dress on. . . ."

Kylie stood up and went to the door. She pushed it open. " Nonie dear, I'm awfully sorry."

" You aren't. I saw Tom Flynn kissing your nose, and you liked it."

Tom had followed Kylie, carrying the bolts of material.

" Talking of noses, young 'un," he said, " you've got the pattern of the wire door right on the tip of yours. That comes from looking in when you're supposed to be looking the other way. Anyhow, why can't I kiss Kylie's nose? Scram off, or I'll kiss yours."

" Come on, Kylie," Nonie said with great dignity. " He's only being funny."

" I'm not understood," groaned Tom. " Here you are, Nonie, this is only a light one. You can carry it for Kylie." He handed her the bolt of white net.

" I'll bring the other two round for you myself," he added.

Tom and Nonie walked up through the sun from the store-room, across the garden, round the corner of the homestead to Kylie's veranda.

Kylie had gone through the front door because she thought it was nearly afternoon tea-time and she had better put the kettle on.

" What goes on here? " said Tom, looking down at the edge of the veranda where Nonie had laid out the pieces of broken china, blue-pink-white floral patterned, that she had washed that day. Beside them, also in a neat row, were Kylie's brush, comb and mirror, their silver backs gleaming in the sun. Last the choicest, lay Kylie's gold bracelet.

" Getting ready for the party," said Nonie loftily. Obviously Tom didn't understand that when there was a party everything had to be got ready. Wasn't all Mrs. Coulsell's china and silver being turned out and polished?

She went inside and put the bolt of white net on Kylie's bed. Then Tom Flynn handed her the other two bolts from the doorway.

Tom turned round and stepped off the veranda. He stooped and picked up Kylie's bracelet.

" You shouldn't leave that lying around, kiddo," he said " Don't you know the magpies pick up gold and silver? "

Nonie didn't answer because she was busily investigating the bolts of material on Kylie's bed and wondering how on earth any one person could use up all that material in a year.

Tom looked at Kylie's bracelet. He turned it round so that the sun could catch it and bring out the lovely glow of its rich yellow gold. He turned it at an angle and read the inscription in it.

"Rosemary Kylie Bentley 1948," he read slowly. He stopped. then read it again. "Rosemary Kylie Bentley . . . *Rosemary Bentley*." He traced the lettering with his finger and let his finger come to rest under *Kylie*.

He stood for several minutes staring at the bracelet.

Then he stepped up on to the veranda and opened the screen door of Kylie's room.

"Here Nonie," he said. "Put this thing away. Put it in the cupboard, or wherever Kylie keeps it. Out there the magpies will take it."

He walked thoughtfully away. For the first time since he had come to Rock Hill eleven years ago he walked past Ray, sitting on the veranda, and did not see her.

Ray, seeing the direction from which he had come, got quietly up. went down the steps of the veranda to the cement path, and followed it round to the side veranda and Kylie's door. She looked with slightly raised eyebrows at the china garden and the display of china on the veranda edge.

Nonie had put away the bracelet and had just taken in the brush and comb set and put it in the cupboard too. At that moment she was picking up her partly made party dress and was about to hold it up against herself in front of the mirror.

Ray opened the screen door.

"Nonie " she said. "What are you doing? "

"This is my dress," Nonie said. "Kylie's making it for me. It's for the party."

"Oh," said Ray. She stared at the child a minute.

"Don't you like it?" said Nonie. "I could put it on. . . ."

"Put it down, Nonie. I don't want to see your dress just now. Where is Kylie? "

"She went inside to make the afternoon tea, I think."

"She wasn't here when Tom Flynn came to see her? "

Nonie was looking at the dress in the mirror and patting

it with one hand. She was longing to put it on and she didn't pay very much attention to Ray.

"He didn't come to see her," she explained, looking only at the dress, thinking only of the frills. "Kylie went to see *him*. Down at the store. I had to go and get her because they were so long. Just sitting on a stool smoking cigarettes. Tom and I carried all that stuff up for her...." She turned and pointed to the material on the bed.

"Oh," said Ray. "Well, Nonie, I think it's time you ran back to Mrs. Craddock. Don't you think you might be late for your own afternoon tea?"

Ray's voice was quite even, neither kind nor unkind, but very cold. Nonie, lost in the transport of joy her dress gave her, came back to earth. She put her dress back on the bed, pressed down her short faded gingham skirt with her two hands and said:

"If you like, Ray...."

"I do like." She held open the door for Nonie to go through. "Leave those broken pieces of china for to-day, Nonie. You can put them away to-morrow. Good-bye now. Run along...."

"Good-bye, Ray," Nonie said.

She walked slowly along the cement path. Then she remembered that she would see Kylie again at five o'clock. Wilson Hendry was going to give Kylie another lesson in driving the jeep. Every day at five o'clock while Mrs. Coulsell and Ray were having their baths, and while Kylie had to wait for hers, Wilson Hendry let Kylie drive round and round the gravel square. To-day he was going to let her drive down the road between the store and the blacksmith's shop.

Nonie forgot Ray and forgot her blue party dress that was not quite finished. She was going to ride in the jeep too. When she grew a bit more and could sit higher in the drive-seat she was going to drive the jeep. Brad had said so. She nearly knew how to do it now from watching Kylie make mistakes.

Nonie sighed, then smiled. She took a little hopping step that was more blithe than carefree. It was a good job for Kylie, she was thinking, that Kylie had Nonie and Wilson Hendry—in that order—to teach her important things about station life.

In the meantime it was quite a good idea to have a cup of

tea and a piece of fruit cake with Mrs. Craddock. Nonie loved Mrs. Craddock's fruit cake best of all.

*

Ray, standing in the middle of Kylie's room, looked around it. It was scrupulously tidy except for Nonie's unfinished blue nylon dress lying on the bed.

Ray looked at the dress for a long minute. She saw the many frills that needed the binding sewn down; the simple neat bodice that if it was tight-fitting enough would make the tiny frilled skirt on the child's dress ruffle out around her like a ballet dancer's dress. To anyone other than Ray, it was a child's delight.

Quietly Ray took out a cigarette case from her pocket, extracted a cigarette and lit it. She puffed it a little until there was a coal glowing at its tip. Then she leaned over and dropped the cigarette in the middle of Nonie's dress.

The nylon did not flare; the cigarette merely left a black hole as it ate its way through a frill, through the front skirt, through the back skirt and the frill that was gathered to the back. Then Ray leaned forward, picked up the cigarette, returned it to her mouth and went out, casually smoking it. She closed the door quietly behind her.

Later, when Kylie took Tom Flynn's tea into him in the office, he stood up to take the tray from her. His manner had quite changed. He was neither the "second best" lover nor the old joking comrade who had made Kylie's first few days on Rock Hill so much easier.

His face seemed serious, a little preoccupied. Perhaps she had interrupted him in the middle of a particularly long column of figures.

" I'm so sorry to interrupt you, Tom. For the second time in an hour too. But tea is generally worth it, isn't it? "

" That's all right, Kylie. Hope the dress turns out all right. By the way, there's a pile of old newspapers there. They've been here a couple of weeks and I was about to throw them out. If you haven't seen them . . . well, there's always something to read even in an old newspaper." He gave her a rather drawn smile. " More fun in the advertisements and agony columns these days than the news. With war here and rebellion there. . . ."

" Thank you, Tom," Kylie said, picking them up. " To tell you the truth I even forgot there is an outside world. I haven't seen the papers. I just might leaf through them."

He came round the table and held open the door for her.

" Good hunting," he said. " And don't forget the advertisements and the agony column——"

" I won't," Kyle smiled back.

She went off along the veranda, the pile of papers in her arm and unconscious of the fact that Tom Flynn still stood in the doorway, watching her go, a strange expression in his eyes.

She thought the newspapers might be a nuisance but she hadn't the heart to rebuff Tom's kind thought. They must be the ones Wilson Hendry brought from the Harveys. He had mentioned them to her . . . she'd forgotten why. Oh well, she'd put them in the corner of her room for a few days, then get rid of them some other way.

She paused.

What was it Wilson Hendry had told her about the papers he had brought with him?

Kylie couldn't remember. So much had happened since he had arrived.

She thought it was strange that her door was closed. Doors were never closed on Rock Hill. The heat didn't permit it. There had to be a free flow of air. . . .

She paused in the open doorway. There was the faint smell of cigarette smoke in the air.

Who had been in her room, she wondered?

Not Tom . . . she had just taken his tea to him in the office. Brad and the others were all out on the run.

Had Nonie been experimenting, as children often do? But what with? Kylie didn't have cigarettes in her room. She rarely smoked and only when someone offered her one in a tense moment.

Something black on Nonie's dress lying on the bed caught her eye. Slowly she went forward, the papers still in her arm. She stared down at the dress.

A minute later she had put the papers down and picked up the dress. She turned it and turned it with unbelieving eyes. Then suddenly she dropped it, ran through the veranda door, out on to the cement path, round the house and down the gravel square to Mrs. Craddock's cottage.

Like every other dwelling in the north, it was wide open to the air, and to visitors. Kylie pulled open the screen door, went through the living-room to the veranda where Nonie was sitting at a table, happily eating fruit cake from a plate with a blue border to it.

"Nonie," said Kylie, sinking down on one knee beside the child. "Nonie, darling. Did you do anything naughty in my room? Do tell me, dear, because I won't be angry if you're truthful."

Nonie stared at her.

"I looked at myself in the mirror," she said. "Why shouldn't I? I'll be grown up soon. You look at yourself in the mirror, Kylie. . . ."

Kylie brushed her hand across her eyes. She looked up again.

"You didn't see any cigarettes?"

"Have you lost your cigarettes?" Nonie asked. "Tom Flynn will give you some. He has them down at the store."

Kylie shook her head.

"Or a match? Or . . . or well . . . ?"

"I didn't see anything except my dress. I held it up against me and then Ray came in. . . ."

"Nonie, listen dear. Did your dress look nice when you held it up against you?"

"Oh, yes. Beautiful. Just like it was this afternoon. Only I don't think Ray liked it much. She doesn't like anything much about me."

Kylie stood up. She asked carefully:

"Was Ray in the room when you went?"

"Yes. She told me to run away. Don't worry about it, Kylie. I never mind when Ray says that. I just go. Mrs. Craddock says she's got *nerves* . . . and to be sorry for her."

Kylie shook her head incredulously, not because of what Nonie said but because of what Ray had done. How bitter was Ray, and did she hate Sara Allen that much?

"Why did you come down, Kylie?" Nonie asked, fitting another large piece of cake into her mouth.

"Darling . . . because I wanted to know if you thought your dress looked nice when you held it up. Well, now you know it does, so don't worry if we don't have a fitting for a day or two. I'll finish the frills . . . and then when it's all done we'll have a last dress rehearsal. Is that all right?"

Nonie nodded.

"A sort-of surprise for me?" she asked.

Kylie laughed. "Well, nearly, because you do know what it looks like, don't you? But finished it will be ever so much nicer. That all right?"

" Okay," said Nonie. " What you really want is me not to bother you while you're finishing it. All right, I won't."

" You're wrong, dear. I want you to let me make a surprise of it *finished*."

She bent down and kissed Nonie's forehead and then turned and went through the doorway and the little house up to the homestead. She hadn't even noticed that Mrs. Craddock was out at the tankstand and she had not even said hallo to her.

*

Back in her room she picked up the newspapers Tom Flynn had given her, rolled them in a bundle without thought and put them in the waste-paper tin that stood on the edge of the cement path a few yards from her room.

She went back, rooted round her sewing-box till she found a razor blade, then sitting on the edge of her bed began slowly and laboriously to cut the stitching between the frills and the skirt.

" Later," she thought, " I'll have to ask Tom Flynn for more nylon from the storeroom. Goodness, I won't have any wages left this week."

*

The next morning, when Kylie, tired through working into the small hours on Nonie's dress, took in the five o'clock tea, Brad had already gone out on the run and neither Tom Flynn nor Wilson Hendry were in the office. There hadn't been a stockman up at the homestead for days . . . they were all out at the muster . . . so Kylie found nothing strange in the silence in the garden below the veranda.

But where was Tom Flynn? Last night at dinner Brad had specifically said Tom would be staying in to-day. Wilson Hendry as valuator didn't only have to examine capital equipment and livestock. He had to see what kind of "book" wealth the Coulsells had too. Tom Flynn was setting everything out in order for him.

Kylie left Tom's tea on the office table in case he had just gone out for a few minutes but when she returned a quarter of an hour later there was only the tea there, undrunk, and no Tom.

Usually at this hour of the morning Kylie filled in time before taking tea and toast into Mrs. Coulsell at a later hour by doing her own room and the little things around the living-room like tidying up the magazines left about the night before, doing the flowers and sorting out Mrs. Coulsell's sewing for her. Mrs. Coulsell was what she called herself . . . a wizard for losing her thimble, her scissors and her needle case. Kylie found the space between the upholstered arms and seats of the chairs a positive treasure trove of lost this-and-thats.

However, this morning, just because things had to be different, and because there was no Brad or Tom Flynn in the office, she turned on the transceiver set herself to get the news. She poured herself a cup of Tom's tea and sat in Brad's chair and listened. The Flying Doctor calls were just finished and the inter-station communication was on for half an hour before the news service.

Two women from far distant stations were talking to one another. Kylie had long since learned that everyone was entitled to listen-in and join in this session so that nothing was confidential. Neighbourly wives, who weren't glued to their stoves or the kitchen sinks at that hour of the morning, were supposed to say hallo to their friends and hear how things were going on other stations. Kylie sat back, drank nearly-cold tea and enjoyed the conversation.

Then unexpectedly came the piece of news that accounted for Tom Flynn's absence.

" Charmian left you yesterday for Harveys', didn't she? Hallo, Mrs. Harvey, are you there? Charmian get in all right last night? "

There was no answer from Mrs. Harvey so she probably had other things to do than listen to the transceiver this morning. The first two voices went on talking to one another.

" Yes, Sam flew her over last night. She got there all right. We got a late call into Brad Coulsell, just caught him before he turned in. He said Tom Flynn would go across to Harveys' this morning for Charmian. She'll be out at Rock Hill for morning tea."

" Hallo, Rock Hill, are you listening? "

" Don't be silly, Eve," came another voice. " Brad'll be out on the run. They're mustering. And Tom Flynn will be half-way home with Charmian. Mrs. Coulsell and Ray don't get up for this session."

" Bet Tom makes a long drawn out drive to-day," someone said, and there was a gale of laughter, like the Luton Girls' Choir, floating round the air of north-west Australia.

" Compliment to Charmian, *that*," said someone.

" Charmian gets all the compliments," another laughed. Kylie leaned forward and turned off the set.

*

So Charmian Dane was on her way to Rock Hill.

Kylie at last had her wish. She had seen Sara Allen and now, in a few hours, she would see Charmian Dane. That, with herself, she supposed completed Brad's " list." If only Charmian Dane and she herself were married like Sara Allen they would be able to call it " Brad's Old Girls' Association."

Suddenly she remembered Mrs. Coulsell and Ray. If Brad had got that message very late last night they probably did not yet know that Charmian was on her way some days before she was expected.

Kylie jumped up, hastily put her cup and saucer back on the tray, picked up the tray and left the office.

In the kitchen she washed up the early tea things and set about making toast and more tea. Ever since Ray had hurt her ankle she had been taking a tray into Ray in the morning too. She found this hard to do cheerfully since the burn in Nonie's dress.

Ten minutes later she knocked on Mrs. Coulsell's door and when she had put the tray on Mrs. Coulsell's side table and had said " Good morning," she added:

" Did you know there was an air-call last night and Charmian Dane is on her way from Harveys'? "

" Yes, dear, I did know," said Mrs. Coulsell. " Brad woke me to tell me but we didn't tell Ray. She would have been in such a flutter none of us would have got any sleep. After all, the spare room is ready, and they'll never get here before eleven o'clock. . . ." She broke off suddenly and sat up. " Goodness me, I forget," she said. " Brad told Tom to take the big car. You know—Brad's Chrysler Royal saloon. It will make time-and-a-half compared with the station wagon."

So Brad arranged for Charmian to make the royal progress to Rock Hill, did he? Well, it must be Charmian after all: not Sara. Anyway Sara was married now.

No station wagons for Charmian, and Kylie was very sure there'd be no bacon and eggs in the Two-way House either! It would be breakfast *de luxe* at the Harveys' for Tom Flynn too.

Kylie could have cried because she made such unkind remarks to herself. But they weren't unkind, she justified herself. They were just true. She had to wake up and face facts. Charmian was an honoured guest and Chrysler Royals —owned by Brad—and breakfast *de luxe* were the proper treatment for honoured guests. Anything else would be *awful*. Now wouldn't it?

To make up for her unkindness she hastily offered to do whatever she could to help.

" You'd better tell Ray, dear," Mrs. Coulsell said. " Then I'll have a bath while she's having her breakfast. And Kylie dear—the flowers! Could you put some fresh flowers in the living-room? And in the spare room too? It's always aired—the spare room I mean—but it needs sheets and things. Use the linen in the best cupboard, dear. It's real Irish linen. . . ."

Kylie was already at the door.

" Don't worry," she said brightly. " By the time you're out of the bath the whole place will be sparkling."

She hastened to the kitchen and poured boiling water into the teapot on Ray's tray. She retrieved from the oven the hot buttered toast. Just to prove to herself she was not unkind, not jealous, and born only to help, she put a bougainvillaea flower on Ray's tray. Ray had been cold as ice and very angry about something for quite a while. Kylie had a feeling it was more than Sara Allen's nearness and Nonie's pretensions to a party dress. The little flower might be received as an act of goodwill.

Here was to trying, anyway!

Brad had not come in by the time Tom Flynn drove up with his charge, though Mrs. Coulsell and Ray were at the garden gate before the car stopped.

Kylie, looking through the wire screen of the morning-room, thought rather wistfully that it was a beautiful car. Long, low slung; with power and sleekness somehow married together in a glossy sophistication. She had only seen Brad drive it once, and that was when he had come home from MacDougalls' station. It had made her heart turn over.

" But that," she told herself this morning, watching Tom come to a stop, jump out and go round to open the passenger door, " was when I was young and foolish. How many weeks ago? Eight. Silly enough to think that all you had to do when you saw a man who bowled you over was chase him across Australia and . . ."

She didn't go on with the thought for after all she hadn't had any thought past the one that, having seen Brad Coulsell, she would take the job at Rock Hill. She had acted blindly and impetuously. She had simply followed a star.

Well, here was another star arriving.

A pair of long slim legs got out of the car first and they were followed by the rest of a tall slim girl. She stood a minute by the car, took off her very smart sun-glasses and looked around, then smiled at Mrs. Coulsell and Ray.

Charmian was tall but used her height to striking advantage. She had dark hair, casually but effectively done in a bouffant style. She carried a hat of cartwheel size in her hand.

She wore a loose cotton jumper of vertical stripes in candy colours and a pair of coffee-brown slacks. Her feet were bare except for fine thonged gold sandals that were mostly sole with very little to hold them on. She looked exactly as if she'd stepped straight off the Italian Riviera.

Even across the distance of the homestead garden Kylie could see her magnificent dark eyes. It was her height, the streamlined elegance of her casual clothes, and her eyes, that told Kylie that no one, absolutely *no one*, on Rock Hill Station would fail to have their attention attracted to Charmian Dane. In some unaccountable way Kylie felt her own height dwindling.

They came up the garden path, Ray smiling delightedly, Mrs. Coulsell talking graciously, pleasure tinged with restrained excitement; Charmian Dane listening but her large dark eyes roaming over the face of the homestead as if looking for something or someone.

" Where's that devastating brother of yours, Ray? " she said when they reached the steps leading up on to the veranda. " Don't tell me I've chosen the wrong time to come? Is he away? "

" He's had to go down to the muster yards," Ray said. " We've got a valuator here—going into Uncle Horace's estate, you know. Brad had to take him down, but he'll be back for morning tea. He promised."

" Stock boots, dust and all, I suppose," Charmian laughed. " One thing I remember about Rock Hill, everyone looks as if he really works."

As Ray predicted, Brad came in twenty minutes later, stock boots covered with red earth dust, and a fair streaking of it on his khaki cotton clothes. It was the only time Kylie had ever seen Brad come in from the run in the morning. Charmian was indeed an honoured guest.

Before Brad came in Charmian had been taken to her room for a wash and a brush-up, and then in the morning-room had been introduced to Kylie.

She was obviously not the handshaking kind. Across the room she had said:

" Oh hallo! Nice job you've got yourself—making tea. You've no idea what a welcome sight is a teacup after that drive."

It was friendly and cheerful, not condescending, and yet her eyes had flicked over Kylie, taking her in and reserving judgment.

Well, that at any rate was better than being dismissed as unimportant.

Yes, those eyes were magnificent. They were large and dark, their lustre increased by the eye-shadow, the touch of mascara and the otherwise simple make-up. Her eyebrows might have been touched up but their arch was natural. Her generous mouth might have been painted, it was so smoothly red, like a Spanish poppy. She wore no rouge so her face was a study in black and white except for that glorious red colour on her lips. It exactly matched one of the finer stripes in her very dashing cotton jumper. Charmian Dane was so striking she knew it, and used it as a power over everyone around her.

How could she help it? Kylie thought, turning to the side table. Being here with Charmian is like being in the same room with a majestic view. Everyone looks and admires. This view, being human, has to be aware of it.

At the moment when Charmian was greeting Kylie, Brad came into the doorway. He smiled across the room at the visitor, the corners of his mouth drawn in a little, his eyes amused, ironic, but definitely appreciative of what he saw in front of him.

Charmian turned round quickly. She held out both hands. " Brad at last! " she said.

With a natural ease and charm Brad walked across the room and took both her hands in his own. He was smiling at Charmian and she was laughing back at him.

Kylie's hand spilled a little tea as she poured some into the next cup in the circle on the tray.

How stupid can I be, she thought, shaking her head sadly.

CHAPTER SIXTEEN

CHARMIAN DANE couldn't help changing the whole atmosphere in the homestead. She didn't have to do anything but stand about for everyone to be aware she was there.

Every day she wore a different cotton or silk jumper—they were waist-length and there was something about the cut as well as the colour that made them absolutely enviable. Every day there was a different pair of slacks and different glittering thonged sandals.

She was quite sweet to Kylie, with a sweetness that made Kylie think Charmian took her in and then dismissed her as having no " flair." " Flair " was in and " chic " was out according to the advice Charmian gave Ray.

Tom Flynn seemed to avoid Kylie, which puzzled her. That moment in the store when he had lit two cigarettes, one for her and one for himself, and kissed her on the nose had been too intimate not to be genuine. True he had said their love was " second best " but it still had been love.

Wilson Hendry was plunged deep into his work. Rock Hill was a big station with an enormous number of ramifications to its outlying provinces. He went off very early in the morning with Brad.

Ray's ankle was sufficiently mended for her to get her foot into a riding-boot and she and Charmian went out on the run nearly every day.

Nonie, who generally loved to button on to anyone going out on the run, made no attempt to attach herself to Charmian and Ray. Actually Nonie was the only person on Rock Hill whom Charmian Dane didn't enchant.

" Why is she always laughing when she talks to Brad? " Nonie asked.

Brad came in a little earlier these days and the sundown drink hour was usually quite a party on the homestead veranda. Even Wilson Hendry seemed to be preoccupied, in an amused kind of a way, with Charmian. He still, however, remained Kylie's friend and they often had a walk together after dinner and before the last cup of tea of the day.

Kylie guessed that Nonie too took her sundown stroll and

came up by the homestead fence to watch the party on the veranda. That was the only way she could have known whether Charmian laughed when she talked to Brad.

" She's a well brought up guest," Kylie explained. " Good guests always make their hosts feel happy."

" Why does she talk to Brad all the time? " persisted Nonie. " There's Tom Flynn and Mr. Hendry too. . . ."

" Darling, I just hadn't noticed. Now shall we try on the dress for the very last time? The binding of the frills has to be sewn down and Mrs. Craddock is going to do that for me. You see I have to get on with my own dress, else I'll never get to that party myself."

Never would Nonie dream, or anyone else in the homestead, that Kylie had sewn far into the nights to repair the damage done to Nonie's dress by Ray's cigarette.

Kylie tried to tell herself that it had been an accident. But then how did the cigarette come to be removed and nothing said about the black holes in the dress?

Kylie did not tell Ray or anyone in the homestead she was remaking Nonie's dress.

Nonie was going to that party, if Kylie had to lie down and die to get her there. The one thing she dreaded was that Ray might, if she knew the dress had been repaired, prevent it by a direct order.

So Kylie said nothing of her sewing ordeals or that through the long hot days she felt exhausted because she had a short sleep at night and no sleep in the afternoon when the rest of the homestead quite literally " passed out."

Oddly enough the person whom Kylie most missed in these busy trying days was Tom Flynn. Gone were those unspoken conversations across the room when Tom signalled things to Kylie that were half in jest, half in earnest.

Once when she was near him she ventured to break the silence between them.

" Hallo, Tom," she said. " You must be awfully busy these days. I don't see you . . ."

" I've been more than busy," he said, looking at her oddly as if he was seeing someone new and a little strange. Kylie was puzzled.

" Did you look at those old newspapers I gave you, Kylie? " he asked.

She had forgotten all about them and shook her head.

" You ought to look at them," he said.

" There's a new batch in now," she offered, by way of excuse.

" The old ones have the best advertisements in the Personal columns," Tom said. " That's where most of the entertainment for readers is to be found."

Kylie thought he had an awfully funny idea of conversation, and she didn't like to tell him how she had come to throw out the papers because it had been when she discovered Nonie's dress had been burned.

All of a sudden a thought struck her. Personal columns? Wilson Hendry had told her that was where the Horace Bentley lawyers had advertised for Rosemary Bentley.

Could Tom Flynn have seen them and associated her with Rosemary Bentley? It didn't seem possible.

As she watched him walk away she felt a twinge of anxiety. She didn't want to leave Rock Hill. She wanted to stay here for ever and ever. But some day someone was going to turn up who would not only know she was Rosemary Bentley, as Wilson Hendry knew, but would make her confess.

Then her honeymoon with the stars would be over. It would be good-bye to Rock Hill.

The more she felt this uncertainty, the more she felt she had only a small bonus of time to use up.

There was something in Kylie that wouldn't let her give up without a fight. She would have one night . . . one dance with Brad. It was all she asked of Fate.

She was on the floor, in her room, cutting out the circles and circles of net to make one of the underslips for her dress, next day when Charmian Dane came in.

" Oh hallo, come in," Kylie said, looking up. She made her voice sound welcoming and friendly.

" The party dress? " Charmian asked, eyebrows arched.

" Sit on the bed," Kylie said as she nodded. " And please don't mind if I talk with my mouth full of pins."

Charmian sat on the bed and crossed her long slim legs. Kylie thought of a ballet dancer out of a French picture she had once seen. Charmian's loose hip-length silk shirt, and her slacks, were all black to-day. Everything was black about her except her white Latin-type face and the Spanish-poppy red lips.

" Who's the dress meant to impress? " Charmian asked. " The Wilson Hendry man? "   She lit a cigarette and expelled a long spiral of smoke that wreathed up into the air like a pencil-fine pathway to the sky.

Kylie snipped bits of net here and there with her scissors. "Why Wilson Hendry?" she asked without looking up, "He's nice. I like him but I'm not trying to capture him."

"Oh, something Ray said. She thinks he's very enamoured of you and wishes to goodness he'd marry you off—to himself."

Kylie put down the scissors, took the pins out of her mouth and looked at Charmian. She would like to be very angry, she thought. But she mustn't show it.

"What a pity for Wilson Hendry," she said with a laugh. "He's much too nice to have me thrust on him like that. It's because he's been teaching me to drive the jeep, I suppose. But then Tom Flynn gave me one lesson, and came riding in the morning with Nonie and me more than once. Why not Tom Flynn, if I've got to be married off to somebody?" She picked up the scissors again.

This was like the business of marrying off Sara to Bill Allen, she thought. How silly could Ray be?

"Hands off Tom Flynn," said Charmian, looking at Kylie out of half-closed eyes. True, the smoke from her cigarette might cause her to close her eyes but it made Kylie feel as if Charmian was diagnosing her and thinking about that diagnosis.

Who had said that about hands off Tom Flynn to Kylie before?

Why, it was Sara Allen!

Why was this warning given! Were the Coulsells afraid they might lose Tom Flynn if some ambitious young woman came along and wooed him away to more lucrative realms?

Kylie bent over her work again.

"What's wrong with Tom Flynn?" she asked, trying to sound impersonal.

"He happens to be Ray's property."

Kylie dropped the scissors with a clatter, knelt up straight and looked at Charmian.

"Ray's property?" she said incredulously. "Why, she's not even very nice to him."

Charmian blew out another spiral of cigarette smoke. She lolled back on Kylie's bed and struck an attitude of amusement at Kylie's naïveté.

"That's why," she said. "He doesn't woo her, or win her. He doesn't even walk in the garden with her at night ... as he does with you, and as Wilson Hendry walks with you, Miss Innocent. You don't mind me calling you that, do you? Half the time I think you are innocent and naïve," she went on. "The other half I think it's your line. Very effective with those grey-green eyes of yours and the young-girl attitude to doing good."

"Just a minute," said Kylie. "One thing at a time. Let's talk about Tom and Ray first. Are you sure Ray feels like that about Tom?"

Charmian, resting on one arm, threw her head back and laughed. Kylie would have thought her pose was very interesting if she had had time to think of anything else but what Charmian was saying.

"She's had feelings for years and years, my dear child. Ever since she left school, in fact. Oh, she goes south and shoots the bright lights with some of the well-moneyed, well-born eligibles in the city, I know that. But home she comes to old Tom Flynn. And what does Tom do? Nary anything. So back to the bright lights ... and the merry-go-round goes round and round."

"Why are you telling me this?" Kylie asked, surprised and a little bewildered.

Charmian sat up and looked at her.

"Because of those nice honest clear grey eyes of yours. I'm not sure they don't shoot a line a more sophisticated girl like Ray never thought of. You just might think Tom is anybody's prize. *I* would if I were in your shoes. So don't."

"Why should you think Tom would be interested in me?"

"The way he looks at you ... when you're not looking. A most curious kind of look. I haven't deciphered it yet. By the same token they all three of them do it. Just what have you got, Miss Clear-eyes?"

"All *three* of them?" asked Kylie, astonished.

Charmian stood up. She stubbed out her cigarette on a pin tray on Kylie's table as if it was an ash-tray. Kylie forgave her in exchange for the information she had just given her.

All three of them, she was thinking. That meant Brad too. Could Brad possibly be looking at her, when she wasn't looking, the way she looked at him, when *he* wasn't looking?

But no, she was star-dreaming again!

" I'd plump for Wilson Hendry," Charmian said, stretching, reaching her arms up and striking another pose. " Brad's my cup of tea for this party."

She went to the door, swung a little on the handle and looked over her shoulder at Kylie.

" Don't worry, poppet! " she said. " Brad's only looking at you to see if you, or someone, *anyone* for that matter, is going to fetch his drink or his cup of tea or whatever-it-is at that hour of day. Very waited-upon is Brad, isn't he? "

On the swing-back of the door she let the handle go and went into the passage. Kylie could hear her feather-light footsteps receding down its polished surface.

" I'm paid to wait on him," Kylie thought angrily. " How do I get out of that? "

Then she fell to thinking about the other things Charmian had said. Ray and Tom? Was it possible?

Tom had said " second best." Could his " first best " be Ray . . . and he'd never told Ray?

But then the Coulsells were station owners. They must be rich. Tom Flynn was the book-keeper. That would be it! It was pride. He couldn't make love to the squatter's sister because it would look as if he was marrying into money.

*

Early after lunch next day, after more sewing in the small hours, it looked as if Kylie's dress might be ready in time for the party. The hold-up over Nonie's dress had made her afraid her own would never get done.

It had to be the dress of all dresses for Kylie. She had never had a party dress before . . . thanks to Horace Bentley's parsimony. The very thought of it enraptured Kylie. When it was all done, except for the starching of the net underslips and the sewing of the hem, she laid it out on her bed and looked at it.

She put her little bead purse beside it and the one hand-made linen handkerchief she possessed. At the foot of the bed she put her pair of lightweight high-heeled shoes. They were white and would pass for evening shoes. She had seen in the magazines that everyone wore them.

She tried one flower after another on the bodice of the dress. First bougainvillaea, then a desert poppy, then a spray of white ti-tree that grew in the Coulsells' garden. None of them quite did and finally it occurred to Kylie that the dress needed no flower. Her only ornament would be her bracelet. Instinct told Kylie that simplicity was the key to success. The soft folds on the bodice of the many fluted skirt was enough.

*

Later that day strange things began to happen. It was like the day of a hundred disasters, Kylie thought. Except they weren't exactly disasters and there weren't so many of them.

First Brad, Tom Flynn and Wilson Hendry came in soon after lunch, an unprecedented thing, and they gave no explanation. They went to Brad's office and talked.

Business! Kylie thought.

Ray and Charmian had gone riding out to Blackfellow's Creek in the morning and weren't expected in till sundown. Mrs. Coulsell was having her afternoon sleep and Nonie was keeping guard over Mrs. Craddock while Mrs. Craddock sewed miles of binding hem round the frills on Nonie's dress.

Kylie left her treasures spread out on her bed because she had heard the men come in, and went to see if she could get them some tea.

She found Brad in the pantry making tea himself.

" Oh, let me do that," Kylie said eagerly.

To her surprise Brad turned his head and looked at her, without smiling, without saying anything, as if he were seeing a strange person, not someone he knew. Kylie felt the blood rising in her cheeks. He looked different, and not very pleased.

" The tea's nearly ready," Brad said at length. " Do you drink tea at this hour too? "

" Well . . . yes," she said reluctantly, then added brightly: " Everyone drinks tea on Rock Hill whenever they're offered it. Haven't you noticed, Brad. . . ? "

Her voice died away on the sound of his name because obviously he was not being impressed by her pseudo brightness.

" Everything seems to be going smoothly . . ." she managed to say. " About the party, I mean. It's only two days before they begin coming. . . ." She was saying anything in order to say something.

She was near him but he watched her relentlessly, knowing she knew it and that it made her uneasy. He did not take his eyes from her face.

She turned to go away. Brad didn't want her, that was clear.

He put the teapot on the tray and turned to lean against the edge of the bench; and folded his arms.

" You have met Wilson Hendry before, Kylie? " he asked unexpectedly.

She was surprised and felt pinned, like a butterfly on a board.

" Yes, I have met him before," she said reluctantly.

There was a small silence as if he was waiting for her to say more. His eyes still did not leave her. In that minute Kylie gained courage.

" He is a very good friend to me," she added simply, looking up to meet Brad's eyes.

There was a restraint and dignity in her manner that was as unconscious as it was natural. The relentless expression in Brad's eyes altered by an imperceptible amount.

He turned and switched off the electric kettle.

" He is devoted to you," he said, then added slowly, that outback, muster yard drawl creeping back into his voice, " and it appears that Tom Flynn is likewise."

Kylie had had too much to do with her dressmaking to think of either Wilson Hendry or Tom Flynn.

" I think you are mistaken," she said clearly. " That is, you mistake kindness and friendship for devotion."

Brad's eyebrows moved and then came back to steady.

" Go on, Kylie," he said. " You interest me."

" A person can be just a little lonely without friendship," she said without emphasis and knowing that the words spoke for themselves.

" Quite," he said. " And of course it is a dangerous thing to abuse such gifts."

Kylie flushed.

" Are you reprimanding me, Brad? Of course I realise it is your right as my employer. You don't want emotional problems interfering with the smooth running of Rock Hill."

" No," he said. " I am simply trying to resolve an enigma. And you are not co-operative."

" I'm sorry," she said, and turned away towards the door.

Brad straightened himself and reached the door before her.

For half a minute they stood, his eyes, expressionless though relentless, on her face, and nothing between them but silence.

What did he want? A clear statement as to her real relationship with Tom Flynn? Didn't he know Tom Flynn hadn't spoken to her for days? Not since the kiss in the store in fact. As for Wilson Hendry . . . perhaps he thought she was determined to have one man if she couldn't have the other. It could look like that to Brad, she thought unhappily.

Surprisingly it was Brad's manner that eased a little now. He stood aside for her to go through the door.

She went quickly out of the pantry, sudden tears almost blinding her eyes. All these weeks, according to Tom's warning and her own instinct for self-preservation where Ray was concerned, she had not allowed herself to look too often at Brad, nor think too much about him. She had done nothing to attract his attention to herself and yet somehow she had managed to do just that. She had attracted his *angry* attention, perhaps his dislike, certainly his distrust.

*

Her next meeting was with Tom Flynn as she retreated hastily down the passage from the pantry after her meeting with Brad.

" Good afternoon," Tom said. His manner was as if speaking to a stranger. There was a puzzled look, almost a hurt one, in his eyes.

Kylie went away down the passage, mystified.

How changed Tom had become in the last twenty-four hours!

Perhaps Brad had really thrown his weight about as manager and owner! Kylie thought she could see it all. Brad believed there was something bordering on the serious between herself and Tom and contrary to the usual Coulsell principles of happily marrying everyone off, he wasn't going to permit it. That would be on account of Ray's feelings, of course.

Ray, and her silly pride!

Kylie wished she could stay on Rock Hill just long enough to make Tom propose to Ray, and make Ray swallow that pride and marry him. Obviously she, herself, wasn't going to stay on Rock Hill very long, if Brad was going to distrust her.

What did all a squatter's possessions, or Tom Flynn's lack of them, matter when true heart-warming love was enough?

But she doubted whether anyone, even Brad, could *make* Ray do anything.

What a strange anti-climax these two meetings were to days that had been full of excitement, and pleasure in hard work. Strange and unexpected. But then balloons always burst suddenly!

The thing now was to keep her own pride. By no word or gesture during the forthcoming evening must she show anyone that anything was wrong: that Brad had quite literally " carpeted " her—even though there was no real carpet in the pantry.

Kylie wiped the unshed tears away and went to the kitchen, instead of her room.

It was a delightful evening, in spite of the cloud of doubt hovering in Kylie's background.

Actually being here on Rock Hill had been a kind of heaven. Work was a panacea for all ills, Kylie decided. In no time, the desolation that had followed Uncle Horace's death had disappeared. She had forgotten her own troubles in becoming absorbed in the human affairs of the people on Rock Hill.

She had been tempted to taste of forbidden fruit when she had followed her star to Rock Hill. Perhaps even that had been fun while it lasted.

Ah well, she would write it all off to experience and start again somewhere else, a little older, a lot wiser!

Perhaps there were other friends to be made elsewhere. . . .

*

That night Wilson Hendry had taken his usual cigarette on his usual walk to the homestead fence. Sometimes, when he had done this, he had said to Kylie, " Coming? " Usually he had gladly gone.

To-night he avoided her eyes as he walked down the veranda steps, leaving the others sitting in cane chairs on the veranda which was festooned with hundreds of hanging ferns that had already been hung from the rafters as decorations for the coming house-party.

He had the air of a man determined to be lonely. He did not want company.

This was not good enough for Kylie who had in odd moments those curious compulsions that made her go out and seek fortune, good or bad. The old sense of following her star.

She ran down the veranda steps after him and caught up with him near the fence.

" Wilson," she said. " Wilson, I haven't really seen you for days. We've all been so madly getting ready for the party. . . ."

" Yes," he said. He had not smiled a welcome. Instea
he had looked away evasively. " We've been pretty bus
round and about the station too. If my luck holds I'll b
able to fold my tent in a day or two and finish the job o
Rock Hill."

" But you're staying for the dance? " Kylie cried in disma
" Why, Wilson, you said you were going to have three danc
with me. And I've got a new dress. It's *lovely*."

He suddenly looked a little sad as he patted her arm. Gon
was the lively fun-making manner. He seemed a differer
man.

" You must dance with somebody younger, Kylie. You'v
got youth. It wouldn't be right of me to take you away fror
people your own age."

People her own age? But she didn't know any of the peopl
coming, let alone those of her own age. They had their ow
sets of friends. They were " station " people and, like th
Levellers, when they didn't talk to themselves they talked onl
to God.

Suddenly she was angry.

She knew what had happened. Brad had more or les
told her not to try and endear herself to Tom Flynn an
Wilson Hendry. And he'd warned them against paying he
attention too. So this was how the Coulsells ran their staf
Brad wasn't any better than Ray. He was *hard*. He wa
managing.

Tears of frustration filled her eyes and she turned and ra
through the garden, around the cement path to her ow
piece of veranda.

When she turned on her bedroom light it shone out ove
Nonie's china garden, making the porcelain dance wit
milk-white gems. Kylie leaned her head against the wal
frame and looked out through the screen at the garden. I
was so pretty. Why did people bother to grow flowers whe
all they had to do was plant china chips in patterns? Wh
did people bother to love other people when all they had t
do was keep to themselves and develop stones for hearts
Like Nonie's garden, they all looked nice, these Coulsells
But really they were only pieces of stone put together to mak
a pattern.

If Nonie stayed with them long enough they would mak
her like that too.

The tears came back to Kylie's eyes.

Dear little Nonie! No, Nonie did know what love and kindness was. She was only seven but she had helped Kylie as Kylie had helped her. Whatever else she remembered about Rock Hill, when she was an old old woman, sitting in an arm-chair with a gouty foot up on another chair, she would remember Nonie.

Suddenly Kylie realised she was dramatising herself. This old old woman business, for instance.

She rubbed the back of her hand across her eyes and went to the mirror. She looked at her own image reflected there. " I'm not exactly pretty," she said. " But I'm not bad. Like Charmian said . . . I do have nice eyes. They're big and they're spaced. And yes, I'm glad they're grey that's nearly green. They're different. And my party dress makes them even better. It sort-of gives them a colour. . . ."

She pressed her lips together.

" I'm going to the party," she told herself in the mirror. " Even if Tom Flynn and Wilson Hendry don't dance with me . . . just because Brad has bullied them . . . I'll make someone dance with me. I'll open my eyes wide, and flutter my eyelashes. . . ."

She fluttered them now and decided they were long.

" And I'll *make* Brad dance with me. Just once. Even if I have to ask him. After that he can give me the sack. I won't even care. I won't care about anything ever again, if only I can dance with Brad *once*."

The tears were nearly back because she realised how illogical he was. It didn't seem to matter if Brad was hard and bossy and interfering in other people's love life . . . she still loved him.

" Yes," said Kylie, dropping her head as she turned away from the mirror. " I still love him. And I don't really know how to flutter my eyelashes. . . ."

CHAPTER SEVENTEEN

KYLIE SPENT the next two days cooking delicacies, pastry-making, helping Mrs. Coulsell prepare rooms and a big sleep-out for the younger girls in the party.

The whole station buzzed. Down at the stockmen's cottages and the bachelors' quarters the same preparations were going

on for such stockmen who, hearing there were to be races
would ride in to try the skill of their own horses against Rock
Hill blood.

Kylie, in between mad huddles with the lubras and vast
cooking utensils in the kitchen, was finishing her dress.

Nonie nearly took to wings when she was finally allowed to
fit on her own finished party frock. Mrs. Craddock covered
some slippers with a piece of blue satin and lo, Nonie had
evening shoes too!

Stockmen, and one or two visitors, had begun to arrive the
night Kylie had shed her tears because she loved Brad
Coulsell in spite of his iron-hard hand in managing other
people's lives. By Friday morning the party had started.

Overlanding cars, station wagons, utility trucks made the
lower end of the gravel square under the trees look like a
city parking area. The saddling paddock was full of tall
silent laconic whip-slim men saddling or unsaddling, and a
dust pall hung over it day and night.

Down at the quarters concertinas vied with mouth organs
and a fiddler. By the creek the natives had half a dozen
camp-fires instead of one.

At the side of the gravel square there was a constant and
tantalising odour of beef grilling or roasting on the open fire
spits as groups of stockmen attended to their own needs, and
the homestead lubras attended to the homestead guests.

The homestead itself was overrun with brown-faced, boot-
legged young men and laughing chattering young women.

Mrs. Coulsell, almost in tears with delight and flurry,
greeted everyone with joy. She had her heart's desire—a
station homestead full of people. Gone was loneliness and
gone the fear of being useless to her beloved son and aggra-
vating daughter. She was hostessing a great party for them.
She would prove to them all this could happen again, and
often.

Kylie did not go to the horse muster on Saturday morning,
nor the picnic races in the afternoon. She was too busy
giving herself and Nonie a face-pack and hair-do for the
dance. So much store had Nonie set on that dance she had
not even *asked* to go to the races. A gathering of horse-riders
without Nonie was almost unbelievable.

" What is Mummy wearing? " Kylie asked as she applied
a mixture of milk, oatmeal and white of egg to Nonie's face.

" She's not coming," said Nonie.

Kylie started.

" But she was *asked* . . ." She bit off the question.

" Oh yes, she was asked," Nonie said airily. " She just oesn't want to come. She says she can't compete with harmian Dane so she's giving her an open field at the ance. She can beat her hands down on horseback, anyway."

" Oh, Nonie," said Kylie, shocked. She hoped the child idn't understand the meaning of what she was repeating.

" Do you know what, Kylie? " Nonie said. " I bet she ries to dance with Brad all the time. Charmian, I mean. ou and I won't let her, will we? "

" Darling, don't talk that way. Actually Charmian is uite nice. It's only because we're jealous of her we think hat way. We are jealous, you know. We should admit ."

" About Brad, you mean? "

" Not exactly, dear. About the way she looks; and she has uch an air of getting on with everybody. It would be nice to e like that."

" Ray loves her, and so does Tom Flynn."

Kylie had finished the face-pack and she was holding Nonie way from her, looking at the result.

" Nonie, whatever do you mean? "

" She talked and talked to Tom Flynn in the garden last ight, then she talked and talked to Ray in her room. Then he took Ray into the garden and when they bumped into om Flynn she walked away. And do you know what, ylie? Tom Flynn kissed Ray and Ray cried and then she issed Tom Flynn some more. And they both said they loved harmian, she was a fairy godmother."

Kylie's heart gave a sudden leap of joy. For the life of her he couldn't have stopped the flow of story but when Nonie topped for breath she did her best to look shocked.

" Nonie, were you spying on other people? That's what istening-in is, you know."

" No, I was just sitting outside the garden fence, in the oad, and looking through the wires. I always do, you know. see you and Wilson Hendry at night-time. And Brad sitting n the veranda. And that's Ray's fault because she won't et me inside. So if people come down near where I sit, hat's their fault, isn't it? "

" Sounds logical," said Kylie, shaking her head, but she was too delighted with what Nonie had told her to scold any

more. So it was true! Ray had been Tom's first best and ¦
had taken Charmian Dane to make him go and confess i
For that Kylie would forgive Charmian anything, eve
stealing Brad. Brad wasn't hers to lose anyway.

Perhaps that was why Tom had kept away from hersel
It hadn't been Brad warning him off, it had been anxiet
that now he had complicated himself with another girl whe
Charmian was telling him Ray really loved him.

That's why Brad was angry too. He didn't want Kylie t
spoil Ray's chances of happiness.

Of course, of course! She could see it all.

She would never be able to tell Brad she hadn't take
advantage of Tom's kindness. But what did that matter
There were an awful lot of things Brad would never kno
about her, anyway. That she was Rosemary Bentley, t
begin with.

But did any of this account for Wilson Hendry's strang
manner?

*

Face-packs were wiped away, hair rollers undone, dinne
over and the dressing begun.

All over the homestead, on the side verandas and in th
camps under the trees people were bathing first and the
putting on their glad rags. Half the fun of the party,
seemed to Kylie, was the getting ready.

She herself was dressed and waiting for Nonie. Now sh
wasn't so sure of herself. What if she was a flop? What
no one danced with her at all?

Wouldn't it be wonderful if she could sweep down tha
polished fern-decorated veranda, the cynosure of all eyes
The most beautiful girl present? The loveliest dress of all
And Brad would step forward and hold out his hand, an
bow. . . .

She was dreaming.

What if no one even noticed she was there?

Kylie looked at her watch. Goodness, Nonie should hav
been here half an hour ago. Already the bush orchestr
was striking up round the corner of the front veranda. Glasse
had been clinking and voices raised in talk and laught
for ages.

It was incredible that Nonie should be late. Kylie ha
expected her to be so early she would be a nuisance with he
excitement.

A quarter of an hour went past and Kylie's surprise turned to anxiety.

What could have happened?

Suddenly she remembered the burnt nylon dress.

Ray hadn't intended Nonie to come to the party. Even in her new-found happiness with Tom Flynn she would still hate Sara Allen. She would be a potential rival to Charmian, and Ray wanted Charmian for Brad. Sara Allen's child had to pay the price.

Fear and doubt became certainty and suddenly Kylie jumped up. She opened the screen door on to the veranda and ran out.

She slipped across the garden, under the wire of the side fence, and ran down the gravel square to Mrs. Craddock's cottage.

All around there were camp-fires, lights in the trees in the garden, stars in the sky. There was laughter, singing, music, voices calling one to another. Kylie ran on unseeing and unhearing.

If she tripped and spoiled her dress she did not care. Nonie was going to that party! If she had to pull Rock Hill down about her ears—Nonie was going to that party!

Mrs. Craddock's cottage was a pool of light but it was also an oasis of silence in the noisy gaiety of the area around the homestead.

Its silence confirmed Kylie in her fear that something was wrong. She ran through the small gate into the tiny enclosed garden, through the screen door on to the lean-to veranda and into the living-room.

Mrs. Craddock was sitting in an old-fashioned rocker, her arms folded, her chin sunk on her ample bosom. The hanger with Nonie's dress on it was hung on the door handle of the inner room. Below it stood the blue satin-covered shoes. On the mantelpiece beside it was a little blue handbag with a gilt chain handle.

Kylie stared at them, then at Mrs. Craddock.

She had pulled up short inside the room and was trying to catch her breath. Mrs. Craddock raised her eyes and looked at Kylie, shook her head slowly from side to side, but said nothing.

" What happened? " gasped Kylie.

Mrs. Craddock did not move her position. She was a woman sunk in gloom.

" Her father came for her an hour ago. He took her down to the stockyards at Wirradonga Dam."

" But why? Why? " cried Kylie.

She hadn't seen much of Bill Allen that day out at the dam. He had been a tall shy silent man and had got on with his job while the others had had their picnic. Yet everything Nonie had quoted him as saying had been good things, often wise things.

" Seems like yesterday, when Miss Ray and that glamour friend of hers . . . looks as if she's out of a picture book or a film, or something . . . went for a ride down there to the dam, Miss Ray told Bill Allen he'd better send for Nonie. A big party round the homestead wasn't a right place for a child."

" But . . ."

" There aren't any ' buts,' Miss Kylie. It was a hint and Bill Allen knew it was. Guess Sara did too. They'd rather drop dead than have Nonie at a homestead party when she wasn't wanted."

" But Ray's not the only one who says what goes on at a party. Mrs. Coulsell was expecting Nonie . . . she wanted her to come. She gave me the nylon for her dress. Brad knew she was coming. Nonie said he'd promised to dance with her. . . ."

" That's as it may be, but Bill and Sara Allen have got their pride. If Miss Ray said ' out ' then they weren't going to lay themselves open to having their child where she wasn't wanted."

Kylie sank down on a chair near Mrs. Craddock's rocker. The older woman had not once moved her position. Her arms were still folded, her chin sunk. Only her eyes were raised to look at Kylie with an expression in them that said she too had had a blow.

Kylie twined her fingers together in her distress.

" How did Nonie take it? "

" She cried. She cried and cried. Bill Allen looked mighty like as if he'd cry too and he's a grown man and the toughest stockman Brad Coulsell ever had on Rock Hill. All the same he wasn't going to budge. No child of his was going to gate-crash a Coulsell party."

" It *is* a Coulsell party, and not just Ray's party," Kylie cried. " I know because I helped get it ready. There are friends of Mrs. Coulsell . . . grey-haired people. And some station owners—married, who'd been to school with Brad. They're *his* friends."

She stood up.

" If Nonie's not going I'm not going. I could never face her again. She trusted me. She let me get that dress made, and put face-packs on her . . . and rollers in her hair. . . ."

" There's no point in you both being out of the party, Miss Kylie."

" There's only point in us both being in it." She dropped her voice and spoke quietly. " And we're going to be in it or out of it together," she said. She turned to go out of the room.

Mrs. Craddock unfolded her arms and heaved herself out of the low-slung chair.

" Where are you going? " she asked.

" To Wirradonga Dam. In the jeep. I can drive it now."

" Good," said Mrs. Craddock with slow precision. " I'm coming with you."

Kylie was at the door but she spun round now.

" Oh no, Mrs. Craddock. I've got to be honest. I can't drive the jeep very well. I've never been away from the station square in it. It's a rough track to the Dam. . . ."

" You just go right along and get that jeep out of the shed. It's all by itself behind the blacksmith's shop. I guess you know that. Don't stand there talking, Miss Kylie. It's over an hour to the Dam. You don't want to be too late. By the time you get it out and turn round I'll be waiting for you under the old boab tree next to the smithy. Now go along . . . I got something to do."

Their two pairs of eyes met across the room, and Mrs. Craddock's did not waver.

Without a word Kylie turned round and ran out of the house.

Ten minutes later when she ran the jeep along the homestead track, away from the gravel square to the boab tree, she had no lights on. She didn't worry about it because the whole homestead environs were lit up. Rising in the east, behind the tall tankstand beside the windmill, the moon was coming up, a huge apricot ball, ready to light the whole plain as if it was daylight.

Kylie had had her jeep driving lessons in the daylight and she didn't know which of the many knobs and buttons on the dashboard was the light switch. She hadn't time to find out and she might pull or turn one that would stop the whole works if she tried.

She stopped the jeep at the boab with a jerk, and stalled the engine.

" You see," she said as Mrs. Craddock climbed in and she herself pressed the starter button and, putting her foot on the accelerator, roared the engine too hard. She let out the clutch and the jeep kangaroo-hopped for twenty yards before Kylie had got the pace and engine adjusted to one another.

" You see . . . I can't drive very well. You shouldn't have come. We might have an accident."

" That's why I came," said Mrs. Craddock. " If you're going to have an accident I'm going to be there to help you." She leaned forward and turned on the light switch.

" Oh," said Kylie, watching the track with concentration. " I wasn't sure which. . . ."

Mrs. Craddock chuckled.

" I used to drive the old station truck myself," she said. " I know a thing or two about cars. Besides . . ."

They were running smoothly now down one of the easier declines to the open paddocks. Kylie glanced at her. There was a large brown paper parcel lying across Mrs. Craddock's knees.

" I had to bring this." Mrs. Craddock tapped the parcel.

" What is it? " asked Kylie.

" Nonie's dress. Maybe if we stand up to Bill Allen and his stiff-necked pride we'll get Nonie to that party yet."

" Do you think . . . ? " said Kylie hopefully. " It'll be awfully late."

" Late for you too, Miss Kylie. Don't forget you're missing the dancing too."

" I don't matter very much," Kylie said a little sadly. " I think all the fun was in making the dress and *anticipating*. When I come to think of it, there isn't anyone to dance with me."

" What? A pretty girl like you? " exclaimed Mrs. Craddock. " And that lovely dress. Look dear, just keep it away from the gears . . . that's right. It might get caught, or get oil on it."

*

It was indeed the full hour before they got to the Dam.

Kylie had driven as fast as she dared, but there had been times when she had had to crawl over the stickier parts of the track and more than once had stalled the engine when she had changed down to bottom gear to negotiate the rocky inclines. However, Mrs. Craddock beside her was a comfort and stalling didn't seem the tragedy Wilson Hendry had made it out to be the first time she did it when she was his pupil.

Occasional kangaroo-hopping didn't do the jeep's engine so much good but by this time Kylie wasn't worrying. Nothing seemed to Kylie to be very important except to get to the Dam and find Nonie.

Even if they couldn't move Bill Allen and didn't bring Nonie back for the last gay hours of the party she wanted the child to know she too would share her disappointment. Something shared was never quite so bad as something one suffered alone.

They'd be able to make a joke about their frocks; call them Cinderellas and think up Prince Charmings that might come some day. . . .

Prince Charming!

Who was dancing with Kylie's own Prince Charming to-night? Charmian? Some of those pretty girls who had ridden, according to account, so magnificently at the picnic races?

Brad would admire a girl who rode well. He wouldn't have to exercise his responsibility as station manager to teach her . . . this unknown girl who could ride so well . . . to suffer bruises and stiffness by a long ride home in order to have everyone on his station proficient.

No room for noodles on Rock Hill Station.

Kylie wondered what he would think if he saw how she handled the jeep on some of these rocky patches on the way to the Dam.

Not much, that was certain.

It was half past ten when they came to the camps high on the lagoon bank. Several of them had lanterns hanging from their canvas roofs and outside one or two other camps there was a fire with figures lolling around it.

Kylie pulled up the jeep, stalling it again! She was past caring now.

She and Mrs. Craddock got out and began stumbling over the broken, burnt-out grassy ground to the nearest camp-fire.

A stockman loomed up, a black silhouette against the yellow gleam of the coals.

" We're looking for Bill Allen, and Sara," Mrs. Craddock said without ado.

" That fire along there by the big tree. Everything all right up at the homestead? Most of the boys rode up there for the races to-day."

" Yes, quite. We've only come down to see Bill and Sara."

Mrs. Craddock was taking the lead now. Beating about in the bush at night didn't mean anything to her. She had been doing it all her life. Kylie stumbled along in her wake, slipping on the rocks embedded in the ground, spoiling her slim white does in the grass that was bedewed with the condensation after the day's heat.

Bill Allen was sitting by the fire, stirring the coals under a billy. The light flickered on his face, making it more gaunt than it really was. Sara lay on her back, her arms under her head, watching the dark figures of Kylie and Mrs. Craddock approach. As they came to the fire's edge she sat up, wrapped her arms around her slacks-covered knees and said, with a touch of cynical casualness in her voice:

" Hallo there! What goes on? "

" I've come down to see Nonie. I hope you don't mind, Sara? " Kylie said.

She was surprised at the sound of her own voice. It was trembling. She hurried on because Bill Allen had stood up and Kylie had a feeling he was menacing her.

" I made her dress for the party," Kylie explained. " I built up all her hopes. I couldn't bear to think she might feel I'd let her down. So I gave the party away too. . . ."

" She's asleep," Sara said. She did not add that Nonie had cried herself to sleep. " To-morrow she'll have forgotten all about it. We're going to take her mustering strays."

" It was mighty nice of you to come, Miss Brown," Bill Allen drawled. His voice was very soft because he spoke through half-closed lips. He sounded like a man who rarely spoke at all. " I guess Nonie will be pleased." He paused. " Maybe it might be the right thing if we woke her up, Sara. We could make some tea for Mrs. Craddock and Miss Brown. . . ."

" And have our own party? " Sara asked as she turned and looked up at the tall shadow of her husband. She gave a low laugh. "Some party, considering the splendour up there at the homestead!"

"Mind if we sit down?" said Mrs. Craddock. "Get off that high horse of yours, Bill. We've come to stay—if we can't take Nonie back with us."

"Yes, please do sit down," Sara said, waving her hand in the direction of the opposite side of the fire. She looked across the coals at Kylie and the firelight glinted in her eyes, making them hard, and just a little bitter. "Wouldn't you get up on your high horse, Miss Kylie Brown?" she said. "By the way, how did you manage to keep on the right side of Ray? You kept away from Tom Flynn and Brad, I suppose."

Kylie followed Mrs. Craddock's example and sat down. She picked up a stick and poked at the edges of the fire.

"Yes, I suppose so," Kylie said reluctantly. She didn't want to talk about Ray, much less Brad and Tom Flynn.

"I'm going to wake that child up, Sara," Mrs. Craddock said. "Whatever happens, whether she comes up to the homestead with us or not, she can sleep in to-morrow. She's young. She can take a late night for once in her life."

Sara did not stop her as she walked away towards the canvas hut. Neither did Bill Allen. He stalked away, probably to get more mugs, and perhaps something to eat.

"Well, go on," said Sara, arms still wrapped round her knees, the light playing on her face as she looked across the fire at Kylie. "What goes on with Ray?"

"Ray seems quite well," Kylie said stiffly, and very embarrassed. Loyalty forbade her to talk to Sara unkindly of any of the Coulsells.

Sara threw back her head and laughed.

"For Ray to be quite well she would have to put a leg-rope and halter on Tom Flynn. That's why she couldn't stand me, you know. Not that she hadn't cause. She was so guardian-like about who was fit to marry Brad that I didn't even try. Like scaling Olympus, that would have been." She unwound her arms and threw a stick on the fire. "I hadn't met Bill then ... he was always at the outcamps, never up at the homestead." Sara shrugged. "So I made a play for Tom. There was nothing to it. Just a bit of fun. Actually I never looked at him again, after I got to know Bill. But Ray didn't trust me. Anyway, she never forgave me."

Kylie stirred uneasily.

" I think perhaps she has been fond of Tom for a long time. Even when she was a schoolgirl, Charmian told me."

" Charmian's all right," Sara said unexpectedly. " Glittering with glamour, of course, and that sort of thing leaves me stone cold. I'd rather have horses. All the same, when you get underneath the grease-paint—she's all right."

" Ray is very attached to Charmian," Kylie said for want of something else to say. " I think—but I'm not sure—that something has happened between Ray and Tom. Perhaps Charmian helped."

" Time someone helped. Tom is about as stiff-necked with pride as Bill. Rears back at the idea of marrying the squatter's sister, you know. As if it matters! Brad would give him a share of Rock Hill, and make him pay for it." She poked the stick into the coals and stirred them into flame. " That's the Bentley-Coulsell strain in them. They do everything the hard way and that's how they'd make it for Tom." She paused. " Tom would want it that way. Who wants to live on wages and his wife's property? Brad knows that too."

" Then why didn't Brad do something about it? " Kylie asked, puzzled.

Sara looked up. The firelight was dancing on both their faces.

" Even Brad wouldn't tell another man to propose to his sister. By the way, I hope you didn't cast those rather attractive eyes of yours at Tom. Brad just wouldn't like that. Ray's preserves, you know. . . ."

Kylie was beginning to see daylight. That was why Brad hadn't liked her friendship with Tom! For a moment she didn't know what to say.

Just then Bill Allen came back to the fire with mugs and a parcel of damper. He unwrapped the damper and began to slice it ready for toasting, Sara watching him.

" There's a husband for you," she said with a laugh. " Gets the supper for his weary wife."

" We share everything," Bill said in his quiet muffled voice. " We ride together and we cook together."

Just then reflected lights from another vehicle swept across the sky as a car, beyond the last rock-strewn rise, began the upward climb.

" Heavens," said Sara. " The whole homestead on leave from the party? Who comes this time? "

At that moment Mrs. Craddock came out of the canvas tent with Nonie. The little girl stood shyly, still not quite awake, in her party dress.

"Oh, Nonie!" cried Kylie, jumping up. "You look heavenly. The firelight's playing all over you and you look as if you've got a fairy dress on."

She went across the space and took Nonie's hand. She looked at Bill Allen.

"May we go to the party, please? You see, I can't go if Nonie doesn't go. You wouldn't have us both miss it?"

Bill Allen stood beside the fire, silent, undecided.

"It's Brad's party, you know," pleaded Kylie. "And Mrs. Coulsell's. They'll be dreadfully upset if Nonie and I don't appear. They'll wonder what has happened."

Nonie stood looking up at Kylie. She was still uncertain, not fully awake, not understanding what was happening.

Mrs. Craddock had gone across and taken the wire toasting fork from Bill Allen. She was holding sliced damper to the flames to brown it.

Sara was watching the big car top the rise and come full belt down the slope. It swerved round to come to a stop beside the jeep. It was the Chrysler Royal. The car door slammed as a man got out.

Kylie, holding Nonie's hand, turned round.

"'S *Brad!*" said Nonie. With a cry of delight she let go Kylie's hand and ran across the space, arms out, to meet him.

Brad caught her, swung her up in the air and then put her down.

"I've come to take you to my party, Nonie," he said. He held her hand and looked across the space at where Kylie stood, very still, shadow and firelight alternately playing across her face. "And Kylie too," said Brad, still looking at her.

There was a moment's silence and then he looked down at Nonie again.

"The two most important people are late," he said. "But then they're very V.I.P.s, aren't they?"

Nonie's face was upturned to his.

"Me and Kylie, you mean?"

Brad looked up at Kylie again.

"You and Kylie," he said.

Bill Allen walked round the fire and stood, hands in his

belt, and looked at the boss. Then he said a surprising thing, right out of the context of what was going on. But then Bill Allen was like that. If he had something on his mind, he had to get rid of it. Time and place meant nothing to him.

" The Whip Man's finished that job, Brad," he said. " He gave it to me to give you round about sundown. Said it was the best whip he ever made, an' he hopes the little lady likes it."

" Ho ho! " said Sara. " You only give the Whip Man's whips to the very best of your pals, Brad. Who's it this time? "

" Nobody you know, Sara. A girl called Rosemary Bentley."

Kylie stiffened. For a moment she thought she would faint. So that was why Wilson Hendry had avoided her. He knew Brad Coulsell was on Rosemary's trail.

But what was this about the Whip Man, and the whip?

Brad was still standing. He swung Nonie round his back so the child now had his left hand. He held out his right hand to Kylie as long ago . . . or so it seemed . . . she had seen him hold it out to Nonie the day he came home from the south. It had been on her own first day at Rock Hill and that gesture —the way he had held his hand out to the child—had brought a lump to her throat.

" Come and sit down, Kylie," he said.

The hand, held out, could not be refused. Kylie, frozen with bewilderment, came forward.

Because that hand demanded it she put her own hand in Brad's. He drew her a little closer as if it was the most natural thing in the world. He went on talking to Sara, easily, casually, as if what he was saying wasn't very important.

" Rosemary Bentley had an aunt," Brad said. " And the aunt had jewels. Years after she died, her will was found stuck between the last pages of an old ledger of her husband's. Now deceased."

" Are you talking about old Horace Bentley, Brad? " Sara asked.

" I am," said Brad simply. " That's how it has come to be our job to try and find Miss Rosemary Bentley. We've even advertised for her. We want to return her legacy to her. Simple? "

He was holding Kylie's hand tight in his own and it seemed

to be conducting some kind of message to her that as yet she couldn't understand.

" Fair enough," Sara said with a shrug. " Anyhow, why are you still standing, Brad? Why don't you all sit down? "

" Mrs. Craddock is making so much toast someone will have to eat it," said Brad. " Bill, is that tea you've got in the billy? By the way, Ray wants me very particularly to bring Nonie and Kylie up to the dance." He looked steadily across the fire at Sara and Bill Allen. " She and Tom Flynn are going to announce their engagement to-night."

His words dropped into a pool of silence.

Brad went on:

" She's very happy, Sara. I'm sure you'll wish her luck."

Sara snapped a stick and threw it into the fire. Then she laughed.

" We'll all turn over a new leaf. Come on, Bill darling! Pour the tea. We'll drink Ray's health out of tin mugs." She sounded as if she was too good a sport to say anything else.

Brad sat with Nonie and Kylie, in their party frocks, on either side of him. He looked magnificent himself in his white sharkskin coat with a black bow tie. Kylie wondered if it did matter very much if Brad got fire smudges on his dinner jacket and she and Nonie got them on their dresses.

This was better than any party, surely.

Nonie was wide awake and excited now. She chattered to Brad at top speed and he spent most of his time answering her, getting a word in now and again when he could.

Sara watched the scene with a funny little smile curling round her mouth. Ray's " happiness " took quite a lot of digesting.

" How's the party going without the host, Brad? " she said at length.

She had noticed Kylie's silence but was beginning to have her own ideas as to the cause. Whoever *Rosemary Bentley* was she didn't care but certainly this girl with the lovely wide-spaced grey-green eyes was bowled over by something. Must be Brad. Any time now she too might be presented with a Whip Man's stockwhip!

Kylie sipped her tea and nibbled at the toast. She couldn't think of anything to say to break her own silence.

" I was there to start the thing going," Brad said across the fire to Sara. " And I'll be back for the last dance. I've got it booked."

Kylie's heart dropped. She had been beginning to wonde
. . . to dream. That whip! Brad had said it was for Rose
mary Bentley. Did he know who she was, and was sh
forgiven? So much was her mind on Brad, that she didn'
have time to think about the jewels.

He had the last dance booked. It would be with Charmian
of course.

*

At length Brad stood up, drawing Nonie up with him
Once again he held out that right hand to Kylie and she pu
her own hand in it. He drew her up beside him.

There was something about the way the fire caught hi
smile that made Kylie's heart turn over.

" I've got two girls," he said, looking from Nonie on on
side to Kylie on the other. " Who am I going to put in th
back seat? "

" You've got the Chrysler Royal, haven't you, Brad? "
Sara said from her ground seat. Her arms were round he
knees again. She didn't think anything so importan
enough to bring her to her feet just now. " There's room fo
a whole family in the front seat, isn't there? "

Suddenly Mrs. Craddock was bustling to her feet.

" That jeep's got to go back to-night. They want it i
the morning. It's many a long day since I've driven a ca
but if Miss Kylie could bring it down then I can take it back.'
She looked at the small girl. " Nonie," she said, " I'm afrai
to drive alone in the dark."

" Oh poof! " said Nonie. " It's not dark, it's moonlight
Look, I could read my book out there. I'll come with you i
you're scarey-cat."

She withdrew her hand from Brad and tilted her face u
towards him.

" I have to look after Mrs. Craddock," she said. She too
the older woman's hand and led her round the fringe of th
camp-fire towards the jeep. Mrs. Craddock suffered herself t
be led.

Kylie felt tears stinging her eyes. She turned back t
Sara and Bill Allen. The stockman was standing beside hi
wife. Sara still sat, knees drawn up and her chin resting o
them, her arms wrapped round them. She hadn't move
all the evening.

" How lucky you are," Kylie said. " You own the nices

ittle girl in the world." They were the only words she had
uttered since Brad had arrived.

Such praise about his daughter rendered the shy stockman
tongue-tied.

"Thanks a lot," Sara said with a laugh.

Brad turned away and taking Kylie's arm began to pick
his way to the big car.

"Happy hunting, Kylie!" Sara called after them. Her
low laugh could be heard rustling in the parched dried grasses
and echoing in the trees that stood stiff and still in the silver
moonlight. Then she added—quite kindly: "Give my love
to Ray."

Kylie was dazed, torn between a painful sweetness that
seemed to pervade her whole being, and a sense of despair
that she should be so foolish as to read any strange meanings
into Brad's actions and Sara's words and laugh.

Had Mrs. Craddock deliberately elected to drive back the
jeep, and take Nonie with her, so that Brad and Kylie could
drive up to the homestead alone?

And what did he know of the whereabouts of Rosemary
Bentley?

As if she had uttered the question aloud, Brad answered her.

"Tom Flynn told me, Kylie," he said. "He read the
inscription in your bracelet. I tried to worry it out of Wilson
Hendry but he wouldn't say a word. He wouldn't say no
and he couldn't say yes. So I knew. He must have made
you a promise?"

He opened the door of the car and put her in. Then he
carefully tucked in the long trailing chiffon skirt and shut
the door. He leaned in the window, looking into her eyes.

"Why didn't you tell us, Kylie?" he said gently.

"I couldn't. You might have sent me away. I loved being
here so much. . . ."

Brad's voice was astonished.

"Send you away? Good God, I went down to that
graveyard-chill of a house in Mosman to get you. To bring
you here. When we found out about you we wanted to give
you a new home. . . ." His voice broke off. Then suddenly
it altered. He put his hand in the window and took hers.
"All Bentleys aren't monsters, Kylie. Did you think we
were?"

She shook her head. She simply didn't know how to
answer that.

He withdrew his hand.

" I've got to go and see Mrs. Craddock and Nonie safel
away. I'll be back in a minute, dear."

Did he say " *dear* "?

Kylie put her hand to her head. Something or someon
must be crazy. It could only be herself. Her aunt had le:
her all those jewels. The Coulsells had wanted her. Bra
had called her *dear*. It was a glorious moonlight night an
yes, indeed, there was such a thing as being moonstruck.

Brad had walked away to the jeep and was seeing Mr
Craddock and Nonie safely stowed in. He watched Mr
Craddock start up, switch on the long-beam headlights an
then turn the jeep before driving first slowly and then faste
away towards the homestead track.

It seemed to Kylie he stood there a long time and watche
them. Then, as if satisfied that the jeep and its passenge
were safe and heading for home, he turned and came back t
the big car. He walked round the back of it, opened th
drive door and slid in. He leaned over Kylie, put his arr
around her and drew her close to him and kissed her.

One leg was still out in the moonlight and he hadn't ye
closed the door.

He lifted his head and looked into her eyes. It wasn't eas
to see. The moonlight was not inside the car, only outsid
in a fantastic fairy world. But the light caught their eyes an
Kylie could see the dark shape of his nose, the firm line of th
lips that had just kissed her lips.

" Good evening, Miss Rosemary Bentley," Brad said softl
" Brad! " Kylie pleaded. " How did you know?   N
about Rosemary . . . but . . . well, that I would love you t
kiss me like that? "

" Charmian guessed where you'd gone, and Charmia
had been talking to Wilson Hendry. She told me to tell yo
. . . when I found you . . . that she loves you because yo
are what you seem to be. And that you'd understand wha
she means. I think Charmian and Wilson have had thei
heads together and they know a lot more about you than yo
dreamed, dear."

" Did you know a lot more about me too, Brad? "

" I know I had fallen in love with a pair of eyes . . . ar
they grey or green, Kylie? I had fallen in love with a gir
who had courage, and kindness, and steadfastness, an
loyalty. Do you want me to go on? "

" I didn't think you even *saw* me."

" Does anyone falling in love ever let anyone know they're
ooking, and noticing, and beginning to wish . . . and thinking
hers too are falling in love with her? "

His arm suddenly tightened round her. He gathered her
o close to him she thought she might smother. Because
is lips were on hers, she thought it was a heavenly way to die.

She had followed him across Australia. Perhaps he liked
hat she had done for the Whip Man, after all. Perhaps he
ked the way she and Goldie had driven that steer out into
he open so he could throw it. Perhaps he liked the way she
ad taken care of Nonie.

And he had said he liked her eyes.

Somewhere up there in the blue-black sky one special star
ould have its lamp lit specially for Kylie Brown. It would be
he star she had followed.

Brad lifted his head, then kissed her eyelids.

" They're grey, Brad," she said. " But sometimes they're
reen. It all depends on what I wear. . . ."

" Darling, what are you talking about? "

" My eyes. You said you liked them."

He laughed.

" Darling, I like every bit of you." He kissed her again
nd in the middle of the kiss he gave a little groan.

" I think we'll get married soon," he said. " Very soon."

" Yes, please," Kylie said. She felt the soft material of his
inner jacket under her hand. She could feel the powerful
eat of his heart.

" Brad, darling," Kylie said. " Could we go and dance?
wanted to dance with you so much. Just once. . . ." She
sted her forehead against his shoulder and closed her eyes
ecause now she saw her dream coming true. She saw
erself waltzing down that polished floor, under the lights
nat were part-hidden in the hanging ferns . . . with a magical
nan. With Brad.

He straightened himself and turned to the steering-wheel.
Ie let the clutch out and moved the gearstick into first.

" If we don't go now," he said, " we'll stay here for ever.
esides, I have the last dance booked."

He looked down at her and the lights from the dashboard
eflected themselves in his eyes as he smiled.

She knew that that last dance was hers, not Charmian
Jane's.

Dear Charmian! Dear Wilson!

The star had brought three wise people to Rock Hill—Charmian, Wilson and herself.

"Is your last dance booked with Rosemary Bentley? she asked softly.

"No, darling. With Kylie Brown."

He had one hand on the steering-wheel, as he moved th car into third gear, and then one arm with which to gathe her close to him.

"She's got stars in her eyes," he added. Then kissed he again.

The car slid up the hill and made at high speed for th Rock Hill homestead party. Kylie's first party.

LUCY WALKER ROMANCES
from
⒝⒝
BALLANTINE BOOKS

▼ **Available at your local bookstore or mail the coupon below** ▼

LUCY WALKER ROMANCES
from
ⓑⓑ
BALLANTINE BOOKS

▼ **Available at your local bookstore or mail the coupon below** ▼